WILL AND TESTAMENT

A novel
by
Vigdis Hjorth

Translated
by Charlotte Barslund

VERSO

London • New York

This translation has been published with the financial support of NORLA

This English-language edition published by Verso 2019
Translation © Charlotte Barslund 2019
Originally published as *Arv og miljø*
© Cappelen Damm AS 2016

1 3 5 7 9 10 8 6 4 2

Verso
UK: 6 Meard Street, London W1F 0EG
US: 20 Jay Street, Suite 1010, Brooklyn, NY 11201
versobooks.com

Verso is the imprint of New Left Books

ISBN-13: 978-1-78873-310-6
ISBN-13: 978-1-78873-312-0 (US EBK)
ISBN-13: 978-1-78873-311-3 (UK EBK)

British Library Cataloguing in Publication Data
A catalogue record for this book is available from the British Library
LCCN: 2019942598

Library of Congress Cataloging-in-Publication Data
A catalog record for this book is available from the Library of Congress

Typeset in Electra by Biblichor Ltd, Edinburgh
Printed and bound by CPI Group (UK) Ltd, Croydon CR0 4YY

You should do something you have to do as something you intended to do all along. Or: If you have to do something, do it as if you meant it.

SLAVOJ ŽIŽEK

Will and Testament

A NOVEL

Vigdis Hjorth

Dad died five months ago, which was either great timing or terrible, depending on your point of view. Personally, I don't think he would have minded going unexpectedly; I was even tempted when I first heard to think that he might have fallen on purpose, before I knew the full story. It was too much like a plot twist in a novel for it to be just an accident.

In the weeks leading up to his death, my siblings had become embroiled in a heated argument about how to share the family estate, the holiday cabins on Hvaler. And just two days before Dad's fall, I had joined in, siding with my older brother against my two younger sisters.

I learned about the row in a roundabout way. One Saturday morning, which I had been looking forward to, when all I had to do was prepare a contribution to a contemporary drama seminar in Fredrikstad that same day, my sister Astrid called. It was a bright and beautiful late November morning, the sun was shining, I might have mistaken it for spring if it wasn't for the leafless trees reaching for the sky and the leaves covering the ground. I was in a good mood, I had made coffee and I was excited about going to Fredrikstad, pottering around the old city centre when the seminar was over, walking on the ramparts with my dog and gazing at the river. After my shower, I saw that Astrid had called several times. I assumed it was about a collection of articles that I had been helping her edit.

She answered her mobile in a hushed voice. Hang on, she said, I could hear beeping in the background as if she were in a room with electrical equipment. Hang on, she said again, still whispering. I waited. I'm at Diakonhjemmet Hospital, she said, her voice louder now, the beeping had gone. It's Mum, she said. But it's all right. She'll be fine.

An overdose, she then said, Mum took an overdose last night, but she'll be fine, she's just very tired.

It wasn't Mum's first attempt, but in the past there had been such a build-up each time that I hadn't been surprised. Astrid reiterated

2

that everything was fine, that Mum would recover, but that it had been dramatic. Mum had called her at four thirty in the morning to tell her that she had taken an overdose: I've taken an overdose. Astrid and her husband had been to a party that night, they had only just got home and weren't in a fit state to drive; Astrid rang Dad who found Mum on the kitchen floor and called their neighbour, a doctor, and he had come over; he wasn't sure that an ambulance was necessary, but had called one anyway, just to be on the safe side, and the ambulance had come and taken Mum to the hospital where she was now on the mend, but very, very tired.

Why, I asked, and Astrid became vague and incoherent, but at length I gathered that ownership of our parents' much-loved cabins on Hvaler had been transferred to my two sisters, Astrid and Åsa, without our brother, Bård, being told, and when he did find out he thought the notional value was way too low. As Astrid put it, he had kicked off and raised hell. She had been in touch with Bård recently because Mum would be turning eighty soon and Dad eighty-five, which was cause for celebration; she had written to invite him and his family to the party and he had replied that he didn't want to see her, that she had wheedled a cabin on Hvaler, that this was the final straw in a long line of financial favouritism going back years, and that she was only ever looking out for herself—as usual.

Astrid had been shocked at his words and accusations, and would appear to have told everything to Mum who in turn became so distraught that she took an overdose and had now been admitted to hospital, so ultimately it was really all Bård's fault.

However, when Astrid had called Bård to tell him about the overdose, he had replied that she only had herself to blame. He's so heartless, she said to me. He uses the most devastating of all weapons, his children. Bård's children had unfriended Astrid and Åsa

3

on Facebook and written to Mum and Dad how upset they were at the loss of the cabins. Mum had always been terrified of losing contact with Bård's children.

I asked her to wish Mum a speedy recovery, what else could I do? She'll be pleased to hear that, Astrid said.

Funny how random it seems, our meeting people who later prove pivotal to our lives, who will affect or directly influence decisions that will cause our lives to change direction. Or perhaps it's not random at all. Can we sense that certain people might nudge us onto a path we consciously or subconsciously would have taken anyway? And so we stay in touch with them. Or do we have a hunch that some people might challenge us or force us off a path we want to take, and so we decide not to see them again? It's remarkable how important just one person can become in determining how we act in critical situations, just because we happened to consult that individual in the past.

I didn't drink my coffee, I was troubled so I got dressed and went outside to feel the wind on my face, to clear my head. I wasn't handling this well, I thought, and called Søren, who of all my children knew our family best. He was surprised about the overdose, of course, but he knew about past overdoses, and it was always fine in the end, his grandmother invariably called for help in time. When I got to the transfer of the cabins and the low valuation, he grew pensive and said that he could understand why Bård was upset. Bård hadn't cut contact like I had done; he had always kept in touch, true, he wasn't as close to my parents as Astrid and Åsa were, but that shouldn't cause him to be financially penalised, surely?

I rang Klara who was outraged. Playing at suicide was just not on. Giving family cabins to two of your four children on the sly and too cheaply was not on either.

My parents had every right to do what they had done, but in recent years they had frequently declared that they would treat their children equally when it came to inheritance. However, it had now become clear that the amount of money Bård and I would get by way of compensation for the cabins was remarkably low. That was what had upset him, I realised, and the fact that no one had bothered to tell him that the transfer of ownership had already taken place. I hadn't been told either, but then again I hadn't spoken to my family for decades. In the last twenty or so years I'd only had

6

contact with my second youngest sister, Astrid, and only with a few phone calls a year. So I had been surprised when, on my birthday some months ago, I'd had a text message from my youngest sister, Åsa, whom I hadn't heard from in years. She wrote that she had texted me happy birthday before, but must have used the wrong number. And then the penny dropped. Up until now they had been two against one, Astrid and Åsa against Bård, but now that I was involved, everything was up for grabs. I'd always said I didn't want to inherit anything and I guess my sisters were hoping that was still my position, but they couldn't be sure. It was what I had said to Astrid every time she wanted me to reconcile with my parents. It felt like Astrid was emotionally blackmailing me; she would tell me how much they suffered as a result of my estrangement, how old they were, how they would die soon, and why couldn't I just turn up at Christmas or for a big birthday? It was probably Mum putting pressure on her, but I wasn't moved by Astrid's talk of old age and death, instead I felt provoked and angry. Didn't she take me seriously? I had already given her my reasons. Explained that being around Mum and Dad made me ill, that seeing them and pretending that everything was fine would be a betrayal of everything I stood for, it was out of the question, I had already tried! I didn't relent, but was provoked into growing increasingly angry, not at the time, but later, at night, on email. I wrote to her that I never wanted to see Mum and Dad again, I would never set foot in their house in Bråteveien, and that they should go ahead and disinherit me.

After I had cut off contact, Mum rang me several times; this was before caller ID so I couldn't tell it was her. She would alternately sob and yell at me, and I felt physically sick, but I had to stick to my guns if I was to survive; in order not to sink or drown I had to keep my distance. She wanted to know why I refused to see her—as if

7

she didn't know—she asked me impossible questions: Why do you hate me so much when you're everything to me? I told her countless times that I didn't hate her, until I *did* start to hate her, I told her over and over, would I have to explain myself—yet again—only for the next conversation to be as if I had never even tried and I felt rejected, would I be rejected yet again?

The first few years after I cut off contact, these phone calls were deeply distressing. Mum would ring with her accusations and pleas, and I would get angry and lose my temper. Eventually they tailed off, then she gave up all together; I guess that she, too, must have decided that certainty and peace were preferable to the misery caused by these pointless conversations. Better have Astrid give it a try every now and then.

In the last few years, however, Mum had started sending me the occasional text message. Sometimes when she was ill, as most old people are from time to time, she would text me. I'm ill, please can we talk? It would be late at night, she had been drinking for sure, I certainly had, and I would reply that she could call me in the morning. Then I texted Astrid to say that I was willing to talk to Mum about her illness and her care, but if she launched into her usual accusations and histrionics, then I would hang up. I don't know if Astrid passed this on, but when Mum rang the next morning, she spoke only about her poor health and her care, and perhaps she felt like I did after I had rung off, that it had been a good conversation. At any rate, she stopped dumping her disappointments and unhappiness on me and, I gathered, dumped them on Astrid instead, and it must have been tough on Astrid to handle Mum's disappointments and unhappiness, so perhaps it was no wonder that she tried to steer me towards a reconciliation.

~

Because of the disappointment and unhappiness I had inflicted on my parents by cutting off contact with them, I was expecting to be disinherited. And, if against all my expectations they didn't, it would be purely because it wouldn't look good in the eyes of the world, and they wanted things to look good.

But all this lay far in the future as they were both in rude health.

So I was surprised when, one Christmas three years ago, I received a letter from my parents. My adult children had visited them just before Christmas as they usually did, as they had done since I cut off contact—at my suggestion because Mum and Dad seeing their grandchildren eased the pressure on me. And my children enjoyed seeing their cousins and returning home with presents and money and three years ago, a letter. I opened it while they stood next to me and I read it out loud. My parents wrote that they had made a joint will and that their four children would inherit equal shares. Except for the cabins on Hvaler, which would go to Astrid and Åsa at the current market value. They wrote that they were happy to bequeath their assets to their children. My own children smiled cautiously, they too had expected to be disinherited.

It was a strange letter to get. Very generous, really, given how awful I had supposedly made them feel. I wondered what they expected in return.

Mum rang me a few months after that Christmas. I was in a market in San Sebastian with my children and grandchild; we were celebrating Easter in a flat I had rented there. I didn't know it was Mum, I hadn't saved her number. Her voice was trembling, as it always did when she was upset: Bård is raising hell, she said. I had no idea what she was talking about.

9

Bård is raising hell, she said again, the same expression Astrid would later use, because of the will, she said, because the cabins are going to Astrid and Åsa. But Astrid and Åsa have been so nice, she said, so caring. They've been going to the cabins with us all these years, we've had such lovely times together that it seems only natural for them to get the cabins. Bård has never used the cabins, nor have you; would you like a cabin on Hvaler?

I would have loved a cabin on Hvaler at the very edge of the rocks with a sea view, except for the constant risk of bumping into Mum and Dad.

No, I said.

That was the answer she wanted to hear, I realised, because she instantly calmed down. And since I hadn't been in touch with Bård, I didn't twig what she was really asking me. I reiterated that I didn't want a cabin on Hvaler, that I thought their will was generous, and that I hadn't been expecting to get anything.

Astrid would later tell me that there had been a major row about the cabins. When during a visit to Bråteveien, Bård found out that Astrid and Åsa had got them, he had stood up and said that Mum and Dad had already lost one child—he was referring to me—and now they would lose another one, then he had walked out. I could tell that Astrid thought he was being unreasonable. He hadn't been to the cabins for years, he had a cabin of his own, and his wife had never got on with Mum and Dad back when they still went to the cabins on Hvaler.

I was taken aback by her strength of feeling, but I didn't say anything. It was a blessing, I thought, not to be involved in the cabin feud.

~

10

However, now it had escalated. Ownership of the cabins had already been transferred to Astrid and Åsa, Bård was furious and Mum was in hospital after taking an overdose.

The first time I saw Klara Tank she was pushing a pram down the corridor of the Department for Literature. In it sat the son of a famous artist. When Klara attended lectures, she would bring with her the child of this artist, who was said to be in the middle of a divorce. I was a dutiful student who read everything I was supposed to read, but I spent little time at the university as I was pregnant with my second child and busy with my family. As a result I saw Klara only a few times at the Department for Literature, but I took notice of her, the student with the pram. The first time she spoke to me was on the pavement in Hausmanns gate some years later, after a talk on literary criticism. She was now the editor of a literary magazine which had mauled a popular author; she had been defending her criticism, bare-legged and waving her arms around, she had meant to say literary trial, but ended up saying literary toilet, had started to laugh and been unable to stop, then she burst into tears, ran outside and didn't come back. When I left, she caught up with me on the pavement in Hausmanns gate, still with bare legs, although it was October, unbuttoned my coat, touched my silk blouse and told me how nice it was. I walked away, I didn't want her eccentricity to rub off on me.

I went for a longer walk than usual although I was due in Fredrik-stad that same evening. I headed into the protected forest, which was still quite green, but it didn't have its usual calming effect on me. Trees that had keeled over during the storms in recent weeks lay with their heavy dark roots exposed and blocked the footpaths. I called both my daughters, but couldn't get hold of them, I called my boyfriend, but couldn't get hold of him, I had an overwhelm-ing urge to share my news and I wondered why that was, after all nothing terrible had happened, in fact things were fine.

I thought about my earlier conversation with Astrid only a few days ago. I'd had more contact with her these last six months than I'd had for years. She was writing a collection of articles about human rights education and wanted my opinion on the layout and division into chapters which I, in my role as a magazine editor, understood. I read and commented, we talked about format and angles, and in our last conversation, only days previously, we had discussed final tweaks and publishers. That had also taken place while I was out walking; I remember shifting my mobile from one hand to the other because the phone was so cold when held without mittens. When we had finished talking about her book, I asked, as I usually did, how the family was. Well, there's this business with Bård and the cabins, she replied, I thought she was referring to the will.

~

I went to Fredrikstad and it wasn't until I drove into the dark, practically deserted, old part of the city that I started to calm down. I found a place to park near the B&B where I would be staying, I had stayed there before, I walked the dog along the ramparts by the river, which glowed copper red in the rays of the setting sun, I tried to focus on the seminar about the lack of contemporary Norwegian drama, but found it difficult to concentrate. I called Tale and Ebba again, but they didn't pick up, I called Lars, but he didn't pick up either, then I called Bo before I remembered that he was in Israel. I asked myself why it was so imperative for me to tell my daughters, my boyfriend and Bo about Mum, her overdose and the two cabins. I called my oldest friend, who was driving and so had to be quick. She had heard about Mum overdosing before, but she was interested in the inheritance dispute, she had experience of such things. They're perfectly entitled to do what they've done, she said, they can dispose of their property in any way they like, but they don't come across as generous as they did in their Christmas letter. Besides she had reflected on the issue of inheritance, she said, when her brother had inherited the family cabin because he was their parents' favourite and she felt that she should have been given it instead as compensation for lack of love and attention.

I left Fido in my room and walked to the ferry which would take me across the river to the centre of Fredrikstad. From there I called Tale and Ebba again, but they still didn't pick up, I called Klara and asked her why I got so wound up, why I absolutely had to talk about it, given that nothing terrible had happened.

It goes deep, Bergljot, she said. It's seriously deep.

I got off the ferry and walked up through the streets, it started to rain, I got wet and felt heavy. It was just as Klara had said, it was how I felt, how deep it went, how it pushed me into the abyss, how it weighed me down, how I started to sink.

The debate went well, I did well. Afterwards I stayed in the café telling my fellow participants all about the cabin valuations and Mum's overdose although I didn't know them personally and, while I told them about it, I thought to myself that I really ought not to. I was ashamed while I spoke and ashamed when I saw the faces of my listeners and I was ashamed on my way home at having whined about cabin valuations and overdoses like a spoilt brat, in a manner that belonged to childhood and self-centred puberty, I was mired in shame the whole night, I couldn't sleep because I was so ashamed that I hadn't grown up, that I couldn't talk about it in a mature and balanced fashion, that I'd become a child once more.

The day after Klara had unbuttoned my coat in Hausmanns gate and touched my silk blouse, she rang me. I was in the hall of the house where I lived with my husband and children and didn't recognise the name. She said it again and then I remembered, then I grew scared, she had caught me off guard. She asked if I would be willing to review a book for the literary magazine she edited, I didn't want to, I didn't have the courage to take it on, but I didn't have the courage to say no either. She asked if I could come over to hers tomorrow morning so we could discuss it, I didn't want to, but I didn't have the courage to say no either. When I arrived the next morning, she was busy trying to put together a bookcase and failing, she wasn't following the instructions and she was drinking gin. I couldn't drink, I was driving, so I took over the bookcase. While I worked on it, she said that the review didn't matter, the magazine was folding, it wasn't making money for the publishers, how would she pay her rent now? I didn't know, I shook my head, I didn't want to get involved with her financial problems. She was in love with a married man, she said, and my heart skipped a beat. She was pregnant by this married man and was having an abortion tomorrow; unless she did so he would refuse to see her again. I couldn't help her, I wanted to go home, I too wanted to drink gin, I put the bookcase together and I left, I never wanted to see her again.

Sunday in the old city of Fredrikstad. Yellow, red and rotting leaves on the cobblestones, cold rain in the air. I walked along the streets feeling morose. I should never have told total strangers about the cabin valuations and the overdose. I had a compelling urge to talk about it, but I didn't know how. Then I bumped into someone who had been present in the café last night and who asked me if I was OK, as if I wouldn't be. She invited me back to her yellow wooden house a short distance up the street and gave me apple cake and coffee, and the tears welled up in my eyes and stories from my childhood poured out of me, and she embraced it all and spoke calmly and dispassionately about her own past. Was it possible for me to ever get to that place?

As I stood in the doorway and was about to leave, she asked me how long it was since I had last spoken to him.

Who?

Your brother.

I couldn't remember, twenty years or more.

Call him, she said, and I had to smile because she didn't understand what it was like. But we hugged one another as if we had exchanged presents and as I opened the gate, she called out: I'm on Bård's side!

~

17

In the car home I was filled with ambivalence. Shame at yesterday's confessions in the café, anger at myself for being so easily upset, gratitude for the invitation to coffee and cake, for meeting someone on a day like that who had given me advice. I asked myself whether my parents or Astrid and Åsa ever sought advice from anyone because it didn't take much insight into human nature to predict that a man who takes exception to being passed over in a will is also likely to take exception to secret transfers at rates well below the market value. If they had taken advice, surely someone would have pointed this out to them. Then again, perhaps they wouldn't have listened. Perhaps they had already made up their mind to do what they had done, regardless of the consequences.

Once I was safely home in Lier, when it had started to get dark and I was walking across the fields with the dog and it had started to snow, I called Tale and she picked up. I told her about the overdose, about the transfer of ownership and the valuations, and my daughter knew me and understood that I was going off the deep end and said that I mustn't take it so seriously, that I mustn't get involved, that it was just my mother creating more drama and casting herself in the leading role as the tragic victim of evil schemes, while her real goal was to silence her critics.

They've seen the last of me, she said, I refuse to take part in that charade any longer.

I heard what she said, I understood it at an intellectual level.

I walked for longer than usual to wear myself out, to be able to sleep, even sleep through the night; I walked a long way and then went home and sat in front of the fireplace. Astrid called and said that Mum was doing well, perhaps she thought I had been worried.

Mum was still at the hospital and was exhausted, but would be going home the next day, and the birthday party would still go ahead next week as planned, she hoped that Søren and Ebba would come.

I said I hadn't heard anything to the contrary. Mum will be so pleased, she said, she was worried that Bård's children wouldn't show up.

He's using the children, she said again. It's the worst thing you can do, using the children! Mum is terrified of losing contact with Bård's children. Mum has always had such a good relationship with them, and now it might be ruined all because of him.

Cautiously I ventured that they might genuinely be sad that the cabins had been transferred to her and Åsa; it was the first time I hinted that I didn't buy her version wholeheartedly. She fell silent. Then she said that if this really was just about the valuations, they could always get new ones. Perhaps it was a silly way to have gone about it, she said. Perhaps the valuations were a little low, she said. Perhaps we should have asked for two quotes, but we didn't think that far ahead.

I opened a bottle of red wine. When I had drunk it, I felt calmer and I took the dog for another walk. It was still snowing, big heavy flakes that melted on my face and soon I was wet through and through. The sky was big and the stars shone with an unreal intensity or maybe it was just the wine. I walked back, I had made up my mind.

I couldn't find Bård's number online so I called Astrid. She said she didn't have it either. But you only spoke to him yesterday? Åsa has it, she said, I asked if she would call Åsa and then call me back, it was late, she said reluctantly, and then it turned out that she had it after all.

When I said my name, Bergljot, he fell silent. Then he said that he had thought about me a lot recently, and it was my turn to fall silent. Then I told him about my conversations with Astrid and he told me how he saw the situation. He seemed sad, I thought. He mentioned a dystopian novel I had once sent him about the decline of a family I thought resembled ours, about a childhood that resembled ours.

It had been like that, he said.

My heart was racing as I drove home from Klara's. Had she told me that she was in love with a married man because she had worked out that I was too? Could she tell from looking? Did anyone else know? I was married to a nice and decent man and I had three young children with him. And yet I was in love with another, a married man. It was monstrous, it was horrible, what should I do, it was impossible, I was impossible. I didn't have a job, no regular income, but three small children and a nice and affluent man and was passionately in love with another, it was terrible, shameful, unforgivable, how could I, what was wrong with me for me to do something like that?

Klara rang the following week; I wouldn't have picked up the phone if I had known it was her. She asked if I would visit her again, she had bought another bookcase she couldn't assemble. I didn't want to, I went there and assembled the bookcase and told her about the married man. She had sensed as much, she said. She could feel things like that, she said and patted my cheek and I started to cry, what was I going to do?

What I was experiencing, I came to realise once I started to understand my life, was that a moment of insight was approaching like the tremors that precede an earthquake, and like an animal I could sense it before it happened. I was filled with dread and I trembled at the painful dawning of a truth which would rip me to pieces, perhaps I was working subconsciously to advance it, to get it over with, given that it was inevitable.

December and fog right down to the ground. Yesterday's snow had melted, there was slush and black puddles on lawns and roads, and it was cold both outside and in because my heating was broken.

I should have been editing theatre reviews and writing the editorial for the next issue of *On Stage*, but I didn't. Instead I made a Thermos flask of tea, got dressed in woollens and wellies and my heavy parka with the hood, it's always a good idea to be dressed properly. I went to the forest where no one ever came at this time of the day, sat down on a fallen tree trunk and let the dog run free. Sometimes I would see deer here, in the spring and summer, and birds and squirrels and frogs, but today it was just us. Fido sniffed and wagged her tail, jumped over branches and stones, blissfully ignorant of inheritance and childhood. Should I write in an ironic style about *The Journey to the Christmas Star* and *The Nutcracker*, about the lovely family shows that theatres staged at Christmas? No, that would be facile; I could feel a lump in my throat.

It grew dark so we went home, I lit a fire, opened a bottle of red wine and took out my editorial notes. I had only just got down to work when Bård emailed me to say that it had been good to talk though the circumstances could have been happier. Would I like to have lunch soon?

I agree and yes, please, I replied.

As soon as I had pressed 'send', Astrid called, wondering if I had spoken to Bård. I said I was meeting him next week. I got the impression that that worried her.

I had closed down my Mac and was getting ready to go to bed when Klara rang to tell me that Rolf Sandberg had died.

Rolf Sandberg. Mum's great extramarital love. A professor at the teacher training college where Mum had been a mature student. The man Mum had fallen head over heels in love with, the man Mum had started an affair with although he also was married. Mum's passionate love affair with Rolf Sandberg lasted several years until Dad found the beginning of a love letter from Mum under an embroidered cloth on a chest of drawers on Hvaler. Perhaps she intended him to find it. Perhaps Mum wanted Dad to know about the affair, perhaps she thought that if Dad found out, he would divorce her and she could marry Rolf Sandberg. But Dad didn't react as she had hoped, but as he always did, with rage and violence, and Rolf Sandberg didn't react as Mum had hoped either. When she told him that Dad had found the letter, he replied that one divorce was better than two. Mum locked herself in a room with pills and alcohol, Dad kicked down the door, called an ambulance and Mum was taken to Fredrikstad Hospital and had her stomach pumped.

Mum tried living on her own, but it wasn't a success. Dad rented a flat for her, but after a week and a half she was back with him, but on his terms. However, she never stopped seeing Rolf Sandberg, and I guess she never stopped loving him either. She told me this. She didn't tell Astrid or Åsa because they would have been horrified to discover that she still was in touch with Rolf Sandberg, and they would have told Dad and sided with him against her. Mum

24

knew that I wouldn't be outraged on Dad's behalf or tell him anything. That was the difference between Astrid and Åsa and me, our relationship with Dad.

Then I cut all contact with my family and heard nothing more of Rolf Sandberg, but I'm convinced that for years Mum kept hoping that the two of them would end up together. When his wife died, I was almost sure that Mum wanted Dad dead so that she could move in with Rolf Sandberg. Then Rolf Sandberg died and Mum took an overdose when she heard that he was on his deathbed— possibly because she realised that her dream had shattered.

I called Astrid though it was past midnight and told her that Rolf Sandberg had died and that Mum's overdose probably had nothing to do with Bård's text message, but everything to do with Rolf Sandberg's death. She began to get nervous, I could hear it.

I wrote to Bård to tell him that Rolf Sandberg had died, and that Mum's overdose was probably to do with his death rather than the text message Bård had sent her.

Klara and I both loved married men who wouldn't get divorced, who didn't want us, who wanted sex with us in hotel rooms, whom we couldn't bear to tear ourselves away from, and we were miserable. Klara lived on her own, it had its downsides, I lived with my husband and three children, that too had its downsides. I had married and had children young in order to be a mother and not a daughter any more, I came to realise once I started to understand my life; now I was deceiving my husband and my children, and I was ashamed. Klara was deceiving no one, but had no money and worked night shifts as a waitress at Renna Bar to make ends meet. My husband earned plenty of money so I was able to study without having to take out a student loan, I was a cheat and a parasite. I visited Klara whenever I could and drank with her friends from the bar who were mentally unstable and alcoholic, intelligent, broke and wretched, misfits and outsiders. Strange, marginal existences with no survival skills, always knocking on Klara's door, as did I, eager to mix with the misfits and the wretched, what was that about? This compelling urge of mine to seek my own downfall, what was wrong with me? I visited Klara and drank in the company of strangers who had failed at life, I spent the night there and woke up the next morning in the bright light of day surrounded by broken, filthy people and I rushed home to hug my children and husband, wanting to live for ever in the big, airy, clean house, I promised myself never to leave it, but I would soon be back at Klara's, drawn to my destruction.

Four days after the overdose, the same day that Rolf Sandberg's obituary appeared in the newspaper, Mum and Dad celebrated their big birthdays in Bråteveien. When Tale heard that Søren and Ebba were going, she was outraged. Why were they playing along with it? Putting on a brave face and accepting the Bråteveien version of events, pretending that nothing had happened? That was why the world was going to hell in a handcart, she said, because people didn't set boundaries, weren't honest and acted hypocritically in order not to upset anyone, why were Søren and Ebba going to Bråteveien to take part in this appalling performance? She herself would never set foot in Bråteveien again, she would tell her grandparents that immediately.

I advised her against it. If she got involved in the inheritance dispute, they would merely think that she wanted a cabin on Hvaler.

On the day of the birthday party I felt twitchy. I knew I was safe, but it made no difference. My doors were locked, Søren and Ebba were grown-ups and could handle themselves, and yet I was on edge as I always was whenever my children visited Bråteveien. I kept looking at the clock as it got closer to the starting time as though a bomb might go off. I imagined Søren and Ebba crossing the threshold, hugging my parents, whom I hadn't seen for years and could no longer be sure of recognising, imagined them hugging or shaking hands with Astrid and her husband and their children, Åsa and her husband and their children, imagined Søren and Ebba's faces and felt sorry for them, or was I projecting and was I really feeling sorry for myself? I wondered what they would say, the usual greetings and congratulations, nothing about the real issues, the inheritance, the overdose, Rolf Sandberg's obituary or the elephant in the room, those of us who weren't there, Bård and I, and Bård's children.

The time passed slowly, I waited impatiently without knowing what for. I knew what my children would say, it had gone well, they had kept to safe topics, updated one another about careers and education, and yet I felt apprehensive. It was just like when my children visited Bråteveien before Christmas and were given presents, and I would be on tenterhooks until they returned. My fear was irrational, it was the non-financial legacy of my upbringing. An irrational sense of guilt because I had opted out, cut contact, because I had done what you weren't supposed to do, refused to see my ageing parents, because I was like that, vile. The party started at six, it was eight o'clock now and my children hadn't called and I didn't want to call them in case they were still there. At eight thirty Søren rang me and said that it had gone well although my Mum had got drunk very quickly and my Dad had just sat brooding in his armchair, more taciturn than usual. Bård and his children hadn't been there, but Astrid and Åsa had been there with theirs, of course, and Astrid had made a speech saying that she and Åsa were happy to be so close to Mum and Dad, how they always had such nice times together, how they saw one another often, several times a week usually, not to mention all the lovely long summers on Hvaler.

Søren remarked and he sounded rather glum, I thought, that perhaps it wasn't surprising that Åsa and Astrid would inherit

28

more than 'us', given how much time they spent with my Mum and Dad and how fond they were of them.

If I didn't know that your parents had two other children, he said, I would think it was a normal, happy family.

The first time I met Bo Schjerven was a Sunday, on Book Day at the Norwegian Theatre. The event included readings from that autumn's new publications in the theatre's several auditoria, and various arts and literature magazines had stands in the foyer including the latest arrival, *Incomprehensible Publications*, founded and developed in the early morning hours in Klara's flat by one of her friends from Renna Bar who had literary ambitions. Klara was staffing the stand between one and three in the afternoon, and I had promised to stop by. When I arrived, I spotted her under a parasol with *Incomprehensible Publications* printed on it and stuck into one of the theatre's big plant pots. She looked uncomfortable, she had had several hostile encounters with authors whose work had been criticized in the magazine, a crime writer had even threatened her with a knife. Writing the reviews had been more fun than publishing them, she acknowledged, she needed a beer. She went to the café and I had taken her place under the parasol when a man came towards me, snatched a copy of the magazine, sat down on the stairs, started reading it and let out a loud sigh, please come back soon, Klara. The man got up, came over to me and informed me that he had translated the poetry anthology which *Incomprehensible Publications* had described as a particularly incomprehensible publication. I said that I had nothing to do with the magazine. The small, bespectacled man looked at me over the rim of his glasses and asked if the editor of *Incomprehensible Publications* knew anything about the political situation in Russia in the 1920s. I said that I didn't know and reiterated that I had nothing to do with *Incomprehensible Publications*, so he asked why I was then staffing the stand of this ridiculous magazine. He asked me if the editor knew anything about the revolutionary ideas popular with literary circles in 1920s St Petersburg; I said I didn't know, that I suspected that she didn't. The pale, stern man then asked if the editor had ever heard of Ivan Yegoryev, the essayist. I didn't know, please come back soon, Klara. He asked if the editor of *Incomprehensible Publications* had read any Russian history or Russian poets, if she knew of the tradition of which the poetry anthology *Autumn Apples* was a part. I didn't know, I suspected that she didn't, please come back soon, Klara. The serious man leaned forwards and declared that the lines which the moronic reviewer in *Incomprehensible Publications* had found particularly incomprehensible were absolutely crucial because they paraphrased the politician V. G. Korolenko's speech at the Communist Party's Fourth Party Congress. The small man, who by now had become quite loud, said that if one was to review a poetry anthology like the one he had translated, one had a duty to familiarise oneself with one's subject, it was the critic's responsibility because if the critic didn't take poetry seriously, who would? He said that if the presumably young and hopelessly arrogant woman who had reviewed *Autumn Apples* in *Incomprehensible Publications* had bothered to get to know her subject, she would have got so much more out of the anthology to the point where it might have changed her life. He studied my face. Changed your life, he said, and my heart sank. Fortunately someone he knew turned up at that point, he put down the magazine and left. I looked around for Klara, I didn't want to sit there any longer. Then the man suddenly came back and asked me to lend him a hundred kroner. His brother had turned up and wanted to have coffee with him in the café, but he had no money and didn't want to say so because he didn't want to worry his brother. I gave him a hundred kroner and he insisted on getting my bank details. The following week one hundred and ten kroner were paid into my bank account, the extra ten kroner being interest.

We had arranged to meet at the Grand Hotel. It was my idea. I went out so rarely that I simply blurted out the name. I texted Bård, please would he book the table?

On my way there I suddenly remembered that Mum always used to meet her friends at the Grand in the old days when they went out shopping and were ladies who lunched. I myself had been out shopping with Mum a couple of times, was it the memory of Mum that had made me pick the Grand? I hoped my childhood wasn't coming back, I hoped I wasn't going back to my childhood, and that that explained why I was shaking. I opened the door, there was a queue to get into the restaurant, the pre-Christmas rush, and many smartly dressed older people, I shouldn't have picked the Grand. I might bump into Mum and her friends, surely there was a woman who looked like Mum, like I remembered her, in the corner, I turned away, I wanted to leave, then I saw someone who looked like him, like I remembered him, his back and the back of his head, Bård, I said, and he turned around and it was him, twenty years older. He recognised me, also twenty years older, we hugged one another like you do when you're brother and sister and there are no inheritance disputes separating you—as far as we knew. A woman who knew him came over, they said hello and hugged one another, and he introduced me as his younger sister, my oldest younger sister, he said. Then we fell silent. We couldn't very well start our conversation while we were queuing, we hadn't spoken for over twenty-three years. The last time we saw one another was when his older daughter was confirmed. That had been ten years after the previous time I'd seen him, I'd worked out on my way here, and both times had been formal events in public venues, restaurants not unlike the Grand. We hadn't, I'd realised, had a private conversation since we left school, and hardly ever even then. We had both distanced ourselves from our family, but not together, not in unison, we had distanced ourselves individually and separately. I heard news of Bård from Astrid on the two occasions every year that I spoke to her, but there was little to report was my impression, his children did well at school. I didn't know that he no longer lived in a house in Nordstrand but had moved to a flat in Fagerborg. Astrid hadn't said anything about that, I learned about the move at the Grand after I had taken our coats to the cloakroom while Bård found the table he had booked for us. He trusted me with his coat because we had once been squashed into the back of a car with our sisters. I hung up our coats in the cloakroom and found him seated at the table, he looked like Dad as he had once looked, Dad had aged a lot, Bård said. We ordered coffee, he had come here on the tram, he said, when I asked if he had driven here by car, and that was when he told me that he no longer lived in Nordstrand, but in Fagerborg, and he was surprised, such was my impression, that I didn't know that, the move was eight years ago, that Astrid—with whom he knew I was in touch—hadn't mentioned it. He served himself first, went up to the buffet with a gait I didn't remember and came back with an open sandwich. I went to the buffet and came back with an open sandwich. So there we were together, at the Grand.

It turned out that the cabin dispute had gone on for much longer than I had assumed. Mum and Dad had decided that Astrid and

Åsa would inherit the cabins several years ago. Bård had learned this from his daughter. She had been visiting her grandparents who told her that Astrid and Åsa would inherit the cabins on Hvaler. Bård's daughter had been taken aback, what should she say, a granddaughter who had been going to Hvaler since she was yea high, but who was too young and shy to voice her embarrassment and disappointment. Was that why they had told her, a young and polite grandchild who wouldn't argue with them, so that they could later say that she hadn't objected? Bård's daughter went home and told her father what his parents had said, and Bård went to see Mum and Dad who confirmed that Astrid and Åsa would indeed inherit the cabins. Did they realise the magnitude of what they were saying? How shocking it was to say this to their only son, who had spent every summer on Hvaler since he was a child and later brought his own family there every summer until his relationship with Mum and Dad became too strained, who had imagined and hoped that when Mum and Dad were gone, he and his siblings might grow close again. He had asked them to reconsider; they had replied that they had made up their minds. Some weeks later he received a copy of their will in the post which made it clear that Astrid and Åsa would inherit the cabins, and if they—contrary to expectations—didn't want to inherit the cabins, they would be sold to the highest bidder. Bård and I would not inherit them.

They don't want us there, he said.

We had probably picked up on that and it explained why we hadn't gone there.

A year later he had written a letter to Mum and Dad, he placed a copy of it in front of me, he had brought all the paperwork, a friendly letter where he argued that all four children should share the two cabins. Because everyone had strong links to Hvaler,

35

because we could then share the maintenance work and the costs, because more people would thus benefit from the cabins, the plots were large, new cabins could be built in the future.

They replied that they had made up their minds.

He had then written to Astrid and Åsa, making the same points, they had replied that it was for Mum and Dad to decide how they wanted to dispose of their property. In the last email Bård had sent on the matter, he wrote that Hvaler was the place that held the happiest memories for him. Why couldn't the four siblings own half a cabin each? It needn't be complicated, he wrote. Several of his friends had inherited cabins jointly with their siblings, and it usually worked out fine. *I ask you to reconsider please. It would mean a lot to me and my children to own half of one of the cabins when one day you're no longer here.* He concluded by writing that he didn't understand why Mum and Dad would rather see their sons-in-law on Hvaler than their own son and his children.

He got no reply. And there was nothing he could do about it. They were perfectly entitled to do what they had done. But did they know what they were doing? The hurt they were inflicting, how they were twisting the knife in the wound? Did Astrid and Åsa understand the consequences of Mum and Dad doing what they were doing with their blessing, didn't they realise that it would impact on their relationship with Bård? Did Mum and Dad think the relationship between the four siblings would remain unchanged? Did Mum and Dad want Bård and his children or me and my children *not* to own half a cabin each on Hvaler? Bård had asked politely and argued his case without knowing that it was already a done deal. Mum and Dad would rather holiday with their sons-in-law than their own son and his family. They didn't want us on Hvaler. They were happy to see Bård and his children, me and my children at Christmas, Easter and big family birthdays, but they didn't want us on Hvaler. They liked having Astrid and Åsa with their husbands and children with them on Hvaler and everywhere else because there was no history with Astrid and Åsa.

Mum and Dad and Astrid and Åsa had decided that the cabins would go to Astrid and Åsa and carried out their plan. They were complicit. Bård had believed that the decision could be changed and had pleaded with them in vain. Some people knew what was really going on, others didn't. It was clearly unfair, but Mum and Dad and Astrid and Åsa continued to act as if everything was just fine, which made it odd that Astrid had never mentioned the matter to me, didn't it?

A catastrophe was looming, didn't they understand or did they understand and not give a damn and were hoping to ride out the storm?

Bård wouldn't be getting a cabin on Hvaler, he would have to learn to live with that, and he did, but the damage had been done.

Bård had popped by in August to see Mum and Dad in Bråteveien to say hi after the summer, and Mum had said that Dad had grown too old to do the things he used to, maintenance work on the cabins, cutting the grass and weeding, and so they had transferred ownership of the old cabin to Astrid and the new cabin to Åsa. Bård, who had accepted that he wasn't going to get a cabin, asked at what price. When Mum told him, he got up and walked out. It was the final straw. The ridiculously low price. The preferential treatment was *deliberate*. They *wanted* Bård and me to receive as little recompense as legally possible. It was *intentional*, and Astrid and Åsa had gone along with it. How would they have felt if it had been the other way round? And would they one day do the same to their children, they had two each. Give the cabins that they now owned to just one of them? No. Of course not. Because it would be awful for the one who didn't get a cabin, they would feel like their parents loved them the least.

As Bård left, Mum called out to him that he should count himself lucky to be getting anything at all.

We should count ourselves lucky to be getting anything at all. The will we had been told about at Christmas three years ago, and which Bård had asked to be sent to him so he could read it, could be changed at any time, presumably it had already been changed, if indeed it still existed, perhaps there was no valid will, in which case the old cabin would be treated as a gift to Astrid and the new cabin as a gift to Åsa and we, Bård and Bergljot, which rolled off the tongue so easily, risked getting nothing at all.

It had rattled him, I could tell, that Mum and Dad had shown such blatant favouritism, that Astrid and Åsa had accepted the injustice apparently without a moment's hesitation, hadn't tried to talk Mum and Dad out of it so that the relationship between the siblings wouldn't be ruined, so that Bård wouldn't feel overlooked and ignored, so that Bård wouldn't be upset as he had been, as he was, because they so very clearly didn't care about his feelings, didn't care enough about him to treat him decently. Bård had had a few knocks along the way and had now been dealt the final blow, he was beaten, I realised. I, too, had received some knocks along the way and was dealt the final blow fifteen years ago when I decided to end all contact.

It happened in the Narvesen kiosk in Bogstadveien on 13 March 1999.

In the years leading up to that date I had tried to have some contact with my family for the sake of my children because they were young and depended on me for seeing their grandparents, aunts and uncles, cousins; so that Mum wouldn't nag, push or tug at my conscience, but it was exhausting to act politely towards people who presented themselves as loving me. If I wrote Mum a simple postcard from Rome, I would immediately get a letter saying how much she was looking forward to seeing me at Christmas and to celebrate Christmas like a normal family. I would then be unable to control my emotions, I would get affronted, hysterical and feel taken for granted because things could never be normal again, they weren't normal, I had explained this to them over and over, but they refused to listen, they didn't want to listen, and how could they celebrate Christmas like a normal family? The mere thought made me want to throw up, I rang them and when they didn't pick up the phone, I left a vicious message saying I did *not* look forward to Christmas, that I did *not* look forward to seeing them, that the thought of seeing them filled me with horror and revulsion, that it was physically impossible for me to be in the same room as them. And yet the next morning I was ashamed of my anger, my aggression, my excessive, uncontrollable, juvenile emotions, so I called Astrid and begged her go to

Bråteveien and delete the angry message, but they had already heard it, she said, her voice trembling, so I realised that Mum and Dad were upset and distraught and that Astrid thought I was a terrible person for upsetting and distressing my aged parents. And I did feel bad, but I was upset too because I wanted Astrid to care about my feelings as well, but she didn't.

When I met Klara by the Narvesen kiosk later the same day and poured out my heart to her, she said I had to cut contact for good. You must stop seeing them.

Are you allowed to do that, I sobbed. Yes, she said, many people do so. And the thought of never having to see them again gave me instant relief. Not having to deal with them, to be free from tears and recriminations and threats, not having to make up excuses, not having to constantly defend and explain myself and yet never be understood, to sever all contact, was that even an option? Yes, she said. I didn't have to say or write anything, just make up my mind and I already had, I'll stop seeing them, I decided outside the Narvesen kiosk in Bogstadveien, and it was done.

Mum tried. Astrid tried, but I stayed silent. Eventually they gave up, the years passed, then Astrid started trying on special occasions. When Mum had surgery. Mum is having surgery, I just thought you ought to know. As if that changed everything. As if it meant that now I had to call them. As if I would change my stance in the light of illness, in the light of death. Would I? It would appear not because I soon forgot about her text message. When I happened to see it again the next day, I was pleased that I had forgotten it, but my reaction also caused me to wonder: Had a part of me always feared that such a message would make me doubt myself? If so that hadn't happened and I was pleased about that, I had succeeded in my efforts to cut the cord, I had silenced their reproachful, threatening, disappointed voices which had existed so powerfully inside me for over forty years. I texted her back saying I was sorry to hear that, that I hoped the operation would go well and that I wished Mum a speedy recovery. I soon gathered from Astrid that she didn't think that was enough, but what more could I do? Call and say what? Go to the hospital and throw my arms around Mum? I imagined myself driving to the hospital, entering the side ward where she lay, and everything in me rebelled. I imagined it again in order to relive the emotion, how everything inside me protested. It was impossible. I had no face with which I could meet her undoubtedly pitiful demeanour. I couldn't sit by her bedside, take her hand in mine and say that I loved her because I didn't. I had loved her once, I'd been incredibly close to her and dependent on her once, she was my mum, but that emotion belonged to the past and couldn't be resurrected because of the impact of what happened later. I felt no love and no longing for Mum and this lack of love and longing for Mum was, I knew, regarded by my family as a character defect in me, something I had to justify and defend. And I justified it and defended myself every time Astrid sent me messages along the lines of 'I just thought you ought to know.' Sometimes I had sent furious replies to such messages because Astrid treated me as though it were a matter of will, as though I could simply decide to turn up, to be nice, to make conversation. But Astrid deleted my furious emails unread, she wrote to me when I apologised for them the next morning, when filled with shame I wrote to her to apologise for my furious emails. Astrid had deleted my furious emails without reading them, she wrote, and that was her right, it was understandable, but it didn't stop me from feeling rejected and disappointed that Astrid didn't deal with their contents, never commented at all on the reasons I gave, didn't seem to reflect on where that

41

enormous rage of mine came from. *I just thought you ought to know.* So that it would be on my mind or I would call or turn up at the hospital. And so I didn't call, I didn't turn up and thus confirmed yet again that I was who they had decided I was, the heartless daughter, selfish and destructive. I just thought you ought to know and realise how bad you are. Forcing me into the role of the black sheep yet again and I was distraught because I just couldn't do it! My legs refuse to carry me! I jumped whenever the phone rang with an unknown number in case it was Mum. I looked her number up and stored it so that I would be able to see if it was her and not pick up. She might well decide to call me when she was ill because surely I wasn't so cruel that I would ignore a sick, possibly dying person?

And, besides, even if I'd managed to get myself to the hospital, even if my legs would have carried me there, then everything I said at her hospital bed—unless it was something furious which it would be inappropriate to say at a sickbed—would be interpreted as remorse and an admission on my part that their demands had been reasonable and my conduct unreasonable, evil, so it was impossible, why go there simply to betray myself?

But if I had truly succeeded in silencing their voices inside me, if their voices genuinely had no power over me now, surely I could go to the hospital and tell white lies? Make hospital small talk with Mum and get it over with. Why did it matter if Mum no longer mattered, why the need for honesty towards someone so irrelevant to me? Why couldn't I just give Mum what she wanted, give the family what it wanted, let Mum think that I repented, let the family think that I repented, perjure myself on this one occasion and be done with it, why was I so stubborn towards someone who no longer mattered. There were so many other lies in my life, what difference would one more make? Why couldn't I just go to the hospital and reel off stock phrases, then leave and be done with my quandary. So I was in a quandary, was I? No! There was no alternative, I knew I wouldn't be able to do it. How weak I was, how trapped.

Could I instead go to the hospital and speak my mind, was that an option? Go there and say that I stood my ground, that I repented nothing, that I had come to say goodbye. No! Impossible! Why? I couldn't work it out! Philosophers, where are you in my hour of need? In my mind I tried to cut contact again by making a decision like the one I'd taken at the Narvesen kiosk in Bogstadveien about not seeing them again, not allowing myself to be emotionally blackmailed, but I didn't experience the relief and comfort I had felt when I made my decisive break at the Narvesen kiosk in Bogstadveien in 1999.

Had it been merely a postponement, a brief respite from an insoluble problem? Because even if Mum didn't express a wish to see me before she died, Astrid would still call me when she died, and I would have to see them at the funeral or before. Surely I couldn't not go—or could I? And their behaviour towards me would be dismissive and disapproving because of my long absence. And Dad, whom I hadn't seen for years, a man I might no longer recognise, who had been poorly for reasons I was unaware of, he would be there, grieving, and I couldn't comfort him, I couldn't take part, but would remain only an outsider. That had been my choice, although I hadn't had a real choice, and now I would suffer the consequences of that choice. But it would also be uncomfortable for them, wouldn't it? So why did they continue to nag me, why was my presence so important to them? Because although it would be uncomfortable also for them, it would be

43

worse for me, was that what they were hoping for? The chance to watch me isolated and squirming, the chance to express their pent-up aggression towards me because I had upset my parents and they had had to pick up the pieces?

Or were my siblings angry with me and did they hate me because, consciously or subconsciously, they had wanted to do what I had done, break free, get away, did they resent me as one who had escaped the parental regime and thus made it more difficult for them to do likewise?

I should have emigrated to America, I thought, I should have sailed around the world and been somewhere on the ocean when it happened, then I would get an email in some port when it was all over, and the ocean would put our little lives, our little deaths into perspective.

But what opportunities for growth and resolution would I then have fled from? What if I was close to an epiphany, I asked myself, perhaps this was the moment, perhaps this was the challenge. And if I failed to meet it, I would never learn the most important lesson of all, but have made only half-hearted attempts and settled for easy answers.

But it hasn't been easy, I protested, it has been a struggle, an ordeal! But what if it's not over yet, I wondered to myself, perhaps this is the last leg of the race and I mustn't give up now.

I didn't sleep the night I had reread the I-just-thought-you-ought-to-know message from Astrid. To be reconciled, to forgive? But surely you can't forgive what people refuse to admit? Did I think they were capable of owning up to it? To finally admit the truth about the very thing they had devoted so much energy to repress and deny? Did I really think they would risk public censure in order to be reconciled with me? No, I wasn't worth that much, they had made that crystal clear to me on several occasions. But what if they admitted it just to me? If I wrote to Mum and Dad that they could admit it just to me, and that I would promise never to tell anyone. No, that wouldn't happen either, I was sure of it, because it didn't even exist between the two of them, they never talked about it, they had entered into a conspiracy to save their reputation, to maintain a level of self-respect; they had entered into an unspoken, unbreakable pact a long time ago in which they were the victims of their oldest daughter's mendacity and callousness, and as long as that version was believed, they remained on the receiving end of compassion, pity and care, and they couldn't manage without that, they fed on it, and it would be harder for them to get it if they ever admitted the truth to me, even if it stayed just between the three of us, harder to keep up their public image of them as the victims. They must be pitied. And there were times when I did pity them because of the mess they had created for themselves, because they were ill and old and would probably die soon, while I was in good health, touch wood, touch more wood, and only halfway through my life. You, too, are going to die, I told myself, by way of consolation. You might die tomorrow, I said, in order to strengthen my resolve. Why do they care, I called out to the sky, what do they want from me, I called out into the darkness. But they didn't care, not really, they hadn't cared for years.

Two days later I got a text message from Astrid saying all Mum's tests were fine. She would make a full recovery and was already feeling much better. As was Dad. I wrote that that was nice and asked her to say hi. I resumed my own life.

~

45

A month later Astrid called. She would be turning fifty soon and was having a party with lots of guests, people she thought I would enjoy meeting. She told me the date and I was free, she was pleased about that, she said, and then she paused and said that Mum and Dad would be there too. They so love a big party, she said, and didn't say 'one final' but it was in the air.

She would appear to think that something had changed. That although I hadn't turned up at the hospital when Mum had her operation, I had wished Mum a speedy recovery and probably realised that Mum could be gone for ever at any moment, and that I'd subsequently had a change of heart. It's merely abstract to her, I thought. But all too real to me. Having to enter a room where my parents were and shake hands? Hug them? Say what? The others had met up regularly during all these years, they were at ease in one another's company, I had chosen to distance myself and be the black sheep. Would I turn up, smiling, with a 'hiya'? As though we didn't see the world differently, in mutually exclusive terms, as though they weren't denying the very fabric from which I was made. Had Astrid no understanding of the reason why I had done what I had done, how deep it went? She talked to me as if it had been a whim, a fad, the result of a child-ish, rebellious urge which I could put aside when something really important happened. That I could 'pull myself together', make an intellectual decision to change my point of view, did she not understand the physical terror I felt at the thought of entering her house where I hadn't been for years, where Mum and Dad came all the time, and seeing them, my parents. To Astrid and to most other people, they probably came across as two harmless, fragile, old folks, but to me they were giants whose grip it had taken years of therapy to shake off, was that the prob-lem? Astrid didn't understand how I could be scared of two stooping, grey, old creatures, but I couldn't go to an airport without quaking with fear of accidentally bumping into them. What are you scared of, I would ask myself on the airport train. I forced myself to imagine seeing them, confronting them like you do to cure yourself of a phobia. What would happen if I reached the airport and they were in the check-in queue? Fear rippled through me! Well, so what? Would I walk straight past them? No. Too stupid, too immature for a woman over fifty to dodge them, to be unable to greet her own parents in a check-in queue. I hoped that I would stop and ask where they were going and they would tell me and then ask me where I was going and I would tell them and smile stiffly and add have a safe flight. A straightforward exchange, perhaps it would be easy to behave like an almost 'normal family', but no! Because afterwards I would have gone to the lavatory and locked myself in a cubicle and sat trembling on the loo seat and waited until they would surely have taken off, even if it meant missing my own flight. It was depressing that I had made so little progress, that it could catch up with me at any time because I didn't want it to catch up with me, I didn't want to be back there again, and yet here I was! I so wanted to be adult and calm and composed. I decided not to go to Astrid's birthday party, I would invent an excuse and forget all about it. But I couldn't do it. Because if my parents hadn't been invited, I would have gone to my sister's fiftieth birthday party to meet the people she worked with, who were likely to be exciting and interesting and possibly useful to me. That was my loss. That I was so inhibited and traumatised that I had to stay away from something that might have been good for me. All because of my stupid childhood. That should be my epitaph: All because of my stupid childhood. Over fifty, but still suffering from that fear of parental authority, which all children have.

Except my siblings appeared to have grown out of it. Perhaps Astrid had invited us all because she thought I was free of my childhood, that I had worked through my traumas and my fear of my parents? Perhaps she thought the only reason I hadn't turned up at the hospital was habit, and decided that it was time for a change. So the invitation could also be regarded as a compliment from Astrid, who thought I had made more progress than I had. Astrid, who believed that I was capable of turning up, all smiles, unaffected by my parents' presence, that I no longer cared about what they thought of me.

I said that I would think about it. I thought of nothing else. I went for long walks in the empty void of the forest and imagined that I was on another continent where no one could reach me. No one can reach you, I told myself, if you make yourself unreachable. Who are you, I asked myself, and who do you want to be and what yardstick do you measure yourself by.

The biggest?

I imagined myself walking through the once familiar streets on my way to Astrid's birthday party, a quiet Saturday afternoon in bright autumn light. Apples hanging ripe on the branches, heavy redcurrant bushes over the fences, bumblebees buzzing, and the smell of freshly cut grass. I inhale it gratefully, the bounty of the earth. Calmly I ring the doorbell and enter my sister's house.

Would I ever get there? No. I so badly wanted to be free, but I was trapped. I so badly wanted to be strong, but I was weak. My heart was pounding and I didn't know how to calm it. I knelt on the ground, pressed my face against my knees and sobbed.

~

That was three years ago.

It was such a long road.

I wondered where Bård was on his journey, and how different it was from mine.

I couldn't ask him that as we sat silent and awkward in the old-fashioned restaurant.

So instead I told him about the time Klara and I went to the old cabin on Hvaler with Tale and her friends, it was many years ago, back when I still had a small amount of contact with my family for the sake of my children. We had been playing music and dancing when Mum appeared in the doorway and asked if I had given the girls ecstasy.

Bård laughed, and I laughed with him, but I hadn't laughed then. Did Mum really think that I would give the girls drugs? I was speechless with shock, but Klara read the situation correctly and offered Mum a chair and a glass of wine. Klara had realised that Mum simply wanted to feel included. Mum had been sitting in the new cabin and could hear that we were having fun and had come up to join in. She probably didn't understand it herself, but that was what she wanted. Klara offered Mum a chair and a glass of wine, and Mum sat there for some minutes before she staggered drunkenly back down to the new cabin in the darkness. Poor Mum. Trapped in the new cabin with Dad. She had heard the sounds of good times coming from the old cabin and had come up to join us, but didn't understand it herself and turned her desire for company into a rebuke: Did you give the girls ecstasy?

Only I hadn't realised it because I was on the defensive.

I asked Bård if he had gone to Astrid's fiftieth birthday party. He hadn't. He had been invited, but he had been abroad at the time.

I said that I had been invited but hadn't gone because Mum and Dad would be there. I'm scared of them, I said, I told him that the thought of Mum and Dad terrified me. It doesn't terrify you, Bård said, but you feel a strong dislike.

Terror and a strong dislike, I said, and we smiled.

I told him that Tale no longer wanted to see the family in Bråteveien, that she refused to keep up appearances. I told him about a time when she and her family spent a summer weekend in the old cabin on Hvaler with another couple. The men went out in the boat and Mum and Dad came up to say hello and asked where the men were. They've gone out in the boat, Tale said, and Mum got hysterical because it was raining and the sea was choppy and it was late in the day and foggy and the water was cold, if they fell overboard they would drown, perhaps they were already dead. And Tale got nervous and didn't know what to do, Mum's anxiety, Mum's catastrophizing histrionics were starting to rub off on her. Dad was upset for different reasons, the men had taken the boat without first asking him, after all he owned the boat and the cabins, because the men had helped themselves and not shown him any respect. Tale stood mute in front of the upset owners through whose generosity she was there. Mum ordered her to come with her down to the jetty, a prisoner of her own anxiety, controlled by her overwhelming fear, which rubbed off on her surroundings, which had rubbed off on me my whole childhood, which had made me just as fearful towards the things that made her fearful such as alcohol and rock music. Tale stood with Mum at the end of the jetty, staring across the sea. I've stood here many times, Mum said. I've stood here many evenings and nights, looking across the sea as I prayed, she said, I've saved lives here!

I mimicked Mum's melodramatic style and Bård laughed. Mum was like that. I mimicked Dad's chastising style, Bård laughed. Dad was like that.

But that wasn't the real reason why Tale went home a day early and found it difficult to be on Hvaler and in Bråteveien. It was because later that evening when the men were safely back from their boat trip, her friend asked her why I, her mother, wasn't in touch with my parents, and Tale had to explain why and saw her friend's reaction. And because the next morning Mum came up to the cabin to ask Tale if she took good care of her child. She had had such bad dreams that night about how Tale wasn't taking proper care of her daughter: I had a terrible dream that you didn't take care of Emma. You do take good care of Emma, don't you?

Mum had had nightmares about Tale not looking after her daughter and had dumped her anxiety on Tale without any sense of shame because she lacked the ability or she was too scared to examine her bad dreams about Tale being a bad mother. Because who was it who had really failed to care for her own daughter, why did Mum have nightmares about a mother who neglected her daughter? She lacked the insight or she was too frightened to ask herself hard questions because then a void would have opened up.

It was Bo Schjerven who reminded me of that story when I was in turmoil once, weighed down by guilt because I had cut contact with Mum and Dad and was refusing to see them.

But they're going to die soon, I cried.

As are you one day, he said.

I had forgotten that.

As I left the Grand and walked up Karl Johans gate towards the metro station, I felt lighter than when I had arrived. It had been good to laugh about Mum with someone who knew her, to joke about our family with someone who knew it. I never laughed about Mum and the family when I spoke to Astrid. Whenever I had contact with her, I was always heavily burdened, I always felt very alone.

I called Klara and told her how we had laughed about Mum and Dad at the Grand. She asked: If you had the choice, which would you pick? A cabin on Hvaler *and* your parents or nothing?
Nothing.

That afternoon Bård texted me to say that every cloud has a silver lining. Love, your brother.
The silver lining being that he and I had found one another again.

December in Lars's cabin in the woods near the river, which was partly frozen and thus strangely quiet. Usually it would babble to anyone who listened carefully. Dark and cold and quiet, the trees black and mourning the summer, which had been taken from them, their branches spiky against the sky, yearning for snow, to be dressed in snow. I tended to work well when I was there, far from the city and the people, where Fido could run free.

December darkness with snow in the air that evening, but the next morning the grass lay green and the sun was strong as though we weren't in December. Then raw December, sudden darkness and red wine in the evening, bad dreams at night, low-lying fog in the morning only for the next moment to be bright and sunny as if it were spring, it didn't make any sense. I couldn't concentrate. I was restless, unedited theatre reviews were piling up. I had intended to write about the risks of dramatizing popular novels, but struggled for hours to find an angle, then I had an email from Bård, who had had an email from Åsa. She wrote that they would obtain new valuations. That the previous ones might have been rather low. However, it was up to the testator to decide how much money should be deducted for presents given as an advance of an inheritance, but by obtaining more quotes and valuations, Mum and Dad would have a basis for a fair estimate. If we were able to agree on a method of calculation, she thought that Mum and Dad would accept it.

It was up to Mum and Dad to decide, but if we could reach an agreement, she thought they would accept the new valuations. The implication being that if Bård continued to object, they would ignore them.

An hour later I received a copy of an email he had sent to Dad, Bård had gone off the deep end now, I recognised the deep end. He reminded Dad how he had always said that he would treat his children equally when it came to inheritance. So how was it fair to give two of his children the cabins on Hvaler as an advance of their inheritance without first having them valued? And presumably many years before the other two, Bergljot and I, he mentioned me by name, would inherit anything at all?

I've never caused you any trouble, he wrote, he was referring to me, who had caused them trouble and grief. You tell me how much you love me and my children, to that he would reply: Actions speak louder than words.

I sat in the forest with no peace. I imagined them gathering in Bråteveien to continue the myth of Bård as a troublemaker and Bård's wife as a warmonger, she had been allocated the role of the woman who had seduced Bård away from his family. I knew exactly how it would play out; once I had contributed to it myself, I had been so completely enmeshed in the family's version of its own story. It wasn't until I became estranged myself, until I had distanced myself, that I started to look at things differently, but still slowly, taking baby steps, such is the power parental stories have over a child's concept of reality that it's almost impossible to free yourself.

And had I managed to free myself? Or was I still stuck, and had the name of the villain merely changed?

I closed the Mac, got dressed, took the dog down to the river and let her off the leash. She didn't run away, she was loyal. I counted the rocks in the river, you couldn't see them in the spring and summer, in my mind I traced the river backwards, to the spring it had come from, its source, I walked along the bank for about an hour and then back in the darkness, alone on the path, as far as it was possible to go without being in another country. I went inside and turned on the Mac, and there was another email from Bård, he was well into it now, he was also tracing the river back to its source. He had received an email from Åsa, who assured him that there was a will which stated that Bård and I would be recompensed for the cabins, that new valuations would be obtained. Some blank spaces followed, then she wrote that it would have been easier to communicate with him if his tone had been less hostile: It's almost scary to receive an email from you.

He replied that she shouldn't forget that his original wish had been for the four of us siblings to share the cabins. We would then have had a natural place to meet with our children. It was sad, he wrote, that Astrid and she were opposed to that solution. He wrote that if she thought it scary to receive emails from him, it must be because she found it uncomfortable to read about how she and Astrid had behaved towards us. He would never understand why they refused him and his children half a cabin on Hvaler.

Lars turned up at the house in the woods. We cooked, we drank wine, I told him about Bård's emails. We went to bed together and afterwards, as we lay close, I told him what Åsa had written to Bård and what Bård had written to Åsa. Lars heaved a sigh and turned over to go to sleep saying that as far as he was aware then I had never shown any interest in getting a cabin on Hvaler. I don't want a cabin on Hvaler, I exclaimed, but I can understand why Bård objects! Don't you see why Bård objects, why he's upset? Lars looked at me, stunned, and sighed wearily: Yes, of course.

What was it like to be a normal human being?

I didn't know what it was like to be a normal human being, an undamaged human being, I had no experience other than my own. When distressing dreams woke me up at night, I would snuggle up to Lars, slip my right arm around his back and try to take over his dreams, which were undoubtedly peaceful. I tried to open my mind towards Lars so that his harmless dreams could flow into mine, I tried to suck the dreams out of his sleeping body, but it didn't work, there was no way in, I was trapped inside myself.

The next day, just after noon, as I tried to write about the risks of making plays based on novels, while Lars sat in the conservatory with coffee and newspapers, I got an email with an attachment from Bård. He had lain awake all night, he wrote, but now felt he had got everything out of his system by writing it down. It was wonderful to have articulated it and sent it, he wrote, he called it the last act in our little family drama.

To Dad

I want to tell you what kind of father I would have been, if I had had a son.

I would have tried to develop a close and strong relationship with my son.

I would have tried to steer him towards activities which he and I could enjoy doing together, both when he was young and also later.

I would have shown an interest in and got involved with his activities.

I would have supported him in these activities even if they didn't interest me to begin with, simply because they mattered to my son.

I would have felt true joy, delight and pride on seeing my son's happiness when he was doing those things I had supported him in, and which I knew he had worked hard to learn. I would have felt and expressed the same sentiments when it came to his education and career.

Once he had grown up and got himself a good education as well as professional experience, I would have asked his advice when it came to business matters where he had more competence than me.

I would have enjoyed some of my finest moments as a father and a human being by sharing experiences with my son.

You and I both know that you haven't behaved like that towards your only son.

I played hundreds of hockey and handball matches. You turned up to watch only one of these matches.

You never introduced me to activities that could have turned into something the two of us could have enjoyed doing together.

I know several of my friends' fathers better than I know you. I have been skiing more often with Trond's and Helge's fathers than I have with you.

I have three qualifications, and I have achieved a great deal in my professional life. Yet you have never said or indicated that you are proud of me or pleased on my behalf.

I have done very well in several types of sport throughout my life, but you have never shown any interest or support.

We can't live our lives over and we all have to live with our choices.

I have never asked much of you as a father, but I demand that you treat the four of us fairly when it comes to inheritance. You and I both know that it hasn't been like that so far, not even close.

Bård

I went to the conservatory. Lars was sitting in his thick, quilted jacket in a chair facing the lawn, the forest and the river, he wasn't reading the newspapers nor was he smoking, he was gazing at the lawn and the forest and the river, and I thought that he felt proud to own it, you can feel joy at ownership, a strange joy, a good and heart-warming if not a politically correct emotion, like the Maasai in Kenya or the Inuit in Greenland probably feel when they gaze across a landscape they regard as theirs although legally it isn't. Like I used to do a long time ago when I was alone on Hvaler as a young woman, alone with my children when they were small, in early autumn or in March, off season when most cabins were closed up and empty, when I would look across the archipelago, the sea and the rocks I knew so well, and feel a sense of belonging and something which could be called pride. Not being able to be on Hvaler had been a great loss, a consequence of my estrangement, but I'd had no choice, and compared to what I had gained in terms of peace of mind by my estrangement, Hvaler meant little.

I tapped Lars on the shoulder and asked if I could read something to him. He looked at me, hoping it didn't have anything to do with inheritance. I sat down and it started to snow. Look, he said. Big flakes whirled in the air, unwilling to settle, like blossom falling from the apple and cherry trees in June. We each chose a snowflake and followed it until it landed and melted. It'll be Christmas soon, he said. I looked at my watch, December 10. Fido chased after the flakes trying to catch them, childhood was unreal. Ice hockey matches and piano lessons unreal. I was loath to look back. I remember thinking on my way to school, in Year Three, when I was wearing a new orange dress which I was so proud of, that I would have been happy if it hadn't been for *that*.

Perhaps Dad was reading Bård's email right now, it had been sent seven minutes ago. I tried to imagine him, but it was so long since I had seen him and I had never seen him in front of a computer, I had no idea what kind of computer he had, where he kept it, in his study, in the living room or in the kitchen. It must be horrible for a father to receive such a message from his son, his only one, his firstborn. Poor old Dad, grey-haired and stooping, his glasses perched on his nose, I'm guessing now, peering at the screen while he clicked on the inbox. To Dad from Bård. A huge amount of compassion welled up in me. The old man who couldn't escape his past, who was forced to carry his past mistakes with him for the rest of his life, and I was overcome with guilt for what I had done by becoming estranged from that poor old man.

Then I reminded myself that the father I pitied wasn't my dad, but an imaginary dad, the archetypal father, the mythical father, my lost father. I reminded myself that my actual father, the person I knew, wouldn't be moved by Bård's letter, but would instinctively go on the offensive. Dad's final words to me, the last time I spoke to him on the telephone seven years ago were: If you want to see a psychopath, just look in the mirror.

It was a sunny Saturday morning at the start of June, I was sitting on the windowsill in a function room after an end-of-year party with a man from the events committee. We had finished clearing up and were enjoying a beer.

He told me that he had studied with my sister Åsa, in Trondheim. I didn't know that, how funny, he told funny stories about their university days in Trondheim. I was giddy and laughing as I called Åsa, to whom I hadn't spoken for years and said: Guess who I'm having a chat and a beer with and handed my phone to the man and he spoke to her, and it was fine, it was good fun. Then I called Bård, to whom I hadn't spoken for years either and said something similar, and he laughed, it was fine, perhaps a part of me had been missing Bård and Åsa since I had called them now that I was drunk and my defences were down. I called Astrid and said something similar and it was fine, although she was more guarded, she knew me better, she was aware that my moods fluctuated and she could probably hear that I had been drinking, then I called Mum and Dad, seeing as I was on a roll, I can't have been thinking straight, I acted on impulse, believing perhaps that it would be fine as it had been when I called the others. Mum answered the phone and I was about to say something funny about the man who had studied with Åsa in Trondheim when I heard her whisper and it must have been to Dad: It's Bergljot. And perhaps she put us on speaker phone, I thought afterwards when the conversation was over and had

60

ended the way it had, she probably put us on speaker to show Dad that she was on his side and wouldn't whisper with me without him being able to hear what was said, or maybe he demanded that she put it on speaker. Mum refused to let me say a word about the man who had studied with Åsa in Trondheim, she went straight to the point, asking aggressively how I could treat her and Dad so badly, be so ungrateful when they had always done their best for me, helped me in every possible way, what had they ever done to me that made me so horrible to them? I was completely unprepared for her reaction, with hindsight it's mind-boggling that I could have been so foolish, what had I imagined, that they would chat light-heartedly with the man who had studied with Åsa in Trondheim? I had been naïve and I came crashing down to earth. When Dad dies, I said, then you'll stop asking those questions, then you'll come round, I said, but by then it'll be too late, I said, and Dad then spoke because Mum had probably put the call on speaker: If you want to see a psychopath, just look in the mirror.

I had often thought that if Dad died first, then Mum would start to see things my way, but also that by then it would be too late. Once he had uttered those words, then it was too late. That was who I had become, who I had chosen to become, merciless. If you want to see a psychopath, just look in the mirror! That was who Dad had become, who Dad had chosen to become or he hadn't had what he regarded as a real choice, he'd had to become merciless. I was convinced that Dad was incapable of feeling what Bård wanted him to feel, and so Bård's email wouldn't have the desired effect. To Dad Bård's email would merely be evidence of his ingratitude, the word he had used about Bård and me. And Mum and Astrid and Åsa would shake their heads at Bård's email, if they

61

ever got to read it. A grown man, almost sixty years old, chiding his old father over nothing.

The email wouldn't be shown to anyone but Astrid and Åsa. Should it become necessary to talk about it, to explain the situation to the rest of the family, they would say that Bård at nearly sixty was so juvenile that he was still cross with his father for not going to more of his handball matches when he was a little boy.

The email would be water off a duck's back, and Bård knew it, he probably had no expectations of ever being understood, but for his own peace of mind he had felt a need have his say as explicitly as he had before it was too late.

I read it aloud to Lars. He listened carefully. Wow, he said when I had finished and then he fell quiet. Lars was a father, Lars had a son. Wow, he said again and grew pensive. The snow fell. We all want our fathers to notice us, he then said. That's what it's all about. The snow fell and the dog ran around the snow to catch the flakes. That's the most important thing for a son, he said, for his father to notice him. That's why Bård wrote to his father, he said.

We sat in silence for a while. Then he said that his father had also been quite distant. That many fathers of that generation were and that back then it wasn't like today where fathers often turn up for hockey and handball games. Had my father merely been a little distant? No, I said. Because even distant fathers were proud of their sons when they won sailing competitions and ski races and would boast about their successful sons to other fathers, but Dad was incapable of giving Bård a single word of praise, of uttering one positive adjective about Bård. Dad was scared. If you're scared, never let them see you tremble, and Dad didn't dare tremble or

62

show any signs of weakness, which is what he believed a compliment to Bård would represent. Dad's regime was sustained by fear. His fear that everything might come tumbling down if he showed weakness. Dad could only accept Bård if he was humble and submissive, but Bård didn't want to be. Dad hated Bård getting rich—although money was Dad's yardstick—because once Bård grew rich Dad lost that power over him, which money represents.

I'm glad I'm not rich, Lars said.

Dad has probably mellowed over the years, I said, that was my impression, but he has painted himself into a corner as far as Bård is concerned. And he isn't capable or willing to come out of it.

Bård hasn't included the worst, I said. He merely lists the symptoms. I'm guessing the worst is too difficult to enter into and express because then he would have to become a little boy again.

December 10 and snow. I gave up doing any work, we went for a silent walk in the snow, the world was quiet and white. Lars left that night in a snowstorm and I was alone once more. The darkness came and with it came more snow. I sat in the conservatory and I smoked, although I don't smoke. There was no wood burning stove there, so I wrapped up warm, I was completely covered up, I smoked and I drank wine, and I looked at the falling snow. I ought to be writing, editing articles, I smoked and drank in the darkness and looked at the snow, which grew higher.

When I went indoors in just after midnight, I saw that Mum had called. I had stored her number, so I wouldn't accidentally answer the phone in case she called. She had left another message. She asked me to call her. It was this business with Bård and the cabins. Her voice wobbled as it usually did when she wanted to tug at my heartstrings, like when I was a little girl and she would sit on the edge of my bed and tell me how much it hurt her, how she would get chest pains when I didn't do what she had told me to, when she doused me with her pain before she left, closing the door behind her, her heart unburdened, I presume, while I lay behind with mine pounding. All the times she had called me, despairing at her relationship with Rolf Sandberg, all the times she had called me to tell me she was going to kill herself and how I would spend hours consoling her and talking her out of it because we loved her so much and needed her so much, she had used me up with that tremble in her voice, which suffered as it expressed her suffering.

She had called because she believed that I would reiterate the statement I had made when she called three years ago not long after I had received the Christmas letter about the will, that I would say what she needed to hear, which was that I didn't want a cabin on Hvaler, that I thought their will was generous—if their will was still the one referred to in the Christmas letter, that is. Because it might have been changed, but whether or not it had been, the circumstances had and were now different from when she had called me three years ago when I was in San Sebastian. I went to bed and slept badly, Bård's email was on my mind. The next morning I wrote to ask him if he wanted me to tell the family that I shared his view of the conflict. It took a while before he replied. He wrote that he thought I should either stay silent or declare that I too felt unfairly treated.

I could see what he was saying. What he was pointing out. That I was offering to back him but was unwilling to enter the fray and express my own opinion.

But I didn't want to argue about cabins and inheritance! I had always said that I didn't care for any of it. I couldn't very well join in now and demand something, it was beneath my dignity!

But then again I did share his feeling of having been let down by Dad, and by Mum who was loyal to Dad, I shared his view that the valuations were laughable, I agreed with him that Åsa and Astrid were behaving appallingly. Should I leave him all alone on stage like the villain, then sneak in and hide in his shadow?

I called Klara.

She said that I had failed to rock the boat for far too long, that it was exactly what Mum and Dad had wanted when they told us about their will that Christmas three years ago, for me not to rock the boat. It left them free to tear up the will or write a new one at any time, while all along I did nothing and regarded them as generous.

I wrote to Bård that I would write to Astrid and Åsa.

Incomprehensible Publications closed after one issue, and financial necessity forced Klara to work evenings and nights at Renna. Klara was exhausted and fed up with guests and staff treating her flat as a late-night drinking den and the married man treating her like dirt. The married man finally ended it with Klara, she was devastated and sinking fast. I need a change of air, she gasped.

I worked on the editorial while the email I had promised Bård came together in my head. When I had submitted the editorial late that evening, I opened a new document and poured myself a glass of wine to strengthen my resolve, then suddenly it couldn't happen soon enough, suddenly it was of the utmost importance to me or perhaps I was scared that I might get cold feet, I wrote as if in a trance and sent it to Bård, although it was late, asking if he thought it was too long.

To Astrid and Åsa
Subject: Cabins on Hvaler

I wrote that, because I had expected no inheritance, I was pleasantly surprised at getting the Christmas letter three years ago which stated that we would all inherit equally. That was why when Mum had called to say that Bård was raising hell because of the cabins, I had said that I thought their will was generous. But that I regretted now, I wrote, that I hadn't phoned Bård, given that I had later learned that he had merely asked Mum and Dad to consider another and fairer solution, namely that the cabins were shared between us four children so that all the grandchildren could enjoy them. This had been dismissed without explanation, and I didn't think it was surprising that Bård had got upset at that or that he was upset now when they had been transferred in secret and at such ridiculously low valuations. After all, Bård had never, unlike me, distanced himself from the family, so why should he be treated differently from his younger sisters?

I wrote that now we knew the cabins had already been transferred in secret and at such low valuations, we must assume the intention was to ensure Bård and me would be left as little as possible in the final will. In other words, more would be given to two branches of the family and less to the other two. Of course this was seen as an injustice and a betrayal. And them blaming Bård for Mum's overdose on top of everything else was particularly nasty, I wrote, making him out to be the bad guy while they themselves looked good and caring at the hospital. I wrote in anger that the responsibility for the current situation really lay with both of them who, if they had wanted to, could have used their influence to dissuade Mum and Dad from doing what they had now done.

I calmed down, poured myself another glass of wine and continued by mentioning that in one of my recent conversations with Astrid she had wondered whether Bård might be jealous of her and Åsa. No, we weren't jealous, I wrote, but we had had a very different childhood to them, our experience of Mum and Dad was very different to theirs. They both had degrees and worked in professions which emphasised rights and equality before the law, the importance of examining both sides of an issue, and the fact that they showed no willingness to understand how Bård and I viewed the situation was depressing. Then I added: *The fact that neither of you has at any point asked me about my side of the story, I've experienced and continue to experience as deeply hurtful.* It needed to be said, I felt. In conclusion, I wrote that throughout our childhood and adulthood Bård and I had been given less than them, emotionally as well as materially, and the fact that we were now passed over so blatantly was distressing to us and our families, especially the realisation that Astrid and Åsa clearly endorsed such discrimination. Regards, Bergljot

Bård replied immediately that it wasn't too long, that everything must be included and he pointed out some typos. I would correct them in the morning, I replied, I didn't want to send it now given how late it was so that Astrid would simply dismiss it as she was wont to do with my angry night-time emails. She deleted them unread, she claimed.

I appreciated that Astrid was in a tricky situation, that she risked being everybody's whipping boy, that Mum probably dumped things on her because she was the only one still in contact with me, that she would alternately be made to pay the price for being in contact with me and then be pressurized to put pressure on me to reconcile with our parents, I appreciated that Astrid was caught between a rock and a hard place, that it was unfair, that she, the only one of my siblings who kept in touch with me, was the one I heaped all my rage upon. I understood, I told her that I understood when I apologised profusely the next morning, and she would reply that she appreciated my apology and that she had deleted my night-time emails unread. Perhaps she said it to reassure me. Did she think that my night-time emails were so awful that she could see why I would regret them and thus she pretended not to have read them for my sake? I did regret my angry night-time emails, I felt remorse when I woke up the next morning and wild panic at the thought of what I had written the night before, but at the same time I was hurt that Astrid dismissed them as trivial, read or unread, because my furious night-time emails were the most truthful, and I regretted them only because I had learned that speaking the truth was against the rules, that speaking the truth would get you punished.

Klara was down in the dumps, Klara had hit rock bottom, Klara was almost broke, she needed a change of air.

I started my theatre degree without having to take out a student loan, I was married to a wealthy, kind and decent man, but unhappily in love with a married university professor who was going to stay married, I realised, although he was having an affair with me, although he had had affairs with many other women, I heard countless stories about how the man I loved was with other women, and it hurt me just as deeply as if he had been my husband, it cut me to the heart like a knife. I couldn't bear the married man's infidelity and I couldn't stay married to the nice, decent man when I felt like this about another man, I wanted a divorce although Mum told me to think about my children. I thought about my children, who were seven, six and three years old, but I had to get a divorce because I couldn't share a bed with the nice man when I was constantly thinking about another man and yearned to be in bed with him, when I suffered due to the married man's infidelity towards his wife and our love. How could I, what was wrong with me, who loved a notorious womaniser rather than my faithful, kind husband, what was wrong with me, who nagged and shouted at my kind, easy-going husband and destroyed him, or so it felt? I was horrible to him and had terrible thoughts about him and told myself that he must have gone to our older daughter's bedroom at night when all he had done was fall asleep in front of the television, what was wrong with me for having such thoughts?

I had to get a divorce, I had no choice. I had lost the married man I couldn't forget and I would lose the nice man I had to forget because he deserved better than me. I braced myself for the loss and went to see Klara who was in bed, shaking, because she had just found out that her father killed himself. She had discovered that her father hadn't drowned *accidentally*, as she had always believed, but had in fact drowned himself. What a difference those twelve letters made. Klara had gone to a family party and overheard her father's sisters whisper while she was behind the door taking off her coat, if only Nils Ole hadn't drowned himself. It was like a knife to Klara's heart and throat, everything fell into place. The fog and confusion of the past cleared, but the realization was painful like a knife slicing through flesh, like sharp glass in the eye, like piercing jets of icy water. He had drowned himself. He had walked into the sea on purpose and kept on going until he drowned, he hadn't fallen from a jetty, he hadn't been drunk. He had been sober and he had stepped out into the sea cold sober, intending to die. Even though Klara was only seven years old, he had drowned himself and she lost her dad, what was he thinking when he drowned himself depriving Klara of her dad, when he walked out into the sea, never to see her again, how desperate he must have been, but how could he have been so desperate when Klara existed and loved him and was only seven years old?

Everyone had known except her. That was the family secret which filled them all with shame and which was never mentioned, which they wouldn't tell her, the daughter. In one respect the discovery set her free because she had always sensed that something was terribly wrong but had concluded that there must be

71

something terribly wrong with her. But there wasn't. He had drowned himself.

She couldn't take any more, she said, she needed a change of air.

The night before Monday 14 December, I couldn't sleep. The clock turned two, the clock turned three, I read my email over and over, tomorrow I would send it, tomorrow I would join the battle.

Monday 14 December. Everything was quiet when I woke up at eleven o'clock, the snow thick, calm and white on the grass outside, on the trees, on the car, all sharp edges were gone, everything outside was curved and soft.

My hands were shaking as I made coffee, turned on my Mac and sat down, but I didn't have the energy to read the text yet again, so I skimmed through it and sent it still with typos just to get it over with.

It had been sent. It could be read. I had joined the battle. I would like to have stayed in the quiet, white forest where I felt more unavailable than in the car, than on the motorway and certainly more than at home where a bus went past fifty metres from my house so that passengers as well as anyone who walked by and the neighbours would know if I was in, if the light was on, if my car was in the drive, if my dog was in the yard, if there were noises coming from my house and, in the winter, when there was snow, when there were footprints in the snow. I could choose not to answer my phone, avoid going online, I could crawl under my duvet and pretend to be out, but if anyone came to my door and

73

saw my footprints in the snow, they would know that I was there. What if someone were to turn up and ring the doorbell and bang on the door and walk around my house to the garden door and bang on it too and shout out my name in a commanding, furious: Bergljot!

I would have liked to stay in Lars's house in the woods far away, I would have liked not to have to ruin the pretty, undulating crust of the snow with my nervous footprints, but the text I needed to edit was at home so I had to go back.

My email had been sent, it could be read, perhaps it was being read right now. I meant what I had written, that wasn't the problem, so what was it?

I cleaned Lars's house and packed my things and dreaded my mobile ringing. I got into my car, restless and troubled, for what, for what? For that which would happen next. Ten minutes later when I had joined the motorway and was doing one hundred kilometres an hour, I heard the email notification from my iPhone on the seat next to me, an act of war, was my guess. I didn't dare open it while I was driving, but neither could I wait to read Astrid's response, I looked for a lay-by, an exit, but there was none, what had she written, what had she replied? Then a sign announced a Statoil petrol station in one kilometre and I accelerated to one hundred and twenty and pulled into it, I stopped the car, my hand was shaking and I forgot the code to my phone, what the hell was it, what had she written?

She wrote that she had seen that I had sent an email about the situation. That she had also written an email about the situation.

Before reading my email, she would send hers first. She felt, she wrote, that hers was an account of many of the facts in the case. She regretted not having sent it earlier, but she had been away. She would also send it to Bård this afternoon, but right now she was on her way to a meeting. She would read my email as soon as her meeting was over.

I called Klara, my head spinning. I called her with the feeling I so often got whenever I was in contact with Astrid. I felt that I had detonated a bomb while Astrid reacted as if I had merely said boo. I felt that I was threatening her with an axe, she reacted as though I was waving a plastic knife in the air. She wasn't scared of me, nor did she respect me or take me seriously. Astrid wants to set the agenda, Klara said. She wants the discussion to be on her terms, not yours.

I drove home and up my snow-covered drive, thus revealing that I was in. I didn't open Astrid's email, I would delete it unread, as she did mine. But perhaps she was lying, she probably was, I too was capable of lying.

Hi everyone, she wrote and apologised for her late response, but she had been away. As she hadn't previously put anything in writing, she had decided to compose this email. She thought it was important that we all listened to one another and so she wanted to have her say.

The situation had taken a very unpleasant turn, she wrote, she had been very angry and upset. The way she saw it, the starting point of the conflict was a valuation which was too low, but then misunderstandings and distrust combined with poor communication had led to accusations and emotional outbursts and the situation had escalated. In order to find a solution we had to get back to the starting point: the cabin valuations. But before she introduced proposals for a resolution, she wanted to comment on Bård's allegations about Mum and Dad.

She wrote that she didn't think that Mum and Dad were being unfair or that they didn't want us to inherit equally. On the contrary, she was convinced that was precisely what they wanted. She had spent a lot of time with them in recent years, and they had said so often. It was also the stated intention of the will. Mum and Dad had repeatedly said that they were pleased to be able to leave something for their children. So she thought we ought to be grateful and mindful of how lucky we were. As a result she was distressed that so much anger and aggression were being directed at Mum and Dad. Nobody is perfect, she wrote, everyone makes mistakes, including Mum and Dad. She had made mistakes in her life, she wrote, as had we probably. She thought it was sad to see our parents upset while we argued about assets we hadn't created, but which were a result of their lifelong work.

Arithmetical equality was straightforward when it came to money, she wrote, but it was more difficult when applied to the cabins. However, people had resolved such issues before and it was usually done by establishing the current market value and then compensating financially those who didn't get the cabins. Mum and Dad's decision that she and Åsa would inherit the cabins was therefore no reason to claim that they were being unfair, as long as Bård and I were properly compensated. The challenge was to establish the correct market price. There was much to suggest that the first valuation had been too low although it had been carried out by a certified appraiser. In hindsight it was unfortunate that they hadn't asked two separate estate agents, since the valuations they got had led to suspicions about Mum and Dad's motives and accusations of unfairness.

She had some sympathy for Bård's argument that he and I had been short-changed, she wrote, yet she felt we ought to understand Mum and Dad's decision, which according to her, was quite natural. It was a simple continuation of the cabin situation as it had been for the last twelve to thirteen years, and with which Mum and Dad were comfortable. That was an important point, she wrote. Åsa and her had spent a lot of time on Hvaler with Mum and Dad in recent years, and they had all really valued that. By Åsa's and her taking over the cabins now, the status quo could be maintained while ensuring that Mum and Dad could continue to spend time on Hvaler in future. Given that this was Mum and Dad's wish and seeing as they were their cabins, she thought we ought to respect it. It was neither surprising nor unreasonable that she and Åsa would inherit the cabins while we would be compensated financially, it was merely the result of how our lives had turned out. Many years ago when we four siblings took over the use of the old cabin, we had agreed usage and the payment of bills. But about thirteen years ago Bård stopped going, and we sisters shared the use and the financial responsibility. Then Bergljot stopped using the old cabin, although she would sometimes borrow Mum and Dad's cabin and her children occasionally the old cabin. Then she and Åsa took over paying the bills and the maintenance and in recent years Åsa and her family had spent more time in the new cabin, either alone or with Mum and Dad, and taken over much of the practical responsibility there. Astrid had taken over the old cabin where she paid the bills and dealt with the practicalities. Ebba and Tale and her family had spent one or two weeks in the old cabin every summer, she wrote, but that wasn't true, she was exaggerating. And Søren had been there in connection with his work, she wrote, and everyone had thought that was great fun. If Bård's children wanted to visit the cabins, that could only be a good thing.

77

She wrote that it could be argued that Mum and Dad should have put off the transfer of the cabins, but she understood their decision because the cabins were old and in need of maintenance and the bills needed paying. After all, Mum and Dad were eighty and eighty-five years old respectively. Given that they also had Bråteveien, it had all become too much for them. It had also suited Åsa and her to clarify the ownership because it reflected the effort they put into maintenance etc. And it was nice for Mum and Dad to know that the cabins wouldn't be sold and that they could continue to go there for the rest of their lives. That was a perfectly understandable sentiment, she wrote. Just as we were concerned with our own feelings in the matter, we had to respect Mum's and Dad's feelings. After all these were assets they had created and had total ownership of, she reiterated. Perhaps they could have communicated the matter better and obtained two valuations, but it wasn't a question of unfairness.

She also believed that the matter should now be resolved by obtaining two new valuations from different appraisers. For information she wanted me to know that the second estate agent had come up with a higher valuation for both cabins than the first one. Four new valuations were probably the closest we could get to an actual market value. Then Åsa's and her inheritance could be reduced proportionally. We were welcome to contribute to the process, she wrote, and if the four of us could agree on a figure and put to Mum and Dad that they used the new valuation as their basis, they had said that they would then do so. Thus the matter could be resolved. She thought it was of the utmost importance that the conflict was resolved. It was not only difficult for Mum and Dad and us four siblings, it might also hurt our children. Her children valued their cousins greatly, she wrote, and had expressed a wish to see more of them; they always had such a nice time whenever they met up. All our children had much to lose if contact between them was made difficult because of us. She also knew that Mum and Dad were anxious not to lose contact with Mari and Siri.

She and Jens had told their children that any disagreement between us in this matter had nothing to do with them, and that it mustn't affect their otherwise good relationship with their cousins.

Even if we couldn't all get one hundred per cent of what we wanted, she concluded, she hoped that we would now do our bit to end the conflict. As she had said earlier, Åsa and she would contact some local estate agents straightaway. Love, Astrid

The elephant in the room wasn't mentioned, the real reason I had stopped coming to Hvaler and Bråteveien; it was as if I didn't exist, as if my story didn't exist.

So you're saying that your personal history should affect the inheritance issue, I asked myself, and the cabin dispute?

Yes, I replied, not entirely convincingly.

Everything is connected. No words are ever totally innocent to someone who is seeking to understand.

An hour after Astrid's email, I got a text message from her.

She must have read my email in the meantime and realised that the problem wasn't quite as simple as she had imagined in her account of the facts of the matter. She happened to be in my neighbourhood, she wrote, and would like to stop by.

But I didn't want to see her, I didn't want to be talked round, I didn't want to be entangled in her therapy jargon now that I had finally found the courage to speak up. I wrote that I wasn't in, that I had gone to Lars's house in the woods. I turned off my mobile and my Mac and went to bed with earplugs and the duvet pulled over my head so I wouldn't hear if she decided to come over anyway and saw my fresh, treacherous footprints in the snow and the dog's paw prints and realised that I was in after all, so I wouldn't hear her if she knocked on the windows and the doors, I prayed to God that it would start snowing again so that our tracks would be obscured.

The last time Klara saw her father was when he drove her to school. She was in Year One. Her mum had given her a big green apple with her packed lunch; back then big green apples were a rare treat. Klara couldn't wait to take the apple to school, placing it on her desk, eating it.

Just as she was getting out of the car, after her father had pulled up in front of the school and they were about to say goodbye, he asked if he could have the apple. Klara was confused and upset, but she gave him the apple. But what if she hadn't?

I stayed under the duvet until the darkness was dense, until the world was quiet, the buses had stopped running and the lights had been switched off in the neighbouring houses, until the least fearful time of the night when everyone was asleep, including human rights activists. I lit a fire and drank to calm myself, then I reread Astrid's email. She wrote that Tale had spent weeks on Hvaler every summer, but Tale had only been on Hvaler two days over two summers, and she had had to put pressure on Astrid to be allowed to stay in the old cabin for those two days over those two summers because it had apparently been difficult for Astrid to find convenient dates, Astrid was already planning her summers as if she owned and could use the cabin as she pleased. Astrid had made Tale feel that she was being a nuisance, and it hadn't been much fun on Hvaler, Astrid herself hadn't been there, and Mum and Dad had interfered with everything.

And then there was Astrid's didactic approach, her desire to lecture us all on the nature of the conflict as if she wasn't a part of it.

And her honest broker attitude, how indirectly and gently she told us to pull ourselves together, to show gratitude. Although we wouldn't get one hundred per cent of what we wanted, she hoped that we would now do our bit to end the conflict, wrote she who had got exactly what she wanted.

But the bit about making mistakes was the worst. How everybody makes mistakes. That Mum and Dad had probably made mistakes. That she herself had made mistakes. How magnanimous of her, how full of self-awareness was Astrid that she could admit that she had made mistakes, unlike the rest of us, Bård and me, so that by admitting her own fallibility, she became the least flawed of us all. If we just examined ourselves and thought carefully, she was in effect saying, then we would discover that we, too, had made mistakes and then we could surely forgive Mum and Dad the odd mistake. She encouraged us to examine ourselves and assumed the role of the mentor, the role of the adult towards us, her older siblings, as though we were uncontrollable, thoughtless children at the mercy of our emotions, who needed to be taught civilisation and psychology. I drank more and got more worked up and ended up at the mercy of my emotions and couldn't not write and didn't want to not write, everybody makes mistakes, are you kidding me, I wrote, incandescent and furious yet utterly clearheaded and I sent my email that evening on 14 December at ten past midnight, although something inside me told me not to do it.

Everybody makes mistakes, you write, wrote I, and that you yourself have made mistakes, that you assume everyone has and so on and so forth in a vague, politically correct tone, thus trivialising what happened to me. Or haven't you understood anything after all these years? Never taken it seriously? It would seem that you haven't. And that feels like an abuse in itself. When you meet victims of human rights abuses, is that what you tell them? Everybody makes mistakes?

I continued still incandescent, hammering on the keyboard: When I was five years old, when you were around two and Mum had just had Åsa, Mum took the two of you to Granny's and Grandad's in Volda for a break, and Dad was left alone with Bård and me in Skaus vei number 22. Bad things happened upstairs. Dad drank a lot. Bård was six years old and probably didn't understand very much, only that something was terribly wrong. Do you want details?

I sent it to Astrid and copied in Bård and Åsa, I didn't get a response, of course I didn't, they were asleep, and we're all children when we sleep as Rolf Jacobsen writes, except that's not true, it's a lie because we relive our battles in our dreams, it's the rule rather than the exception, and so I was reluctant to fall asleep and I drank in order to sleep and read and reread my own text over and over, I read it and I drank myself to sleep. I woke up late the next morning, the clock said five, but it wasn't true, it was light outside. I checked on my Mac, it showed ten past noon, my watch had stopped, the battery must be dead. I hadn't got any emails from Åsa or Astrid, nor had I expected any, well at least not from Åsa, what could she say, I had never written like that to her before. If she had heard the story, as she must have done, from Mum and Dad, who needed to explain my absence, then it was their version that she would know and I had no idea what that was like, but I presumed it was about my overactive imagination, which I'd always had even as a child, how good I was at making things up and telling tales, as well as me probably wanting someone to blame for my unhappiness, my outrageous behaviour, my divorce, or it was something a therapist had planted in me, the possibilities were endless. Perhaps she had deleted my email unread on advice from Astrid, who had probably deleted hers unread. Astrid was waiting for an apology, only this time she wouldn't get one, she wouldn't get one because I still felt angry the next morning despite my hangover. No, I didn't want Astrid to become estranged from Mum and Dad as well, her defending them worked to my

85

advantage, it set me free; if Åsa and Astrid hadn't sided with Mum and Dad, my cutting off contact would have been far harder, my sense of guilt far greater, and it was bad enough as it was, but it provoked me that Astrid had never been open to the truth and thus the gravity of what I had said, and that she wrote that Mum and Dad could make mistakes like everybody else. That was her mistake, Astrid's mistake. She claimed to be neutral, but deep down she wasn't because sweet-talking everyone isn't being neutral if one party has hurt the other, only she didn't factor that in or she didn't believe it. She didn't seem to understand or be willing to accept that there were conflicts which couldn't be resolved in the way she would like them to be, that there are situations which can't be balanced out, talked over and round, where you have to pick a side.

Klara needed a change of air. Anton Vindskev had the answer. Klara first met Anton Vindskev at Renna. He had ordered lamb kebabs, but they had run out and his girlfriend got uppity and insisted that they serve lamb kebabs to Anton Vindskev because he was Norway's greatest poet. Klara said she refused to believe that. So who, in your opinion, is Norway's greatest poet, he asked her. Stein Mehren, Klara said, or Jan Erik Vold, she said, but definitely not you. And that was how Klara and Anton Vindskev became friends. He later moved to Copenhagen because he wrote well there. When Klara realised that her father had killed himself and she was feeling at her lowest and needed a change of air, Anton suggested that she rent a room in his flat in Copenhagen. Klara went to Copenhagen for a breath of fresh air.

I divorced the nice, decent man. I moved from the big airy house to a smaller house, I carried tables and chairs and plates, the whole of my half of our marital assets to my car and drove from the big house to a smaller one. I was hurting. I had lost the decent, nice man, and before that I had also lost my great passion, the married professor, I suffered from the loss of two men, but knew that I was doing the right thing, that it was the first step on the road to an inevitable destination. It was something I had to do, I carried tables and chairs, I carried it all in the certain knowledge that I was doing the right thing even though I couldn't explain my certainty to anyone, not even myself, or rather least of all to myself. I had lost, it was my own fault, had I wanted to lose? But why? It was my fault that the children had lost their home. Mum had begged me not to get a divorce, had pleaded with me to think of the children, my poor children, but still I left.

Klara was in Copenhagen. I was divorced, I was alone, it was my choice, I had made my bed and could lie in it.

The married man had found himself a new mistress, I couldn't blame him. My ex-husband soon found himself a new girlfriend, another woman to be kind to, I couldn't blame him either. I had to grin and bear it, I had chosen this myself. I didn't complain to my family, they had warned me, told me to think of the children, and I had thought of the children, but not in the way that they wanted me to think of them, and I got divorced. Dad helped me renovate the bathroom in my new house, sometimes I would drive back to my new home, see Dad's car parked outside and feel alarmed. Dad couldn't have a key to my new home, it was unacceptable, Dad couldn't be allowed to come and go as he pleased, turn up out of the blue, no way, I grew scared that he might suddenly be there, turn up unannounced, in the middle of the night even. I didn't dare tell him, but I had to say that he couldn't have his own key, I hoped he would finish the bathroom soon. The bathroom was finished, I still didn't dare ask Dad if I could have my key back, but as long as Dad had a key, he could walk into my new home at any time.

I existed in a trance of fear, of loss, it was fog and confusion, I did the laundry. It felt like I was drowning in laundry, I hated doing the laundry, back when my life was normal, that is to say numb, I used to regard it as the dullest, most exhausting chore, having to do the never-ending laundry. The contents of the laundry basket and the mountains of clothes lying next to the overflowing laundry basket, the heavy bedsheets and duvet covers and tablecloths as well as curtains, piles of underpants and socks and dirty tea towels, I would curse all that laundry back when my life had been simple and undramatic. If it hadn't been for all that laundry, I used to think back then, then I would have been more content, I would have been able to read the books I ought to read and longed to read, but rather than read them, I was forced to start yet another load of washing and when that was finished, I had to hang up the heavy, unmanageable sheets to dry, and it would rain or it would be winter so I had to drape them over doors and chairs because the clothes horses were too small and already covered with socks and pants and shirts and tops, I cursed the laundry. But now that my world had imploded and I was raging and grieving, it was the laundry that kept me going, the time it took to do the laundry and hang it up and when it was finally dry, to fold it, put it away in the cupboards when the children were asleep at night, and then fall asleep myself knowing the laundry had been done and dried and folded and was ready, clean and waiting in the cupboards, I'm surviving on laundry, I thought to myself.

I did the laundry, I cleaned the house, I wrote my final year essay on modern German drama as well as theatre reviews for small newspapers, I started writing a one-act play, I tried to live a normal life, to appear normal, to repress the dizzying sensation of falling. One bright Sunday morning in May when the children were playing in the garden, I was struck down by a feeling of pain that defies description. It wasn't centred on any specific part of my body, but it was physical rather than mental, I couldn't move, couldn't stand up, couldn't talk, couldn't do anything other than curl up in bed. It lasted three hours, then it passed and I started feeling like myself again, but still numb. Three days later, one sunny Wednesday in May while the children were at school, it happened again, it came back, a three-hour episode of pure agony. And again on the Friday and on the Tuesday the following week. The fifth time it happened, once I had recovered, I looked in my diary where I had noted down the times of the attacks to see what I had been doing in the hours leading up to them. I had been working on my one-act play. What had I written? I went to the Mac and read my text, and there it was, in between all the other words, and I had a shock, I was floored, and at one fell swoop I turned into someone else, forever changed into another by this moment of truth. I had lived a life characterised by routines, sustained by routines, and then this happened, a brutal encounter with the truth that upended my life.

I couldn't bear the anguish that followed or process the discovery, the horrific realisation, I couldn't deal with any of it on my own, but neither could I talk about it. I read poems about pain, poets that usually soothed me, Gunvor Hofmo, Gunnar Ekelöf, Sylvia Plath, but they didn't soothe me, I prayed to God, he didn't respond, I wanted to surrender to him although I didn't believe in him, anything as long as it might help, I needed help, I need help! I cried out from the void. At night I wrote pleading letters to the country's psychoanalysts. I had read a great deal of psychology in an attempt to understand and heal myself, I knew about Freud, of course, I had read Freud, I had read Jung, I knew a couple of psychologists about the same age as me, but I wouldn't dream of contacting them because they were no wiser than I, at least that was how I saw it. I knew that if I were to trust and open up to another human being, it had to be a psychoanalyst.

~

I told no one about the letters, I hid the letters because the children needed taking to school and packed lunches and Constitution Day decorations and new football boots and lifts to swimming lessons and basketball practice, and I had to do the laundry and shop for groceries and cook dinner and put the children to bed and I was holding it together, just about. Then a Thursday afternoon at the start of June, a man called just as I was about to take Søren to football practice and said he had read my letter, I had no idea what he was talking about. Then I understood and the pain came back and I collapsed on the floor, unable to speak, I heard how he heard, how he realised that I had repressed my letter, that he was speaking to a human being driven to repressing things. He offered me an appointment and when I sat in front of him in his consulting room, trembling with guilt and shame, he said with a grave face that he had interpreted my letter as a cry for help. He understood. He took it seriously.

I was sent to Rikshospitalet for strange tests. The man conducting them said that ultimately analysis might change my life, he warned me that I risked breaking ties and shattering relationships, I understood, but it was too late, I had nothing left to lose. Two days later I was informed that I qualified for state-funded psychoanalysis four times a week for as long as was necessary.

This was a new development. My desperate unhappiness remained the same, but I had taken one step towards change.

Four days a week I would lie on the couch and not see my listener, not know if he heard what I said. I couldn't scan his face or body for reactions, indications of acknowledgement, understanding, surprise, compassion, there was no point in gesturing, smiling, fluttering my eyelashes, making myself attractive, adding a grimace or waving my hands about, there were only my words and my voice that carried them and they would often linger in the air and I heard what I said, how I lied. My first sentence on the couch was: There were four of us, I was the favourite.

As I said it, in the embarrassing silence that followed because I got no reaction and was unable to carry on, a bolt of lightning shot through my whole body. The words with which I had so often begun the story about myself, revealed me in all their mendacity. It wasn't true, it was the exact opposite! But this obvious fact hadn't dawned on me until this moment. Why would I have made myself believe something like that? Was the rest of my story equally untruthful?

Four times a week. Before I turned up for a session, I wondered what I would say when I got there; when I left, I wondered what I had said, before I started thinking about what I would say the next time, I existed in a state of pain and shame, which couldn't be undone, but which I couldn't live with unprocessed either.

When I was a little girl, I would often be alone with Dad, I would go with Dad to the sweetshop and Dad would buy me sweets. I don't remember much of what happened before or after we went to the sweetshop, but I remember the sweetshop trips, it was wonderful that Dad bought sweets just for me. Once when I was in the sweetshop with Dad, a boy I was in love with turned up, I fell in love with boys from an early age, I was unusually interested in boys, a boy I was in love with came in and I blushed, mortified that he saw me in the sweetshop with my dad.

Once I had grown up, I was rarely alone with Dad, but occasionally Dad and I would be on our own in Bråteveien and the mood would be strained. Once Dad told me about a dream he had had. Dad was interested in dreams, in Jung. He had dreamt that an alcoholic woman in a shabby old dressing gown was staggering through the house in Bråteveien, and it had been a frightening sight, a nightmare. My first thought was how strange that he had dreamt about me, that my future self so terrified Dad. Dad was interested in Jung and in dreams because he knew they couldn't be controlled.

December 15. My watch had stopped, it said five o'clock though it was ten past noon. I checked my inbox, no new emails. I couldn't stand being at home constantly checking my emails, I dressed up warmly, put the article about Elfriede Jelinek into my bag and walked seven kilometres to the watchmaker who fitted my watch with a new battery. I went to the café by the railway station and drank coffee and edited the article with my pen in my hand, without the Mac so I wouldn't check my emails all the time, but I checked my emails on my mobile instead and found that I'd had a reply from Bård, who wrote that he would like to hear what had happened to me. I said that he would get to hear it one day. I didn't want to tell him about it, I wanted him to know it, wanted them all to know it, but I would rather not have to tell them because it was disgusting and telling it made me ill. I checked my emails on my mobile, at ten minutes to two Bård had replied to yesterday's email from Astrid and copied me in. I put the article about Elfriede Jelinek aside, I couldn't concentrate anyway.

Bård began by pointing out that if Mum and Dad really wanted to treat us equally, they needn't write a will at all because the inheritance law would deal with the issue of fairness.

He listed circumstances with which I wasn't familiar because I had been apart from the family for years, while Bård had done his homework. It concerned the transfer of flats and various forms of financial assistance, matters he had mentioned to Dad several times, and Dad had always assured him that everything had been written down and would be accounted for and that interest would be calculated at a future probate meeting, but that had now turned out to have been a lie to make Bård accept what he had regarded as only temporary preferential treatment, so that he wouldn't rock the boat, he wrote, using Klara's expression.

He pointed out that if Astrid really had paid the bills for one of the cabins then that was only fair given that she had enjoyed the use of it for all these years. He pointed out that Mum and Dad had just had the cabins connected to public water and sewage, and not transferred the ownership of them until this considerable expenditure had been incurred, that Dad had paid the stamp duty, that the new valuation was forty per cent higher than the original one, what kind of mandate had the first estate agent been given? To come up with the lowest possible valuation so that Astrid could have the cabin transferred at the lowest possible price to Bergljot's detriment, there was my name again, and his?

When it came to the children, he wrote in conclusion, they were adults and didn't need telling what the conflict was about, they could make up their own minds.

Astrid's reply came just one hour later, at ten to three, as I sat in the café at the railway station with a new battery in my watch. She wrote that Bård had misunderstood, he replied immediately that he hadn't, unbeknown to me they would appear to have had a fierce exchange about financial and practical matters. In her email to me Astrid wrote that of course she took me seriously, that she had always taken me seriously—so she hadn't deleted last night's email after all, that was good although I was guessing the reason was that it had been sent to other people as well as her. She wanted us to meet in person, she had asked me for that only yesterday, she pointed out, if we could meet face to face, she would be happy to come to my place.

It was a brave effort, but I didn't want to, everything in me protested. Nothing good would come from it, nothing ever had, I invariable ended up being the one who had to be understanding and listen to how badly my behaviour was affecting everybody else, how terrible it was for Mum and Dad, I knew her language only too well and it usually left me sad and angry. Astrid meant well, but the good she wanted wasn't for my benefit. She acted in good faith, I didn't think otherwise, she probably had the best of intentions, she sought reconciliation and cooperation, but there are opposites which can't be cancelled out, there are times when you must choose.

The second time I met Bo Schjerven was at the check-in counter at Fornebu Airport. Bo Schjerven and I were flying to Slovakia to talk to newly established writers associations about how we organised things in Norway, Bo was representing the Norwegian Writers Association, I had been despatched by the Association of Norwegian Magazine Publishers to whose board I had been elected after being proposed by Klara, who was deputy chair of its electoral committee, the last thing she did before she moved to Copenhagen. The Slovakian invitation was tabled at my first board meeting, but no one else was free to go; I was happy to go, I wanted to get away.

In the seven months since I first met Bo Schjerven in the foyer of the Norwegian Theatre, my life had changed completely. I was now living on my own, I had shared custody of the children, I had had my terrifying epiphany, confronted my parents, lost my birth family, and started psychoanalysis. I came straight from a psychoanalysis session to the airport, on edge and flustered, Bo Schjerven and I checked in together, and in the café inside, in the departure hall, I poured out my heart while Bo listened.

I was basically in deep distress, in shock and grieving, but I had started psychoanalysis, I had taken a step towards change, begun the process although it was painful and fraught with danger. I had been able to get out of bed, shower and dress, clean my teeth and pack, I had remembered my passport and some money, it was uncanny, it was just like doing the laundry. With Bo Schjerven at the airport, I managed to check in and get on the plane to Slovakia with him, the plane was white. The clouds were white and the sky above the clouds blue and white, we drank white wine and became light and almost as transparent as the air. We landed and were picked up by a white bus and driven to a white castle in a park surrounded by blossoming cherry trees. The room was white, the bed white, the morning white and the bread and the nights were white, the Slovakian poets pale-skinned, how would they manage, how would any of us manage? We drank clear schnapps and lay awake in the grass, which was white with cherry blossom, while the Slovakian poets recited incomprehensible poetry, undoubtedly also white, Bo danced under the trees, Bo turned into a white angel. When we woke late in the morning there was white cheese and milk along with white bread on the white tablecloth in a large bright, white-painted dining room. It was possible to exist in two states simultaneously. To be fundamentally unhappy, shaken and rattled to your core, and yet still experience moments of happiness, and possibly experience them more intensely because of the fundamental unhappiness, and not just moments, but hours, or as in Slovakia two whole days.

Wednesday 16 December in the morning. The snow had melted, it was dark and rainy, sleeting and grey, I drank coffee and edited the article on Elfriede Jelinek while I wondered whether I ought to reply to Astrid. In spite of everything, she was reaching out to me, she believed that was what she was doing and she couldn't know that her gesture would be interpreted by me as more of a command than an invitation. It would be unfair of me not to explain to her how I saw her olive branch. I put aside the article on Elfriede Jelinek and wrote to Astrid that yes, we could talk and have contact, but that it was difficult when she wouldn't address the most important thing for me, when she never commented or touched upon it, and this had become very obvious in situations like the one that had arisen now. It wasn't, I wrote, that I expected her to choose between Mum and Dad and me, she had always had a different relationship with Mum and Dad than I had, a different childhood to mine. But she couldn't act as if what I had told her didn't exist, even if she found it disturbing or impossible to deal with. That was her challenge, I wrote. If she wanted a relationship with me, the things I had told her had to be recognised as essential for that relationship.

We could talk again, I wrote in conclusion, when the row about the cabins was over, but it was conditional on the above. Merry Christmas and a happy New Year.

~

I felt I had made my point and could look forward to a good Christmas. I read my email to Klara, who thought I was being too soft as usual, but suggested that I send it anyway so that I could get on with my life. I sent it while I still had Klara on the phone, I could hear that someone else was trying to call me, but I was busy talking to Klara. When I rang off, I saw that it was Astrid and I was pleased that I hadn't taken her call, but had sent her an email which stated my position.

Then Søren rang me. Astrid had called him because Dad had fallen down the stairs in Bråteveien and was in the ICU at Ullevål Hospital.

Dad? Klara would cry out at night in Copenhagen, but he didn't reply. Dad! Klara raged in the dark night, but he didn't hear. If you hadn't killed yourself, how might I have turned out? Probably much better, Klara grumbled, before she apologised. Sorry, Dad, forgive me, she pleaded, for thinking of myself, and not about how terrible you must have felt as you walked out into the cold water.

I rang Astrid immediately. Her voice was grave, different from when she had called me from Diakonhjemmet Hospital. Dad had gone to let in two plumbers at eight o'clock that morning but must have tripped on the stairs and bashed his head against the concrete wall; he never reached the front door. Mum, who was still in bed, thought it strange that she didn't hear any sounds, Dad's voice, the plumbers' voices, plumbing noises, so she got up and found Dad lying twisted, covered in blood, seemingly lifeless on the landing. She ran down to the hall to open the door to the plumbers, scream-ing that she thought her husband was dead. The plumbers entered, ran up the stairs and put Dad in the recovery position, they tried mouth-to-mouth resuscitation, one physically, the other consult-ing an app that told you how, after twenty minutes they got Dad's heart going again. An ambulance had been called, the plumbers had called the ambulance and Mum had managed to call Åsa, who fortunately had taken the car to work that day, had turned around immediately and reached Bråteveien before the ambu-lance which took Dad to Ullevål, where he was now in the ICU hooked up to a ventilator.

It sounded serious. And yet the family had so often cried wolf that I didn't know how to react. They were at Ullevål with Dad, Astrid said, she, Åsa and Mum. The doctors didn't know if Dad had suffered brain damage, they would carry out an MRI scan in a few hours, then they would know more, for the time being all they could do was wait.

I called Klara. They're exaggerating, she said, they're using your dad's fall to silence and marginalise Bård and you, she said, but the hours went by and I heard nothing from Astrid. Had it been only exaggeration and game playing, she would have rung me by now, I thought, she would have milked this for all she could, made hay while the sun shone. But she didn't call, she had things other than me on her mind.

I told my children, we didn't know what to make of it. I had meetings, I was busy right up until the evening when I was going to the Nationaltheateret to see *Peer Gynt* with Lars. When my meetings were over, I still hadn't heard from Astrid, so it had to be serious, she must have other and more important things on her mind than me. I texted her asking how he was, she replied that he was in a bad way, that it was very serious, that Dad's heart had stopped beating for twenty minutes. It was untypically matter-of-fact for her, so it had to be serious. I stood in the December darkness at Storo metro station after an editorial meeting, struggling to buy a ticket when I received a call from Bergen Student Union, asking if I could give a talk on Peter Handke on 22 March next year, and heard to my astonishment how I replied in a thick voice that I couldn't deal with this right now because my father was in hospital and that it was serious. The train arrived, I got on without a ticket and wanted to cry. Dad had been such a huge presence in my life these last few days as a result of the cabin feud, my seeing Bård, Bård's emails, my childhood coming back to me, my memories of Hvaler, the lavatory which was now connected to mains drains, the well which was no longer in use, I had imagined Dad with the estate agent going through the rooms of both cabins to point out weaknesses, imagined Dad reading Bård's email when I read Bård's email.

I got off the train at Nationaltheateret and called my younger daughter, Ebba, and said I thought it was serious. I was still on the verge of tears, and she heard it and became tearful herself, we were both tearful without knowing why. *Peer Gynt* started in three quarters of an hour, I decided to have a beer at Burns before I went to the theatre, I texted Lars that I would be in Burns having a beer, he was already there, he replied, with a beer and a cigarette under an outdoor heater. I bought a beer and couldn't drink it quickly enough, I wanted to buy another one, and Lars couldn't deny me a beer or three or more given that my dad was in the ICU at Ullevål and might be dying.

I visited Klara in Copenhagen. I was now working as a theatre critic for a national newspaper and I had asked for, and was given, permission to go to Copenhagen to review a highly acclaimed production of *Ghosts* at the Kongelige Teater. The production was ruthless in its treatment of both the late Captain Alving and the still-living Mrs Alving, I wrote a feverish review and faxed it home, dreading the thought of my words being printed in a Norwegian newspaper where they could be read by many people, including my family. But I was far away, in Copenhagen, drinking with Klara at Eiffel, Anton Vindskev's favourite pub, grateful for Klara's existence and for the existence of dark pubs where you could drink yourself senseless because when everything else was so brightly lit all the time, you had to carry the darkness around within yourself and that was unbearable. Anton Vindskev told funny anecdotes and made us forget our unhappiness. He talked about a time when he and Harald Sverdrup went to a poetry convention in Sweden and were put up in a castle with a huge park outside Stockholm, and they went out drinking in Stockholm and Harald Sverdrup got so drunk that he had to be sent back to the castle to sleep it off, while Anton managed to pick up a woman who collected plants, who carried around a bag with a pair of secateurs to take cuttings. When the woman entered the park, she saw many fine specimens: Oh, that's wonderful! Oh, this is wonderful! She opened her bag and took out the secateurs and helped herself to some cuttings.

Anton had eventually got the woman inside the castle and into his room when Harald Sverdrup knocked on his door wearing just a T-shirt with his genitals dangling below the hem, he wanted to join in the fun, but Anton had just managed to shove the bag with the secateurs under his bed and didn't want to share his fun with Harald Sverdrup, so he gave him a bottle of vodka instead and Harald Sverdrup left holding the vodka bottle and with his genitals still on show, and the next morning they found him lying in the park next to a fork on which he had speared a note reading: Help me. Halald! He had misspelt his own name.

It felt good to laugh.

On the Sunday we took the train to the Louisiana Museum of Modern Art where they were showing a recording of Marina Abramović's *Rhythm 0* from 1974. Seventy-two different objects were laid out on a long table, a feather, a pistol, a chain, a rose and on the wall behind the table a video of the six-hour-long performance was playing. Visitors could use the objects on Marina Abramović, who was standing in front of the table, to do what they wanted to with them and her, she would continue to stand there for six hours taking and tolerating it, no matter what, that was the experiment, she wanted to see what they would do. At first the audience stood still, they were shy and expecting her to make the first move, but she didn't. Then one person came up to her tentatively, then another, then a third person broke though the intimacy barrier, then another moved closer, then the next person touched her, people became intrusive and tore at her shirt, they ripped her shirt to pieces, egging one another on, encouraging each other's audacity, wanting to outdo one another in daring, they became menacing, someone pulled the torn shirt off her and humiliated her, and the audience turned aggressive as if her passive and possibly thus increasingly powerful presence provoked them. One placed the pistol in her hand and raised it so the barrel was pointing straight at her head, and did he also whisper 'fire!'? When the performance was over, when the clock struck, when she finally moved, when she took a step towards the audience, they retreated in horror and disgust: 'They could not stand my person because of what they had done to me.'

Peer wore a white suit, Peer drank champagne and got high on his own ego, Peer was a stranger to moderation, Peer was hubristic and arrogant, he knew no boundaries and helped himself to women and adventures, power and sensual pleasures, Peer wanted to get ahead, to become emperor, he focused not on limitations, but possibilities, Peer told himself that the sky was the limit, that he could get away with anything, a man after Dad's own heart, a man who wanted to become rich and became rich, and knew how to use his wealth to his advantage when it became necessary. When Peer's mother, Aase, was dying, when she lay in a modern hospital bed connected to an ECG machine, like the one to which I knew Dad was connected along with the ventilator now, right now, I started to cry. Dad was in a similar side ward to the one Aase was lying in now, right now, that is if he wasn't already dead, but then Astrid would have called, and I would have seen it on my phone, I kept checking my phone. If Dad had died, Astrid would have called me, and I would have left the auditorium to call her back. So Dad was still alive, hooked up to machines like the ones Aase was hooked up to on stage and I started to cry, I sobbed inconsolably throughout the whole of her death scene.

In the final scene when Peer returns to Solveig and expects the same warm welcome he has always been given, she walks out;

Solveig leaves Peer with Nora's words, the words of a modern woman. She takes off, she leaves Peer, she does what Mum never did, what Mum had never been capable of, dependent and impotent as she was, a woman who had never paid a bill in all her life. Solveig leaves Peer, and it dawned on me when I saw Peer standing there alone, incredulous and weary, that Dad's life hadn't been an easy one. A deep compassion rose in me at the thought of Dad and Dad's life, poor, poor Dad, who had done some stupid things as a young man which couldn't be undone, which he couldn't fix, and he didn't know how to bear them, how to live with them. So he tried to forget and repress them and for a long time it looked as if the person he had hurt had forgotten them and repressed them, and anybody who might have known what had been done and to whom, also acted as if they had forgotten them, repressed them, but what had been repressed and forgotten could come back at any time, it might rise up from oblivion, from repression, then what? It must have been a difficult life, a life lived in fear, a life lived in terror. Dad avoided and feared his two older children because they reminded him of his crime, he couldn't stand them because of what he had done to them.

Peer didn't understand that he went too far, Peer didn't understand when he went too far, Peer didn't know where the line was and so he crossed it, but even if he had known where the line was, he would probably still have crossed it, chosen to cross it, for the hell of it, for the irresistible thrill of crossing lines and because he thought he could get away with it, he thought he would be forgiven because he didn't take seriously the consequences his actions would have for other people, because he thought that things would always work out well for him, only now they were no longer working out well for Peer.

109

It's too late, Peer, Solveig said to him, and it was a moment of catharsis. It's too late, Peer, Solveig said. Sometimes it is too late. Sometimes you can't make amends, sometimes the damage is past repair.

When I came back after visiting Klara in Copenhagen, I discovered a cryptic card from the married man in my postbox. He wanted to keep me on the hook. I didn't reply, but I was already hooked. All through that autumn, all through that winter, all through that year and the year after I got cryptic postcards and hints from the married man, I didn't reply, but I was hooked. Am I elegant or elephantine, he wrote. You're an elegant elephant, I wanted to reply, but I didn't, I devoted myself to psychoanalysis, which wouldn't in itself prove anything, but which might change something. However, it demanded that I devote myself to the psychoanalyst, to him and no one else, as wholly and faithfully as if it were a love affair, while I was already in love with a married man, I already had my love object although it was unobtainable.

I dreamt that a war was raging, that I was standing with another soldier among some trees on the outskirts of an open area which we had to cross. It was risky because we would be visible to the enemy, who was close by. It was night and we had to get moving before daybreak, which was soon, I peered across the plain, shaking with fear, I tried to steel myself for the coming advance while my fellow soldier had sat down against a tree. I checked the time, we had to go now, I turned to my fellow soldier who was still sitting up against the tree. He's useless in war, I thought, and then I ran.

~

I told my psychoanalyst about the dream and how I thought that the other soldier was the married man who didn't dare get a divorce, who stayed passive while I was on active service and had divorced, I talked about the married man for a long time. But the psychoanalyst thought he was the other soldier, immobile on his chair behind the desk while I battled it out on the couch. How conceited he is, I thought back then, but now that my feelings for the married man are history while my feelings for psychoanalysis still live within me, I'm tempted to agree with him. And whether or not it was him or the other man or the two of them combined, it often felt like being isolated in a combat situation. I didn't let, or wasn't able to give, the psychoanalyst that space in me, which he needed in order to operate at an optimum level, the transfer failed to happen although for a few moments it was beautiful and we came close, like once when I had undoubtedly reproached him for something or other, he said that the two of us were in this room together, to help me, united in the name of psychoanalysis.

When we came back from the theatre, we drank, I drank. Astrid texted that they had been sent home from the hospital and told to return the following morning and that Astrid and Åsa were spending the night at Mum's. I thanked them for turning up.

I drank and spoke maniacally, I couldn't relax, I stayed up after Lars had gone to bed, topping up my red wine glass to the brim and draining it. Had it been serious, Klara reassured me, I had called Klara, the hospital wouldn't have told them to go home. I circled the floor, knocking back wine to calm myself down, to be able to sleep, but became increasingly agitated and nauseous and threw up and spent the night hunched over the lavatory bowl. I called Astrid in the morning. They were on their way to the hospital. It was Thursday, I had no appointments in my diary except a reminder to take bottles to the recycling bank, buy a pork joint and change the bed linen as Tale and her family would soon be back from Stockholm, but I didn't leave Lars's place, I stayed with him, pacing up and down. Astrid called at twelve noon. They had met with the doctors, Mum and Astrid and Åsa and Aunt Unni, who was a doctor, and Aunt Sidsel, also a doctor. They hadn't asked me to join them and I was glad that they hadn't because I wouldn't have gone, but it made everything crystal clear to me. This time it really was serious and when it was serious, they didn't want me there, my presence would upset the unity and harmony, they wouldn't invite an agent provocateur like me into such a situation, even though I was Dad's, the dying man's, daughter, they didn't ask me to come, to take part, fortunately, because what would I have said if they had urged me to come? Everything became crystal clear. It was the reality of the situation. The thing that Astrid on all previous occasions had pretended wasn't the case, which she under all other circumstances ignored and blanked out. When push came to shove, as it had now, when it was serious, as it was now, it became perfectly clear that Astrid and Åsa and Mum did in fact share Bård's and my view that we were a very long way away from harmony, that we weren't a 'normal' family.

The doctors at the hospital had said that Dad couldn't breathe unaided. Dad's neck was broken. It was highly likely that Dad was paralysed from the neck down and that if he were to regain consciousness, which was highly unlikely, he would probably be paralysed from the neck down and unable to speak. The question was whether to turn off the ventilator. In their discreet and professional manner, the doctors had hinted, I gathered, that it would be in Dad's best interest to do so, that that was what they would have done, had he been one of their relatives. And Aunt Unni and Aunt

113

Sidsel, who were themselves doctors, had agreed with the doctors at Ullevål, and Åsa and Mum had agreed with the doctors, the only one who hesitated, I later found out, was Astrid. Yet eventually they all agreed that the ventilator should be turned off. That was what she was calling to tell me. As it happens I had no objections, however, she didn't ask if I had, she had called merely to let me know. It would be done in the next hour.

I rang the children with an update, saying the ventilator would be turned off within the next hour. I called Klara, I emailed my closest friends. Astrid called three quarters of an hour later and said: Dad's dead.

Four times a week I lay on the couch talking in turns about pain, shame and the minutiae of everyday life, and every now and then we would suddenly experience a breakthrough. I dreamt that I picked up a hitchhiker who was going to Drøbak, as was I. Then I took a wrong turn, I went off the main road to Drøbak, I got lost and couldn't find my way back to the main road, and I felt guilty on account of the hitchhiker who was inconvenienced by my uselessness and would be late getting to Drøbak. Then I thought I saw the main road, the lights from the main road; if I drove under the garage door in front of me, I would get back on it. I had accelerated to drive under the garage door when it started to close, I stepped on the gas to get through before it closed completely, but didn't make it, it came down too quickly and it slammed into the car, we were startled and shocked, but at least we were alive, the hitchhiker ashen-faced and with his trouser pockets turned out and the car a complete write-off. Then Mum showed up and said in her usual cheerful manner that it could probably be fixed, although everyone could see that was impossible.

Then I spotted a five-øre coin on the road and bent down to pick it up because finding money brings good luck, and I told myself by way of consolation that it might turn out to be my lucky day after all. I picked it up only to discover that it was just a button.

A five-year-old? he asked.

No, a five-øre coin, I said.

You said a five-year-old, he said.

I meant a five-øre coin, I said, and repeated my dream: When the garage door came down, it felt as if I was crushed.

Almost as crushed as a five-year-old, he said, and I felt an electric shock go through me.

Åsa and Astrid, Aunt Unni and Aunt Sidsel took care of Mum. They organised a rota of sleepovers in Bråteveien so she wouldn't be alone. I thanked Astrid for their turning up, I asked her to give my best to Mum. They were at Bråteveien, she replied, I was welcome to come over. I didn't even consider dropping by. I soon started to feel relieved. And I soon concluded that my nausea and vomiting during the night between the day of Dad's fall and the day of his death had really been about my subconscious fear of a prolonged illness. Dad paralysed in a care home for years, how would I have coped with that? Dad summoning me from his sickbed and my having to choose between not going and disappointing him or going and being disappointed myself. I didn't believe that Dad would ever give me what I wanted, an admission and an apology. If I went to Dad's sickbed with that hope, I would be disappointed, as I had been so often in my encounters with Dad. I had been hoping for so long, but all in vain, I had knocked on the imaginary door to Mum and Dad so many times, I had stood in front of their imaginary door, hoping they would open it and that what had happened to me would be accepted, that I would be accepted, invited in, but it didn't happen, they never let me in, the door remained firmly shut and I was frustrated, upset, I had stood on the threshold, knocking on their door, then I stopped knocking, I stopped hoping, I turned around and left and I became free to some extent. I wouldn't have gone to Dad's sickbed, I would have been strong, I hoped, and like Solveig to Peer Gynt, say: It's too late. But Astrid and Mum would have pressured me and pestered me and accused me of tormenting a sick, paralysed and helpless man who had no greater wish than to be reconciled with his oldest daughter and for it to happen in such a way that the daughter would pretend that what he had done to her hadn't happened, would I really deny him that? As if I were on some sort of crusade, as if it wasn't about feelings, the deepest ones. They would blame me and it would be unpleasant, and if he was bedridden for a long time, there would be pressure to help Mum and Astrid and Åsa with the hard work of looking after him, and I would refuse, and they would be outraged and tell everyone, including the staff at the care home, about my indifference, my selfishness, my callousness, but then it didn't happen, then Dad died, then Dad was gone. I felt relieved, I had been so scared of Dad, I realised, and what had gone was my fear of this unpleasant scenario, which could have arisen from that side of the family at any time, but not anymore. Dad was dead. Recriminations and accusations and barbs, if you want to see a psychopath, just look in the mirror, but not anymore, Dad was dead. Dad couldn't hurt me ever again. Strictly speaking Dad hadn't been able to hurt me for years, I hadn't walked around every day terrified of Dad, or maybe I had, maybe this fear of Dad lived inside me. It's hard to conquer your fear of an unpredictable, aggressive lion while it lives, but now the lion was dead.

Freud wrote somewhere that it is unfortunate that no description of psychoanalysis can ever reproduce the impressions you get during its actual operation, that the most definitive experience can never be conveyed through reading, but only through the experience, and I agree with that, it's impossible to explain. It's equally impossible, I think, to explain why you end psychoanalysis, how it is you realise that the time has come.

After more than three years of several sessions a week, I rushed in for an appointment one day when I really needed it. I had got drunk the night before, slept with a man I shouldn't be with, I wasn't wearing my own clothes, I had lost my contact lenses, I was desperate to get on the couch, pour out my heart, cry and despair, but the psychoanalyst didn't come out to get me at the usual time. Thirty minutes later I knocked on his door, but he didn't reply, he didn't come, I tried the handle, but the door was locked, I shook it, I think I screamed and was vaguely aware of how the psychology students who occasionally frequented the waiting room at the Institute for Psychoanalysis noted my desperation: So that's what they look like when they turn up. One of them patted my shoulder and pointed to a notice on the noticeboard stating that my psychoanalyst was on holiday for three weeks. He had probably told me and I had repressed it, as I still did many unpleasant things. What would I do now? I had always suspected that I might go mad one day, and now the day had arrived. My knees buckled, I collapsed on the floor, still vaguely aware of the students studying my break-down. I expected to become psychotic, but I didn't, so somewhat surprised I got up, looked around and then I left, what else could I do? It was a clear and sparkling August day, I hadn't noticed that until now. The air was warm, I hadn't noticed that before. I walked down Bogstadveien, what else could I do? I was surprisingly calm. It was late summer, the air was warm, the weather lovely, I hadn't realised that until now, three weeks without analysis lay ahead of me, I turned into another street, what else could I do? I walked past a shop front and saw someone who looked like me in the window, but it couldn't be me because she looked well. I stopped, retraced my steps and studied myself, a seemingly functioning woman. Could I see myself through her eyes? You're clever, I said to her, and you don't look too bad, I said to her. Shouldn't you be out in the world doing things?

I survived those three weeks and decided to end my treatment although I understood that the psychoanalyst thought I ought to continue, enter more deeply into the pain to get a better perspective. With hindsight, it's easy to agree with him, but back then I thought I had experienced enough pain, spent enough time being in pain, the married man had finally got a divorce and would be mine, I wanted to be happy!

During the twenty-four hours that Dad was ill, in the twenty-four hours he was in hospital, I replied to all of Astrid's text messages. She kept in touch with me, while Åsa kept in touch with Bård. Her messages were mostly about practical matters, information on the extraordinary situation which Astrid and Åsa were dealing with at the front line. Astrid wrote that she was at Bråteveien with Mum and Åsa, and that I was more than welcome. I asked if Mum was alone at night, she wasn't, they took turns sleeping at the house, including Aunt Unni and Aunt Sidsel, Mum was scared of falling down the stairs. I thanked them for turning up and asked Astrid to give my best to everyone, especially Mum. Astrid sent warm regards and hugs back. You're always welcome, she wrote. Perhaps it was a figure of speech, perhaps they thought, Astrid, Åsa and Mum, that things were different now, that it was possible for us to be a family again now that Dad was dead. Except I don't think that they really wanted me there unless I broke down in tears, having suddenly had an epiphany of how deeply I had loved Dad and was willing to express remorse for my behaviour. I didn't think they wanted me to be a part of their intimacy; they were probably more raw and vulnerable now than ever and wanted to be with people they knew and with whom they felt comfortable, it was natural, or perhaps they wanted a sign, perhaps they wanted me to pay a symbolic visit, an indication from me signalling fair weather and a positive outlook. I'm sure many people were visiting Bråteveien now, more distant relatives, neighbours and friends with flowers and warmth and compassion, I could come as a friend or a neighbour. They were still going ahead with Christmas, Astrid wrote, they had decided to throw a big party, to be together all of them, to have a big Christmas party in Mum and Dad's house in Bråteveien, which now belonged entirely to Mum, but somehow also to my sisters. Åsa and Astrid would be there with their husbands and children, there would be lots of people, perhaps also Aunt Unni and Aunt Sidsel. I replied to all the text messages and responded with warm hugs back but didn't comment on the invitation to stop by. It didn't even cross my mind to do so, I wrote 'thinking of you all' and it wasn't untrue, it wasn't a lie, I was thinking of them, and I saw them in my mind's eye, and I wrote again that I was happy that they were there, taking care of Mum and everything.

Dad?

Are you out there somewhere?

What's it like to be dead?

It felt wrong for me to want to summon him, but he was just as much my dad as the others'.

Dad died on Thursday 17 December. He would be buried after Christmas on 28 December. Two days after his death, on Saturday 19 December in the morning, Astrid emailed me asking if we could talk. I was about to put my bag in the car to leave Lars's house in Oslo and I asked her to call me back in ten minutes when I would be in the car.

I had been feeling relieved and as I walked down the steps from Lars's place to clear the snow off the car on a bright and quiet December morning, I felt light. Astrid called while I was waiting for the lights to change at the Smestadkrysset junction, asking me how things were, she sounded expectant, even hopeful. To be honest, I said, disappointing her, I feel relieved. She fell silent. Perhaps she had hoped that I would be in despair, distraught because Dad had died without our being reconciled, that I now repented being so stubborn and pig-headed, that I regretted being estranged, that I would be guilt-laden now that it was too late for me to apologise to Dad. My being relieved rather than repentant made my story more credible, and if my narrative was true, then she had erred. Astrid's position had been difficult, impossible even, and I had never wanted her to pick a side, only her acceptance that the situation was impossible. Not to have wanted me to turn up to her fiftieth birthday party and be pleasant, not to have put pressure on me, not to have acted and treated me as if I could make the impossible possible.

~

Mum would like to meet with you before the funeral, she said. Mum hadn't seen me for fifteen years and Astrid was scared that it would be too much for Mum to see me at the funeral. That Mum wouldn't be able to bury Dad, see me for the first time in fifteen years and meet Bård, who was angry because of the cabins, all at the same time. Astrid was afraid that Mum would break down at the funeral. Astrid and Åsa and Mum wanted the funeral to be dignified. They had asked Bård to meet with them as well, but he had refused. Yet it was more important that Mum saw me because the issue with me went far deeper than the inheritance dispute with Bård. We could go for a walk, she said, they could come over to my place. I didn't want that, it would be too intimate, we could meet at a café. Tomorrow morning, Sunday, she suggested, I agreed.

I called Søren and asked him if he wanted to join us. He said yes, he came over to my house that same evening and saw that I wasn't dissolved in tears because my dad had died, but that I was twitchy at the prospect of meeting Astrid and Åsa and the mum I hadn't seen for fifteen years the following day.

We were sitting in front of the fireplace when I got a text message from Bård, who asked what the point of the meeting was. Perhaps he was worried, Søren said, that I might falter and soften and change sides in the inheritance dispute now that Dad was dead. Mum had wanted to meet with Bård as well, but he had asked what the point of the meeting was and Åsa had replied that it was just to talk about what had happened, Dad's death had been so dramatic, and so that Mum would see him before the funeral, she hadn't seen him since the start of the inheritance dispute. Åsa and Astrid didn't want Mum to dread the funeral, they were afraid that Mum might break down at it, if she didn't meet with us before it. Bård had replied that he knew everything he needed to know and that Mum was much stronger than they thought. He was right about that, it turned out that Mum was much stronger than Åsa and Astrid thought, than Mum herself pretended to be, Mum had always played on her pseudo-fragility, possibly subconsciously or maybe she genuinely believed it. But I wouldn't back down in the inheritance dispute when faced with the grieving family. I replied that we wouldn't be discussing the inheritance, that I had said to Astrid that if there was any drama or the inheritance was brought up, then I would leave.

It reeks of drama, Bård said.

I didn't have the energy for Mum's drama, Mum's tears and violent, overpowering, invasive emotions which made it impossible to know your own. I started to dread the next day and sent Astrid an email rather than a text message because I knew they were together and showing each other their phones every time they beeped, I'm sure the mobiles at Bråteveien beeped constantly, condolences ticking in and how-are-you and our-thoughts-are-with-you messages from near and far. I wrote that I hoped Mum didn't have any great expectations of the meeting or for the future, that I was going purely because these were extraordinary circumstances and I felt sorry for Mum. I wrote that I hoped that there wouldn't be any drama. She replied immediately that she agreed, there wouldn't be any drama, nothing much was expected, we would deal with one issue at a time.

Meet at the café, the funeral and then what?

We left in plenty of time. We ate a quick breakfast and left in plenty of time. We couldn't find a space where we had intended to park. It was Sunday but coming up to Christmas and the shops were open, cars and people everywhere. I suggested another place we could park, Søren had different ideas, we fell out, we started arguing, then we found an empty space, parked and got out. The café where we had agreed to meet was packed with families with young children, steaming coats and Christmas shopping, there were no vacant tables, would we have to wait for them outside in the cold? We waited anxiously in the chaos, hoping that someone would leave, but no one did, and anyway this wasn't a place for sad conversations, I had picked the wrong venue. Should I call Astrid and say that I had picked the wrong venue, that the venue was packed, that we would have to find another place, or should we wait until they turned up? The pub by the river was one option, but people were probably drinking beer there already, the ice cream parlour inside the shopping centre wasn't cosy. We stood in the chaos at the café, fretting about it. A little girl came toddling towards me, her mother hobbling behind her, bent over her daughter, her arms ready to catch her if she fell, like Mum must have walked behind me when I took my first steps, it must have been like that although it was hard to imagine now, Mum was probably a good mum back then, to begin with, intuitive and physically present, in tune with her instincts and her body, that was a long time ago, but I was still walking, I could still walk. We went outside the café and waited in the cold, Søren towering in his big quilted jacket, we discussed alternative venues in order not to have to think about what was coming, the unpleasantness awaiting us, I didn't know what Søren was expecting, nor did I ask, we didn't want to talk about it, just to let it happen, it was good not to be alone, it was good that Søren was an adult, Søren should always be there.

Should I call Astrid and tell her that we had to go elsewhere even though I hadn't found anywhere else, perhaps it would be better to go for a walk in the cold as she had initially suggested, along the river, then Astrid called, they were by the pizzeria across the bridge, we had forgotten about that, we crossed the bridge, and there they were, outside the pizzeria, three uncomfortable figures, Mum as I remembered her, only less spectacular, everyone was as I remembered to the extent that I remembered them, to the extent that I looked at them, they looked like themselves, all three of them, only less spectacular. I wasn't spectacular either, but I had dressed with care, I had decided last night what I was going to wear and laid out my clothes on a chair, I was wearing my face for facing the world. They weren't wearing theirs. We hugged one another. I hugged Mum first, she said: My girl, as in the old days, like some of my boyfriends had said, my girl. Then I hugged Åsa, then I hugged Astrid. Søren hugged Mum and Astrid and Åsa, and we entered the pizzeria and looked for a quiet table, who would take the lead here? Not me, I hadn't issued the invitation. Åsa found a quiet table, they walked with Mum, one on either side, Astrid and Åsa stayed close to Mum in order to protect her and they also sat down on either side of her. Søren and I sat down opposite them, Astrid, Åsa, Mum sat on one side of the table, Søren and I on the other, who would start and how? Looking at me, Åsa asked what we wanted, I wanted coffee, no beer for me if that was what she thought, that deep down I was distraught, crushed and burdened with guilt because I had cut off contact with Dad, who was now dead, and thus I was in need of a beer. Åsa asked if everyone wanted coffee, everyone wanted coffee, Åsa went to the counter and ordered some coffee.

We've cried and cried, Mum said, we're all cried out, said Mum as if to apologise for them not crying now, they didn't look tearful, they looked agitated and slightly manic. We drank our coffee and they told us what had happened from beginning to end, talking

128

over each another, they were utterly consumed by it, from beginning to end. It had been so dramatic, they said, none of them had ever experienced something quite that dramatic before. Åsa asked if we had ever been at the scene of an accident. Åsa had once been the first person at the scene of an accident, a car crash, the driver had died from his injuries, there had been blood everywhere, that was when she realised she was squeamish and no good with blood, but she had directed the traffic, someone had to do that, there was a job for her too, everyone had a role to play. The plumbers were due at eight o'clock and Dad had got up when the plumbers rang the doorbell and gone downstairs to let them in, but he must have fallen on the stairs, tripped and fallen or had a dizzy spell and fallen or suffered a heart attack and then fallen, no one could be sure how Dad had fallen, but when he fell, he banged his head against the concrete wall, and it wasn't until Mum thought it odd that she couldn't hear plumbing noises, voices, Dad's voice, that she got up and found Dad on the landing, bleeding and lying in a contorted position with his head and neck twisted unnaturally backwards, and she ran down to the plumbers who had rung the bell again, wearing nothing but her underwear, she said, and they all giggled and Mum repeated that they were all cried out, as if to apologise for the laughter, they had cried and laughed and cried again, Mum said. Søren and I hadn't cried, hadn't laughed, Søren and I were outsiders, Søren and I weren't in the same place as them although we were drinking coffee in the same pizzeria.

Mum had screamed to the plumbers, two very young men, that she thought her husband had died, and the young plumbers raced up the stairs and put Dad in the recovery position and started mouth-to-mouth resuscitation, two very young men, it had probably been tough for two such young plumbers to find themselves at the scene of an accident, but they had been great, Mum said, and

Mum had managed to call Åsa, who was fortunately taking her car to work that day, and she turned around immediately and reached Bråteveien before the ambulance. The plumbers managed to restart Dad's heart, the plumbers carried on for twenty minutes and got Dad's heart beating before the ambulance arrived. The ambulance arrived and drove off with Mum and Dad and Astrid and Åsa, and the plumbers had stayed behind to do their plumbing, they had been great, Åsa said, they would send them flowers as a thank-you once they had the energy, there was so much to do. The plumbers had been fantastic and stayed behind to fix the hot water tank. Dad had announced, Mum said, a long time ago that he was never leaving Bråteveien, that he would be carried out of Bråteveien with his boots on, and that was what had happened, Dad was carried out of Bråteveien with his boots on, or rather with his slippers on. Dad fell while he was on the go, Astrid said, yes, Mum said, that was well put, Astrid, Dad fell while he was still on the go. Typical Dad, that's just like him, Åsa said, he died as he had lived, Astrid said, always in a hurry. Yes, Åsa smiled and was about to add something, but Mum interrupted Åsa and asked me if I had any wishes for the funeral. Wishes for the funeral? No, I had no wishes for the funeral. Mum told us the kind of music she wanted at the funeral, Dad had been very fond of a song they played on the radio, Dad used to listen to the radio when he sat in his armchair reading journals, all kinds of difficult journals, Mum said, looking at me, I want you to know that, Bergljot, that Dad read all kinds of difficult journals. I said nothing, I didn't know what to say. They hoped that it would be a good funeral, Astrid said, one of their neighbours from their cabins on Hvaler was going to play the violin, it would be in good taste, there might also be a singer. It seemed as if everything that needed doing, anything they could think of, all the decisions that they had to make jointly, agitated them, this state of emergency in which they lived made them quiver. The undertakers would handle most things, Mum said, food and beverages and so on, Mum said, but no function room, they didn't want to hire a function room, she said, looking at me, they wanted to have the reception in Bråteveien, they had lots of room in Bråteveien, there was no point in hiring a function room when they had Bråteveien and Dad had loved Bråteveien, he had always loved Bråteveien. Did I have any thoughts about the death notice, Mum asked, I shook my head, I hadn't even thought about it. The Norwegian health service was amazing, Åsa said. Pay your taxes with joy, she said. There had been two doctors with Dad all the time. Or perhaps not all the time. They looked at one another and agreed that two doctors had been with Dad pretty much all the time, they nodded in unison, most of the time two doctors had been with Dad, and Aunt Unni had been there and Aunt Sidsel had been there, and both of them had been great and asked the doctors complicated medical questions. All sorts of tests were carried out, but the blood supply to Dad's brain had stopped for twenty minutes and he never regained consciousness, every detail repeated over and over, they were utterly consumed by it. And no wonder, it had been dramatic, that's how you process dramatic events by retelling them over and over. Astrid took a clementine out of her pocket, peeled it, popped a segment into her mouth and passed the rest of the clementine to Søren, who was at a loss before he realised that he was meant to take a segment and pass it on to me. Søren took a segment and passed the clementine to me who took a segment and passed the clementine to Mum who took a segment and passed the clementine to Åsa, just like the chair of the Association of Norwegian Magazine Publishers had done when we were in tricky negotiations with our publishers, peeled an orange and passed it round the table so that everyone could take a segment, an old African custom intended to lower the conflict level; when people shared food and ate from the same thing, their mood would soften. When the decision to stop the ventilation had been taken, they had gone to say goodbye to Dad. Åsa had said to Dad that they were disconnecting the ventilator for his own sake because the alternative was undignified for him, a man like Dad, paralysed and possibly unable to speak, dependent on a ventilator, he was always on the go. Åsa was great, Astrid said, but Mum said Astrid had been great because she had sat with Dad until the end and had seen how the life ebbed out of Dad, how the pulse stopped beating in his neck, how serene Dad's face was when he died. In contrast to the day before when his face was distorted by alarming and uncontrollable twitches, Astrid's daughter hadn't felt able to visit Dad that day because he looked so alien, all bloodied and bruised. Mum had been great, Astrid said, so calm in spite of everything, so composed in spite of everything, for her, Astrid said with a smile to Mum and Åsa smiled, and Mum smiled and looked gratefully at her daughters; they admitted, they said and laughed in unison, that it had taken a fair number of sleeping pills and quite a lot of red wine. Aunt Unni had been great, Astrid said, so calm and composed as well, Aunt Unni had spoken to the doctors about medical matters, and Aunt Sidsel had been great and asked the doctors complicated medical questions, and the doctors had been impressed, they thought, with Aunt Unni and Aunt Sidsel, and Dad's brain had showed no sign of Alzheimer's they wanted me to know, and Åsa had been great, Mum said, in one way or another they were letting me know that I should repent my estrangement and my absence because if it hadn't been for that then I, too, would have been able to take part in this momentous experience and Søren could have taken part in this momentous experience as well, as it was he had to sit there and hear what he had missed out on because he had a mother like me.

They were meeting with the undertakers tomorrow, Monday, it was all happening so quickly. They would celebrate Christmas, they said, with a big party in Bråteveien, they had decided that, they weren't the kind of family that was knocked out by something like that, they would throw a party to celebrate Dad, even in death. It would be a big party and everyone was invited, Aunt Unni and Aunt Sidsel, as well as Astrid and Åsa and their children. And the night before Christmas Eve would be celebrated as usual, and surely my children would be coming to Bråteveien as usual? Søren nodded in a subdued manner, he always went to the gathering on the twenty-third, as did Ebba. Tale and her children will be coming as well, won't they, Mum asked, how old is her youngest, little Anna, and what does Emma want for Christmas, she asked, after all, she's almost five years old now. While we, Søren and I, knew that Tale and her family wouldn't be going to Bråteveien on the twenty-third, and that after those two days on Hvaler in the summer when Mum had asked if she took good care of her daughter, Tale was refusing to play happy families any longer, although I had asked her to carry on because the pressure on me was reduced when my children played along. Tale was an adult now and made her own decisions, and she had considered writing to Mum and Dad to tell them that she didn't want to see them again, but had dropped the idea when I advised her against it because Mum and Dad would simply assume that she was joining the inheritance dispute, that she wanted a cabin on Hvaler, and then Dad had died. Tale felt the need to state her position, Tale wanted to take a stance because it was because of people who didn't, who didn't put their foot down, who didn't have the courage of their

133

convictions, but tagged along without a word of protest that the world was going to hell in a handcart, because people swallowed camels in order to please others, to avoid the unpleasantness that would follow when you took a stance, that was why the world was going to hell, she refused to play along any more, but Dad had just died and now wasn't the right time to ram home a point of principle, so what was the right thing to do?

They've been delayed coming back from Stockholm, I mumbled, I haven't spoken to them, I said, I think they'll be back sometime tonight, I said.

Well, then they'll be back in time for our party on the twenty-third, Mum said, what would Emma like for Christmas? She was addressing Søren, who grew uncomfortable and hesitant. Don't worry about that now, I said, don't waste your strength on that now, I said.

Such things don't waste your strength, Åsa said, they give you strength, she said.

Yes, Mum said, how true, Åsa, such things don't waste your strength, they give you strength, what does Emma want for Christmas, a doll, a dress?

You can't go wrong with a dress, Søren said.

A dress it is, Mum said, beaming.

Dad loved living in Bråteveien. Dad was delighted to move from Skaus vei to Bråteveien, as was Mum. Mum once said that she had never regretted the move from Skaus vei to Bråteveien, that she hadn't missed Skaus vei for one second. And no wonder. Who wants to live at a crime scene?

The married man got a divorce and became mine. In the years I was with him, I didn't see a lot of Bo and Klara. I devoted myself to the man who was finally mine, my salvation. Since then I've thought that if I had seen more of Bo and Klara in the years when I was with him, my salvation, then I might not have been with him for as long, perhaps our relationship might have ended before it became destructive for us both. In the years I was with him, my salvation, I spoke to Klara on the phone and sent postcards when I was abroad, when the professor, my salvation, lectured at universities and colleges in Norway and abroad and I didn't have the children and could come with him and work on my Ph.D. on contemporary German drama. Klara organised poetry recitals at Café Eiffel in Copenhagen and had started writing a book about Anton Vindskev. But when my relationship with the professor, my salvation, ended, when I finally lost him after many good years and some destructive ones, I went to see Klara in Copenhagen. When the relationship broke down, when it foundered at last, I went to see Klara. Before I went, I had a session with the psychoanalyst because the pain of my broken heart felt unbearable. When I told him that it was over, my relationship with the professor about whom he had heard so much, my fellow soldier who wasn't one you would take to war said: So you finally put your foot down?

I understood that he saw it as a sign of health and that was what I wanted to hear, that my pain wasn't an illness.

My pain wasn't an illness, but it was all-consuming. I went to Copenhagen to see Klara and Anton Vindskev, who knew what to say to someone like me, what would help. Being an outsider makes you resourceful. Loss makes you resourceful. Poverty makes you resourceful, as does fighting with the tax office, being oppressed makes you resourceful. If you're lucky enough to be successful, you mustn't forget that, the skills you acquired when you were utterly miserable.

We put on our coats and went out into the cold, it was growing dark already or maybe a storm was brewing, it got darker as we stood outside the pizzeria and said our goodbyes. It was the kind of darkness that falls, the kind of darkness that flows and spreads, that penetrates buildings and houses and takes over no matter how many lights you turn on, no matter how many candles you put on the table and in the windowsills, no matter how many torches you light and put at the entrances to shops and malls and along the drives of houses throwing Christmas parties. A darkness that didn't come from above, from the sky, but from below, from the cold ground where the dead lay rotting in the darkness, a darkness that poured out from the icy, shivering, black, stiff branches of the trees and the small ugly bushes, a darkness full of knives, a darkness that cut body and soul, a darkness that didn't leave visible injuries but knotted scar tissue and lumps which prevented the blood, the lymph and the thoughts from flowing, which chopped and stopped and built up in tight, unsolvable puzzles. I wanted to go home, Søren wanted to go home, Åsa wanted to go home, the darkness was upon us, we were outside the pizzeria saying good- bye, but Mum and Astrid dragged it out. It was nice of you to meet with us, Mum said. Don't mention it, I said, we know this is important, I said, something along those lines, carried away by the moment. I hope it'll be a good funeral, Mum said. I'm sure it will, I said, I wanted to go home, I had to get out of there, Søren wanted to get out of there, I could feel it, the darkness was getting to him, Åsa wanted to get out of there. Do you think so, she asked, looking me in the eye. Yes, I said. She looked me straight in the eye again and repeated as if seeking reassurance. Do you think so? Did Åsa think that I would ruin the funeral, make a scene, make a speech? Yes, I said, I wanted to get out of there, I wanted to go home, I had reached my limit, the darkness had got right inside my brain. I'll stay close to Bård, I said. It'll be fine, I said, the darkness reached my bone marrow, penetrated it and spread out, I had sacrificed enough.

We hugged one another and walked back to our respective cars. It's done, I said. I've seen her now, I said. She hasn't changed, I said to Søren, but you've seen her more often than I have.

He said he would be willing to take Emma and Anna to Bråteveien for the party, if Tale refused to go.

When my relationship with the man I had longed for for so long and lived with for so long ended, I went to visit Klara in Copenhagen. My pain wasn't an illness, but it was all-consuming. Klara dragged me through the parks of Copenhagen and stuffed food into my mouth. When I wanted to call the man who was the cause of my grief, she hid my phone, and she hid pills and knives and anything else people use to kill themselves, and she wrote invitations to a New Year's Eve party and sent them to sixty-three people in my name. Sixty-three people accepted an invitation to a New Year's Eve party in my house, comprising a three-course dinner and fireworks at midnight. I had to hire tables and chairs for sixty-three people and shop and organise, I spent six weeks planning and organising the party and woke up on 3 January after a three-day New Year celebration with Klara and three remaining guests from Renna in a trashed house. Klara and I spent three days tidying up and cleaning and woke up on 6 January to a clean and tidy house. I woke up on a cold, clear and fresh morning, and realised that I hadn't thought about my pain for six weeks and six days and that now it had come back, but it was noticeably weaker. Klara had given me a New Year's Eve party as medicine.

That morning, that cold, clear, new January day as we sat in my neat and tidy kitchen drinking tea, Klara learned that her book about Anton Vindskev had been turned down. She hadn't heard from the publishers since she sent in the manuscript several months ago and she had been reluctant to call them because she knew what their silence meant. But this cold, clear January day as we sat in my clean kitchen drinking tea, she called them and was told that they didn't think her book about Anton Vindskev would be of interest to the Norwegian market. She buried her head in her hands: What am I going to do?

She had hoped for a big advance from the publishers, had based her finances on it, she was broke, what was she going to do now? If it wasn't one thing, then it was another. As soon as one problem was solved, another would rear its ugly head no matter how hard she worked, she would never be safe no matter how many New Year's Eve parties she organised, rejection slips and tax bills were waiting to ambush her, danger lurked around every corner, soon she would probably fall in love unhappily or get hit by a car, there was never any respite and how would it end—with death, of that at least she could be sure.

Well, she said. Endurance is the first duty of all living beings.

Mum was pretty. Of her sisters, Mum was the pretty one. The others had different talents, Mum was pretty. That was what people said about Mum, that she was pretty. She knew that it was true, it's hard to dismiss objective expressions of beauty. Mum's identity was tied to her beauty, she staked everything on it. Mum was shapely. Shapely was Dad's word. Beauty and shapeliness were Mum's aces. But those are the very cards a woman is sure to lose, so she can never become complacent. The young and pretty woman knows it; whenever she photographs herself naked or half-naked because she's proud of her body, she's also pained and haunted by this fact obvious to everyone, that the very thing that makes her visible and desirable is transient and will be lost one day, then what? That's the fear beautiful women live with, especially this beautiful woman whose only asset was her beauty. She doesn't feel good about herself. Mum didn't feel good about herself. Mum was pretty, but had no education, no experience, no money, Mum was Dad's possession, Dad was proud of his pretty possession, Mum radiated fear. Mum was innocent in the sense that she was inexperienced and naïve. Many men prefer and are attracted to inexperienced and naïve women, simple, childish ones who are easy to impress, awestruck, devoted, sincere, needy, those who don't use irony, who don't hold back. Mum was inexperienced, childish and chose to remain a child. If Mum had chosen to grow up, her reality would have become unbearable. Mum was the kind of woman many men wanted women to be back then, a skylark at the end of the skylark era, and the dilemma which Mum faced and which could have made her grow up and become a free human being was harder to resolve than the one faced by Nora. Did Mum make a choice? Did she decide not to jump ship, but hope for the best, not to react, is that a choice? To be like a child and not understand too much. Try to stay buoyant, put on a smile, do the best she could, given where she was, knowing she didn't have the strength to leave, after all, she had tried. Nora had the strength, Nora left, but Nora wasn't real, Nora was a man's invention. Mum was real, a vulnerable, shapely woman for as long as that lasted, it doesn't last, it fades and younger, more attractive women appear; she can even give birth to them herself.

Tale and her family arrived from Stockholm. Tale hugged me as though I might be upset and possibly tearful, but she soon realised that I wasn't, that I was relieved but still anxious about what lay ahead, the party on 23 December and the funeral. Ebba arrived in the evening and hugged me and she was tearful and wondering whether I might be upset because I might have been waiting my whole life for an apology from Dad and had realised now that I wouldn't get one. But I'd had no such hope. I told her that I was relieved and hoped she didn't think my words hard and cold, didn't think me hard and cold, as Mum had found me hard and cold, who had called me hard and cold ever since I was little because I had always disagreed with her.

We did the usual Christmas things. An excess of shopping, organising and wrapping. The day of the party arrived. Tale didn't want to go to Bråteveien. Søren offered to take Emma and Anna, but Tale didn't want him to. I was secretly wishing she would let him take Emma and Anna to Bråteveien because then something which would have been seen as an issue could have been avoided, but I didn't say anything. She doesn't want to be infected by Bråteveien, I thought.

You're making it more difficult for us, Ebba said. What do we say when they ask us why you're not there? Do you want us to lie?

I agree, Søren said. You're making it more difficult for us. You make it easier for yourself by not going, but harder for those of us who bother turning up.

You don't have to lie, Tale said. I'm happy to tell them why I won't be coming.

My children argued about going to Bråteveien. The sins of the father, I thought.

Ebba and Søren went to the party. I wasn't nervous as I had been the last time they went to Bråteveien, on the day they celebrated Mum turning eighty and Dad turning eighty-five, five days after her overdose, the day that Rolf Sandberg's obituary appeared in the newspaper, because Tale was with me as was little Emma who was almost five, and little Anna who was almost two, and my dog. We went for a walk across some open ground which the pram could handle, it was snowing and everything turned white again. The dog chased the falling snowflakes and the approaching darkness didn't hurt like the sharp darkness from the other day. This darkness felt like soft fabric that erased us and the forest around us, it covered everything in a cool, protective cloak and it felt fine, light.

By the time Søren and Ebba came back, we had lit a fire and opened a bottle of red wine, Emma and Anna were asleep. It had been fine, they said. It had been like it always was, they said, except that Dad had died. Mum had found some old family photos and they had looked at them together and laughed and cried because everyone looked so young all those years ago and wore such funny clothes. Somehow the mood was lighter, Søren said, when Dad wasn't sitting silent and glowering in his armchair. I wondered if Mum was relieved that Dad had died. And that perhaps she wasn't the only one. What if Dad had been a problem for people other than me, maybe Astrid and Åsa were somehow also relieved that Dad was dead after years of him sitting in his armchair silent, depressed and gloomy, dampening the mood. What if all of them, but especially Mum, believed that Dad was the cause of the problem when it came to Bård and me, and so they thought that when Dad was gone, we could start over, perhaps it wasn't just Mum but everyone who was hoping for that. The mood had been good, Søren said, it had been light, he said, and although they had shed some tears when they looked at the family photos, they had mostly laughed.

As Søren and Ebba were about to leave, Mum had followed them out to the hall and asked after Tale and her great-grandchildren, Emma and Anna. She had tried calling Tale many times, she said, but never got an answer and Tale never rang back, she never heard from Tale. It's probably her phone, Ebba said, it might be because it's a Swedish number, because she's on a Swedish network. Try her again, Søren said. Mum had played dumb, he said, as they stood in the hall covering up for Tale, pretending and lying.

The street of my childhood, Klara said, quoting Tove Ditlevsen, is the root of my being. It anchored me on a day I was utterly lost. It sprinkled melancholy into my mind on a rainy night. It threw me to the ground to harden my heart, before raising me gently and wiping away my tears.

On the morning of Christmas Eve I stopped off to see Karen and Klara as I always did. They both treated me with kid gloves. I told them I felt relieved because now there could be no more unpleasantness from that front. They said they knew what I meant. I told them I dreaded the funeral, they said they knew what I meant. We discussed the best way to handle it. When I came home the aroma of roast pork was wafting through the house, Søren and my son-in-law were bent over saucepans in the kitchen, the tree had been decorated and my grandchildren were toddling around the presents, I asked for the music to be turned down, for silence, there was something I wanted to say before we sat down to eat. I wanted them to know that I accepted whatever position they adopted towards the family in Bråteveien. That as far as I was concerned, it made no difference which stance each of them took, if they chose to see a lot of the family in Bråteveien, a little or nothing at all, that I loved them all the same, that I hoped that in return they would accept each other's choices. And now, let's talk no more about it, I said. And so we talked no more about it, we celebrated Christmas and I felt grown up.

Klara had no father. No children and no siblings, but she had Anton Vindskev and she organised poetry recitals for him and some Danish poets at Café Eiffel in Copenhagen, she thought things were going quite well. I visited her in Copenhagen and attended a poetry recital with Anton Vindskev and his Danish colleagues; apart from Klara and me the audience comprised only two paying members. It's back-breaking, she whispered, but meant ground-breaking. Aren't we lucky, she whispered, elbowing me in the side as Anton read aloud, and she glowed.

My children were having dinner with their father on Christmas Day and I was due to have dinner with Lars. His son, twelve-year-old Tor, was there when I arrived. I realised immediately that he had been told that my dad had just died. He looked sad and anxious, curled up in the far corner of the sofa, he was reluctant to look at me and come near me although I knew him well. How was he meant to treat someone who had just lost their father, the worst thing that could happen to you, how do you greet someone who has just experienced the worst that can happen? He was desperate not to get it wrong. And then I turned out not to be in the state that he had imagined. Because Lars had never told him how I felt about my dad. Tor was relieved that I didn't looked distraught, that I was myself because then he was free to be himself, too, and enjoy his Christmas dinner, but he continued to peer furtively at me, what kind of person was I really?

Astrid wrote to tell me that Dad's death notice would be in Monday's newspaper. It'll be in on Monday. Bård wrote to tell me that it was short. It was short. No adjectives other than dear. They were meeting Bård and me halfway, I thought, they didn't want to provoke Bård and me, they wanted the funeral to go well, with dignity. Astrid wrote to tell me not to worry about flowers. I hadn't been worried about flowers. Were they afraid that I might turn up with a wreath with inappropriate words? Were they dreading the funeral just as much as I was?

The night before the funeral I had a dream about going to the funeral. I sat in the front of a car next to Astrid, who was driving, Åsa was in the back. She said: We must remember to hug one another. It mustn't look as if we're hugely relieved.

My window was down, Dad was standing outside, I said while I looked at him: But I am relieved.

His face contorted in anger and pain.

I realised that I had laddered my tights and that I was wearing a white jumper, I had to change my tights, change to a black top, did we have enough time? Yes, if I went straight from Skaus vei to the church. I got out of the car, Dad saw me leave and thought I was walking away from it all, he said: Is that the kind of daughter I raised?

I turned to him and with forced calm I said: Yes!

Then I carried on, still with forced calm, with forced confidence, but dreading him coming after me. I made myself walk slowly, but all I could think about was whether he would come after me, I turned around after a while to see if he was coming after me, and he was. But there were people about, surely he wouldn't hurt me when there were other people around? He came after me, getting closer all the time, gaining on me, he was right behind me, he bent down and picked up a heavy metal pipe, he raised it ready to strike me and I thought: Surely those people will stop him! And then: If he hits me, I'll die.

By the time the Balkan Wars broke out Bo Schjerven and I had become good friends. Bo loved Yugoslavia and it broke his heart when Yugoslavia fell apart, when people who had lived peacefully side by side started killing one another. How could it have happened? Every morning he would run down to the Narvesen kiosk on the corner and buy a copy of every single Norwegian newspaper, but he didn't buy their coverage of the Balkan Wars. Something didn't add up. He tried working out what it was, he sat tirelessly in the University Library from morning till night reading foreign newspapers, German, French, British, Russian, and became increasingly agitated and morose, drowning in copies of articles from foreign newspapers which he had underlined and commented on in the margins. He submitted outraged articles to Norwegian newspapers criticising their coverage of the Balkan Wars, but they rarely published them. I edited quite a few of them and toned them down, and occasionally some made it to print. Then important people would write that Bo's observations were pertinent, and that made it all worthwhile, Bo said, although it didn't change anything. Bo Schjerven's articles being published changed nothing, but he said citing the philosopher that he didn't write to convince those who disagreed with him, but so that those who agreed with him would know that they weren't alone.

~

Bo's perspective was different. Bo considered things from another angle. Bo didn't just say: This is true. But he went on to ask: What else is true?

We mustn't be late. I begged Søren and Ebba not to be late. Tale delayed her return to Stockholm in order to attend the funeral, we mustn't be late. We left in plenty of time, but I didn't want to get there too early either, I didn't want to stand on the steps to the chapel, greeting people and making small talk. I mustn't be late, I must get there right on time, I was dreading it. When we were nearly there, we were much too early, we didn't want to be at the chapel as early as that so we drove to the nearest petrol station and got some coffee. We sat in the car, drinking coffee. We didn't leave the petrol station until we absolutely had to, so we got there as late as possible while still on time, I was terrified. We pulled into the car park, I dreaded who I might meet there, I spotted Bård with his wife and their children. I imagined they had also wanted to get there as late as possible, but still on time. We got out and said hello, Lars arrived, I was fraught. Karen arrived, Klara came running, my ex-husband and Ebba arrived, I wanted to tell them about my dream and the iron pipe, I talked too loudly about my dream, together we walked towards the door, but I didn't want to go in straightaway. Other people went inside, most of them must be inside already because there was no one chatting on the steps outside, a couple I didn't know rushed past me and went inside, Søren rang and said he couldn't find it, I had to explain to Søren how to find it, Klara said I had to go in now. Bård and his wife and children had gone inside, my ex-husband had gone inside, I

155

grabbed Tale's arm. Klara said I had to go inside, but Søren didn't know how to find the chapel, I had to explain to Søren how to get here, I wanted to tell Klara about my dream, Klara snatched the phone from my hand and said that she would explain to Søren how to get here, she insisted I went inside, they dragged me inside, Tale, Lars and Ebba dragged me inside, I didn't look right or left, but marched as quickly as I could up the central aisle to the front where I was forced to sit so that everyone could see me. Bård sat with his wife and daughters on the first pew to the right, Mum sat on the left side with Astrid and Åsa and their husbands and children and the pew behind them was full as was the pew behind it, most pews on the left were full, but there was no one sitting next to Bård and his wife and children, nor on the pew behind them and only one man was sitting on the pew behind that, but then I came, then the rest of us came. I took a seat next to Bård, Bård's wife and Bård's daughters, and my children sat next to me and Lars squeezed himself down between Bård's children and me, we filled the first pew to the right, while the pew behind us remained empty, people didn't want to sit on our side, people didn't want to side with us, but those who had come in last, my friends, who would have preferred to sit in the back because of their peripheral relationship to my dad, were told by the chapel usher to take the second pew to the right, which she had noticed was empty and it didn't look good that it was empty. My friends came and sat in the pew behind Bård and me, on our side, siding with us, and Søren arrived in time in his thick quilted jacket and was the tallest one there.

Lars nudged my side with his elbow: Someone's trying to get your attention. He nodded toward the first pew to the left, towards Mum who was staring intently at me, around her neck she wore a scarf I had given her one Christmas. I had no choice but to go over and say hello to her and hug her in full view of everyone, I went over there and I hugged her and I hugged Åsa and Astrid as quickly as I could, then I stopped, enough was enough, I wasn't willing to hug the whole pew, Astrid's and Åsa's husbands and children, so I returned to my seat to the right, now it was all about surviving the service, getting myself out of the chapel, back to my car, driving off and being done with it, then heading out to Lars's house in the woods, surely it couldn't take more than an hour. The photograph on the order of service taken maybe thirty years ago had Dad sitting bare-chested in a boat on Hvaler with his hand on the outboard motor, I didn't like seeing him so undressed, so much exposed flesh; on the back page there was a poem which Mum had written for Dad about how she liked lying close to him. Now he was lying in a white coffin under the flowers, they had organised the flowers, four floral hearts from his four children lay around the altar, our names and those of our children printed on pink silk ribbons, I visualised Dad wielding the metal pipe.

A funeral celebrant entered, welcomed everyone and read aloud Mum's poem to Dad, which was printed on the back of the order of service. She had written it on an early January morning, he said, Mum had woken up before Dad, got up and sat by the window and written this poem, which was about her longing to lie close to him and about spring in January. The celebrant would return to this theme many times, spring in January, as the time that would follow Dad's death, to the month of January, which was nearly upon us, as soon as the day after tomorrow. Mum's life after Dad, about everything that would start over, the celebrant talked a lot about that, I'm guessing on orders from Mum, who was probably hoping for spring in January. We sang 'The Day You Gave Us

Lord, Is Ended', and I joined in to show that my voice wasn't trembling, I wondered if the family thought I was going to be a part of this new life-after-Dad that had just been announced, spring in January, Mum's, Astrid's and Åsa's life after Dad's death, if they really thought that we could start over, as if history didn't exist, as if history could be forgotten, erased, even though every war ever fought on this earth has proved that you can't ignore history, sweep it under the carpet, and that if you want to reduce history's destructive impact on the future, everyone's version of what happened must be brought out into the open and acknowledged. Åsa gave the eulogy and said that Dad had loved Mum. I think she was right about that, that Dad had loved Mum, given how furious Dad would get whenever he doubted that he was loved back by Mum, given how furious Dad would get whenever he thought he detected signs of a lack of devotion from Mum, and how furious he would get if Mum rejected him sexually or in other ways, Dad loved Mum to the extent that he hated and got furious with Mum and all other women, anyone female, if he felt rejected by Mum, Dad was so vulnerable in his relationship with Mum that he reacted with rage and aggression whenever he felt rejected by her, Dad loved Mum so much and so obsessively that he wanted to own and rule over her and control her, and Dad had pretty much succeeded in that respect, but he could never know what Mum felt in her heart of hearts and it tormented Dad that Mum's private thoughts couldn't be completely controlled one hundred per cent. It caused Dad to suffer and to hate Mum for it, as he had hated his own cold mother he could never reach, who had rejected him, he had said so many times, whom I had myself experienced as cold when I was a child. That was my analysis of Dad, strongly inspired by Freud, but I believed it to be true, I felt it. Mum would be made to pay the price for the coldness Dad's mother had supposedly exhibited, unless she surrendered one hundred per cent to Dad and so she tried to do that, she had no choice, but Dad could never feel safe, he could never be sure that the surrender was complete, there might still be half a percentage point in Mum of distance towards him and he couldn't bear that, deep down Dad hated Mum and all women because they eluded his total control and because he needed them so badly. Poor Dad.

Mum had undoubtedly been the love of Dad's life, Åsa said, but she also said, phew, that having Mum as the love of your life could be something of a challenge, she was referring to Mum's affair with Rolf Sandberg, which everyone knew about. Then she came to us children, Dad's four children. She said that Mum and Dad's genetic mix had produced very different children. She didn't want to be compared to Bård and me, so she took us in turn. There was Bård, who had excelled in many types of sport and made a career for himself as a lawyer and investor, she must have read Bård's email to Dad and was now giving him the recognition Dad never had, they were hoping for spring in January. Then there was Bergljot, she said, getting to me, number two, I tensed up. Bergljot, she said, had always been very keen on theatre, on drama. Bergljot had directed all the kids in the neighbourhood in her own theatre productions. Bergljot was creative and imaginative and was now a theatre critic and a magazine editor. Then there was Astrid, she said, number three, who like Bård, had also been very good at sport when she was younger, but now she worked with human rights, while she herself, the youngest, who had always been shy and was therefore regarded as the most intelligent, she said, she meant it as a joke and we laughed, she now worked for the civil service drafting legislation, she liked being in the background, analysing, reflecting.

159

Then she talked about how kind Dad had been to Granny, towards his mother, when she got ill in her old age. It was true, I had completely forgotten that, how Dad had visited his old mother when she fell ill, how Dad would drive to the care home where she lived several times a week to help care for her. Åsa went on to say that Dad had arranged for a family member to visit his mother every day. I didn't remember that either, I hadn't been a part of it, or perhaps that had happened after I had left home as quickly as I could after finishing school at eighteen, when Astrid and Åsa were still living at home, perhaps it had been the four of them as early as that. Why had I forgotten that Dad took such good care of Granny, of his mother, when she fell ill and had visited her in the care home several times a week? Was it because it didn't fit my image of Dad? Hadn't I just concluded that he hated all women because of his cold mother, because she had rejected him? I had tried to analyse Dad, but did he elude analysis? Or was Dad making amends, not to those he had betrayed, but towards a harmless, sick old lady he no longer feared? Dad was given an opportunity to be kind, to show that he cared, and he needed so badly to be kind and to show that he cared, and it was simpler to care for his sick old mother than those he had betrayed, whom he feared, who were growing up, who had become adults and might one day prove dangerous, isn't that often the case?

Åsa turned to the coffin, to Dad, and said goodbye to him in a thick voice, I looked towards Astrid, who was sat leaning forwards with her head turned away, Mum seemed composed.

Åsa's daughter came up and placed a red rose on Dad's coffin, the celebrant, who had so far resorted to neutral terms now employed Christian ones, earth to earth, ashes to ashes, dust to dust. He threw earth on Dad's coffin three times with a spade and must have pushed a button because the coffin was then lowered and when it had disappeared, the floor closed with a thud. We sang another hymn, and I sang loud to prove that my voice wasn't trembling, surely it had to be over soon, then when we had finished singing, the celebrant walked from wreath to wreath reading aloud the names on the ribbons, he walked from heart to heart and read aloud our names and those on the other flowers and bouquets, the names of people I didn't know as if to point out that many people had loved Dad and were now missing and mourning him. When he had finished reading the names it was over, the bells started tolling and the doors behind us were opened, Mum, the widow, left first down the central aisle, then Åsa and Astrid followed with their families, everyone seated on the first pew to the left, then it was our turn, our pew, Bård with his family and then me with Lars and my family, there was no way of getting round it, I grabbed Tale's arm and headed down the central aisle in plain sight, people were staring at me, I guess, but I didn't meet anyone's gaze, I walked as quickly as I possibly could with my eyes fixed on the back in front of me, Bård's back, towards the light beyond the door, the clear December light outside. The celebrant was standing on the steps waiting to shake hands with us, I shook his hand and said it was a fine service although I didn't think so, I said to Åsa, who was standing on the steps that I thought it was a fine eulogy, I told Mum that it had been a fine service and continued down the steps so they couldn't ask me if I was coming to Bråteveien, so I wouldn't have to say no, so they wouldn't implore me, to avoid shocked and horrified reactions from the mourners pouring out of the chapel, greeting and hugging Mum, Åsa and Astrid, I clutched Tale's arm and we walked towards the car as quickly as we could without running, we reached the car and I got in on the passenger side, Tale would be driving because I had drunk too much wine last night, I asked her to start the car and leave, then I remembered that Klara had my mobile and I asked Tale to go get my mobile, quickly before anyone came, but fortunately Klara had already come down to the car with my mobile and said it was right for me to leave, and Karen came and I hugged them and thanked them for coming, but that I had to leave now, and we left.

One Easter, I might have been eleven, the whole family was crammed into the tiny cabin my parents used to rent before Dad bought the ones on Hvaler, we were listening to the radio, to a programme about telepathy. We tried to read one another's minds. Bård pulled a card from a deck, looked at it and thought about the card while the rest of us had to guess which one he was thinking of. None of us could guess it. Astrid chose a card and thought about the card, but none of us could guess which one she had chosen and was thinking of. Dad took a card, looked at it and sent thoughts about the card to all of us and his thoughts reached me loud and clear: The ace of hearts.

I was right. Dad turned over the card, it was the ace of hearts, I was so happy! The ace of hearts from Dad to me.

Klara rang me on the night of the funeral, I was alone in Lars's house in the woods. What a bizarre performance, she said. Whose idea was the floral hearts? And reciting Mum's poem about lying close to Dad. And the reading aloud of the names on all the wreaths and bouquets and Åsa's eulogy describing you as someone who liked drama and directing everyone, while painting herself as the insightful analyst who prefers quiet reticence. She has no idea what you're having to deal with, Klara said.

That night I dreamt that our extended family was carrying out an experiment where we would be sharing a house for three months. The house was full of relatives, my sisters, nieces, nephews, aunts and uncles who talked and laughed and were effortlessly together, while I was ill at ease, an outsider who was trying to drag an awkward suitcase up to my room. The others were busy planning trips, everyone was excited, animated, all except me, everyone was looking forward to it, all except me, they worked closely together, but ignored me, no one offered to help me with my suitcase. I decided to ask Bård for help, but I couldn't find him.

That's how I was with my family, I thought when I woke up, especially during the holidays when there was no school, when the family would gather together in the evenings on Hvaler. Bård had gone out in the world, Bård wanted out, he was always off sailing, dating girls, while I stayed at home with my family because

Mum worried about me to the point of hysteria and her anxiety rubbed off on me. During the day I would run around alone on the rocks, finding caves where I could hide and make my own, I knew Hvaler like the back of my hand, but in the evenings, I had to stay inside with my family, confined to my family, my tummy hurt, I had a lump in my throat, my chest felt tight, I used to watch Mum and my sisters, but they couldn't possibly have felt the same way. I didn't watch Dad, we never looked at one another unless we had to, but Dad was always on the periphery, Dad probably felt the way I did, alone with his unmanageable baggage.

Freud believed that dreams expressed a repressed desire, a desire that is camouflaged and distorted. Jung, however, believed that if he didn't understand a dream, it was because his own spirit was distorted and preventing him from truly seeing the dream. Jung didn't want to view things from an angle other than the one his instinct encouraged him to adopt because if he did that, his snake would turn on him. Freud believed certain things which Jung's snake couldn't accept so Jung broke with Freud; Jung wanted to follow the path his snake prescribed because it was good for him.

Dad was a good-looking man. Dad was just as good-looking as Mum was pretty. Mum and Dad made a handsome couple. They looked good when they went to Christmas festivities and other events they had to take part in. They would always leave such events as soon as they could, talk as little with the other parents as they could, Mum wanted to socialise, but Dad was awkward and uncomfortable and wanted to go home. Dad was good-looking, I thought Dad was a bit like James Bond as played by Roger Moore, but without the easy charm.

I lost my birth family twenty-three years ago. It was my choice, I was alone at Christmas when my children were with their father and I would rather be alone than lose myself in my family, but I had lost my family. I was scared of dying and my family organising my funeral and Mum or Dad giving a eulogy and lying about me, lying about us. I was scared of dying, for my family to take over and thus lose my true self in death. I rang Klara and told her that if I died, she and Karen were to organise my funeral. She agreed. I called Karen and said that if I died, she and Klara were to organise my funeral and to prevent Mum and Dad from giving a eulogy. She agreed.

Bo tried to understand wars without simplifying them like the media did, to avoid black and white thinking, good and evil, victim and aggressor, like the media did, like people often do, like I do.

We met at a patisserie at least once a month to discuss global conflicts, and Bo explained their backgrounds to me as he saw it, he made a point of saying that they could be viewed differently.

At least once a month I would sit in a patisserie waiting for Bo and he would arrive with his characteristic forward leaning gait, his old knapsack on his back filled with copies of newspaper articles from foreign newspapers, he would leaf through them and aim his bright light on what lay in darkness and spot connections where others claimed there were none, see patterns the authorities claimed didn't exist but were merely coincidences that, by a happy chance, benefited the powerful, but sadly nobody else. Bo would come from the University Library with Goebbels's diaries and speeches in his knapsack and show me their similarities to contemporary orators, the lengths to which we go to protect civilians. Bo studied Goebbels's rhetoric and highlighted how today's Norwegian politicians were adopting Goebbels's pre-war rhetoric to justify the wars they were about to join. Bo was beside himself when Norwegian politicians went to war having used Goebbels's pre-war rhetoric, which the country swallowed raw, we must save the civilians. Bo turned up at the patisserie with the evidence in his knapsack, the gift of the gab and his intellect in his heart.

Lars came to the house in the woods in the snow and we celebrated the New Year together. We tried hard to have a nice time, but I could talk about one thing only. I tried talking about other things, but I invariably ended up talking about The Thing. Dad, his funeral, my childhood. Lars had had enough of hearing about my dad, his funeral, my childhood, what good will it do, there's nothing you can do now apart from putting it behind you. I knew he was right, but how did you do that, how did you put something behind you? I knew I was being tiresome, but I couldn't help myself. And that's no excuse. Dad couldn't help himself either, nor could Mum help being who she was, Astrid couldn't help being who she was, I took after them in that I couldn't help being me: destroyed and destructive.

On 1 January Bård wrote to wish me a happy New Year and asked me if I had received a notice of the meeting with the executors, a firm of accountants. I hadn't. You should have got one, he wrote back, along with a copy of the will. The meeting was being held on 4 January at five o'clock. Lars left the next day and I was alone in the woods.

I went for long walks. I had managed to extend the deadline for *On Stage*, I had explained to the editorial staff and the printers that my dad had just died and that I wasn't able to work with as much concentration as usual, they understood and expressed their condolences and told me to take as much time as I needed, no wonder that losing a parent had knocked me sideways.

I went for long, contemplative walks along the river and despite my misgivings, I texted Mum and wished her a happy New Year. She responded immediately by thanking us for turning up at the chapel in full force. I suspected Astrid and Åsa were helping her text, *in full force* wasn't in Mum's vocabulary. They took turns with her, I guessed, they probably spent every other day with her, it must be exhausting. She wrote that she thought it was a dignified end. It was, I replied.

Then I received a notice from the accountant, 4 January at five o'clock.

From time to time I had wondered how I would react when Mum or Dad died or if they died together, say, in a plane crash. I had always believed that it would be impossible for me, mentally and physically, to turn up for a meeting about money and property, to sit with my siblings distributing Mum and Dad's assets. Given I hadn't wanted to see my parents while they were alive, it would be hypocritical to turn up when they were dead in order to get their money or some of their things. I had previously made up my mind not to turn up for such a meeting, not to participate in the distribution of their estate and had felt relief at my decision. But it had then occurred to me that I might be being unfair to my children. I had called their father and asked if, should my parents die, say, in a plane crash, he would represent our children's interest at the reading of the will, and he had said yes. Once our children were adult and could represent themselves it was no longer an issue, but subsequently I had got in contact with Bård and sided with him in the inheritance dispute, so now I was duty bound to show up, wasn't I?

I had also become aware that the thought of such a meeting no longer filled me with the same dread as before Dad's death because it was Dad, I realised that now, I had been scared of, although I had tried my best to imagine him being dead. But now he really was dead, and I wasn't scared of Mum, Astrid or Åsa the way I had been scared of Dad, I didn't fear their voices as I had feared Dad's voice when he raised it, Dad's stare when he wanted to terrify me into silence. The meeting with the accountant was on 4 January at five o'clock. How should I behave there? What was I trying to achieve? What am I trying to achieve, I asked Klara. Justice, she said. Restoration, she said. But they can't give me justice or restoration, I said. They'll have no choice but to listen to you, she said. They shouldn't get away with their underhand behaviour. They've never supported you, never listened to you, they've silenced you for all these years, and now they want to cheat you as well whereas you should have been awarded damages, as should Bård, the neglected son, but instead you'll both get less, instead they'll profit from your misery. She insisted on seeing me before the meeting with the accountant on 4 January at five o'clock, she refused to accept that I would accept being conned, that I was ashamed to demand something when it was Astrid and Åsa who ought to be ashamed.

But it's already on Monday, I said.

Come over Sunday evening, she said, she insisted, and we'll prepare you for that meeting.

172

Once many years ago after a long day at a café with Bo's articles, we were walking down dark city streets, it was late October and raw, and we talked about our insomnia. We kept slipping because the streets were covered with slimy, rotting chestnut leaves, our legs got wet, but we didn't go home, we put off going our separate ways, we walked in the dark autumn streets under the chestnut trees, telling each other what we did when we lay awake at night. Bo would occasionally use sleeping aids and take sleeping pills, but he was scared of getting hooked on them, he put a lot of energy into planning what kind of sleeping aids and what kind of sleeping pills he would use and how often, I drank wine. Bo had had trouble sleeping ever since he was little as had I, I had always dreaded sleep, longed for it, but dreaded it, dreaded falling asleep, falling in general. I had made up a story when I was little, when I lay in bed and couldn't sleep, didn't dare fall asleep, that I was Jewish and lay close to other Jews in a railway carriage heading somewhere during the Second World War, that I was close to other people in a railway carriage, surrounded by other living, warm bodies in a shared destiny, not alone but together with others while the train rolled along with its rhythmic, calming chugging, I imagined that I could hear other people breathe around me, near my ear, my neck, and I tried breathing in the same rhythm as them, as the train, I imagined that I lay as close to other living, warm human

173

beings as it was possible to lie, that we were one big body morphing into the train.

You identify with victims, he said.

But, he then said with a wry smile, every victim is a potential aggressor; don't be too generous with your compassion.

Astrid rang Sunday afternoon just as I leaving to see Klara. There were two things she wanted me to know before the meeting the following day. One was that Mum's overdose had nothing to do with Rolf Sandberg. She had asked Mum and Mum had said that it had nothing to do with him. On the contrary: Mum had attended Rolf Sandberg's funeral with Dad's blessing. The other thing that wasn't true was that Mum and Dad had given her money over the years, which Bård seemed to believe. Mum had paid her office rent for some years, but that had been Mum's contribution to human rights and she was perfectly entitled to spend her money as she wished.

And Mum was doing well, by the way, all things considered. They took turns staying with her, day and night, but of course that couldn't carry on.

When I got pregnant with my first child at the age of twenty, when the pregnancy test was positive, I called Mum and Dad to give them the good news and Mum invited me to Bråteveien. When I arrived, she met me, smiling and secretive, at the door. She too was pregnant, she told me, and that was exactly what she and Dad needed after the upheaval with Rolf Sandberg, a new baby. We could go shopping for baby clothes together, she said, go for walks with our prams, she said, and my heart sank, I would never be free. She wanted us to buy pregnancy tests and I was ambushed into going with her to the chemist where she bought two Prediktor pregnancy tests, and we went back to Bråteveien and peed into the jars and if there were two blue circles at the bottom of the jar in the next hour, we were pregnant, but during that hour we mustn't touch the glass. After one hour blue circles at the bottom of the jars proved that we were pregnant. Aunt Unni, who was a doctor, dropped by and Mum told her that we were pregnant and that we had the pregnancy tests to prove it. Aunt Unni looked at her, my childish mother, and said: You tampered with the glass, didn't you?

Yes, she confessed, she had touched the glass.

How desperate she must have been. There was no way out. Every door was shut to her.

Lars told me about his unhappy grandmother who lived on Fagernes in the 1960s. Granny Borghild had toiled from morning till night for years, Granny Borghild had cooked the food and done the laundry and cleaned the house for years, until one afternoon Granny Borghild said to her husband, who was sitting at the kitchen table reading the newspaper, Lars was there and heard it himself: No, I can't do this any longer. I'm leaving.

But where will you go, Borghild, her husband said and made himself comfortable on the sofa.

I sat in Klara's study the night before the meeting with the accountant.

Oh, Bergljot, she said. If it's not one thing, then it's another.

Yes, I said.

The street of childhood, she said, quoting Tove Ditlevsen again, taught you to hate, taught you hardness and defiance, it gave you your strongest weapons, you must learn to use them well.

Yes, I said.

Whatever happens tomorrow, she said, is a once in a lifetime opportunity.

I took it to mean that she wanted me to mention the unmentionable.

Wouldn't it be inappropriate? In those circumstances?

No. If you don't speak up now, then when? If you want to speak up, it's now or never. You won't get another chance, your mum might die soon, you know now how quickly, how unexpectedly a death can happen. When will the five of you be together in one place again, and with an outsider present? If there's no outsider present, a witness, they'll walk out, you know they will, they'll stop you, they'll scream and shout and drown you out and throw you out or walk out themselves, and you know it, but they can't do that tomorrow with the accountant present, this is your moment if you're ever going to speak up, say what you want to say to them, what you've always wanted to say to them, all together, but which you've never managed to say when they were all together, with you being sober, without you being emotional or angry, surely it has to be tomorrow?

I had never said anything when we were all together. I had never argued my case to anyone other than Astrid and then always in the throes of emotion, of rebellion. If I were to finally speak up, get it off my chest, my case well prepared and my being composed, then it had to be now. And it wasn't inappropriate, Klara said, because what had happened to me was relevant to the terms of the will because Mum had justified favouring Astrid and Åsa by saying they had been so nice, so kind, so present, so helpful and close, but whose fault was it that Bård and I weren't present, weren't close, warm or helpful, why weren't we? Were we naturally cold, less helpful and warm, or was our coldness the result of Mum and Dad's treatment of us. Why would two out of four children be cold and lacking in empathy, while the other two were loving and considerate, was it perhaps the result of the various genetic mixes Åsa had mentioned in her eulogy in the chapel? Or might there be another explanation?

Klara was right. Tomorrow, Monday 4 January, was my chance. It would do me good, I thought, it felt like it when I sat with Klara, the day before, on Sunday the third.

Tomorrow.

I wouldn't be ruining anything for myself, I thought, because it couldn't get any worse, any more ruined for me than it already was. I didn't believe in spring in January. If Mum and Astrid and Åsa believed in spring in January, in more temperate weather now that Dad was dead, was it simply because they didn't understand the extent to which I felt betrayed by them? In the twenty-three years which had passed since my estrangement none of them had ever contacted me and asked to hear my side of the story. No amends could be made, it was impossible. A vase smashes onto the floor, you glue it together, the vase smashes onto the floor a second time, you glue it back together again, it doesn't look as nice, but it still works—just about, it smashes onto the floor a third time and lies shattered at your feet and you can see immediately that it's lost for ever, that it can't be fixed. That was how it was. Destroyed. My family was gone.

But then why did I care? Why go there to cause a scene and experience one in return? To have my say when for once I was calm, composed and prepared, because I needed to speak my own carefully chosen words just the once, for my own peace of mind, for the sake of my honour, for the sake of my self-respect, get it out into the open, the rot, the rumours, the knowing nods, the glances they would sometimes exchange, to end this game of Chinese whispers; it felt as though if I didn't do it now—and it had to be now—then I would have allowed myself to be bought off with the promise of an inheritance. Tell Bergljot she'll inherit something, that'll probably stop her telling tales about what she claims happened to her, promise her some money and she'll change her tune. That was why they wanted me to inherit, that was why they preached treating their children equally, to shut Bård and me up. They wanted to buy our silence and the benefit of our company, but only on their own terms.

In *Memento*, Larousse writes that mourning the death of a parent lasts eighteen months.

But Roland Barthes writes in his *Mourning Diary* that this is not true, that time doesn't lessen grief, that grief is never-ending.

Barthes writes that time doesn't heal anything, apart from the *emotional* side of grief.

Have I always been grieving? Is grief my default setting? And is it only the emotional side of my grief that has lessened? Deep down have I always been sad? Only when I'm calm, when I'm alone, when I work intensely, is my sadness less painful. That's why I'm calm, that's why I work so hard, that's why I'm alone.

Roland Barthes said to a friend that the feeling will pass, but the grief remains. The friend replied: No, feelings come back, just you wait.

Feelings come back.

The night before Monday 4 January, I couldn't sleep. The words from the draft I had written with Klara in her study kept going round my head. I finally nodded off around one o'clock, but woke up at four and couldn't get back to sleep because the words from Klara's study kept going round my head. It turned five o'clock, I couldn't sleep, but had to sleep, so as not to turn up sleep deprived on this critical day, with just a few hours' sleep under my belt, I had to sleep, but I couldn't sleep because the words from Klara's study kept going round my head, I got up and downed a bottle of wine in order to sleep, but I couldn't sleep, I dozed off and woke up around eleven in the morning and didn't have as much time as I had hoped for and expected to have to write a brief summary. I was still drunk, but I had to get up and write a short, concise text. I used the draft from my meeting with Klara, but expressed in my own words, I was more economic in my vocabulary than she was, I wrote a draft and went for a walk with the dog to clear my head, to get some snow on my hair, I called my children who could hear that I was drunk, who said that I mustn't for anything in the world be drunk at the meeting with the accountant, no, no, I said, I promise, I said, it would be disastrous if I were to turn up drunk for the meeting, I knew that, I said, that's why I had gone for a walk, I said, to sober up, to clear my head, to get some snow on my hair, it's coffee only from now on, I said. Once I was home again I edited my draft, making what I needed to say as short and succinct

182

as possible, I felt as I wrote that it was crucial for me to say it, I became increasingly convinced as I wrote that it was the right thing to do and increasingly anxious about the unmentionable, which would be mentioned with everyone present. I rang the children when I was done and read my text aloud to them. Tale said do it, Ebba said if that's how you feel. Søren was more hesitant, perhaps it wasn't a smart move to bring such matters up at an executor meeting, perhaps it would harden positions, make us real enemies, he said, but I defended my text, I had made up my mind. I called Klara afterwards and read it aloud to her, she said she would have been blunter, but OK. I called Bo and read it aloud to him, he said the text showed that I also cared about my brother. I called Lars, who was exasperated that I was in such a state, so het up and agitated and on edge as if I cultivated and wallowed in my pain, rather than working to put it behind me. You're going to get a drubbing, he said, but I had made up my mind. I called Karen to get the assurance I needed, then I caught the bus because I was meeting Ebba afterwards at an Indian restaurant, I would be needing a beer, someone to talk to, I would be shaking. I was shaking now, I caught the bus and then the train into town, and I felt that everyone could tell from looking at me that I was shaking, that I was on my way to the front and that I was in mortal fear of the upcoming battle, and I was reminded of the opening scene in *Festen* where the central character walks through golden, undulating fields knowing he is on his way to the front, how did he manage to appear so calm, and why couldn't I? I got off the train and went to the café where Bård was waiting as we had arranged, and I said to Bård that I was shaking and that I had written a text, it feels unreal now, but it was unreal at the time as well, I gave the text to Bård and asked if he thought I should read it aloud at the meeting. I went to the loo while he read it. I was thinking, as I sat on the

183

loo, now he's reading the text, its contents. I had considered not letting him read it in advance, to surprise Bård as well because if I asked him to read my text before the meeting, he might say that I shouldn't read it aloud and I *wanted* to read it aloud, it had become crucial for me, I didn't want to risk missing my moment which would never come back and I would never get a chance to say something which it was now essential for me to say, but when I saw Bård, when I entered the café and saw Bård's grave face, I realised that I had to let him read the text first, that I couldn't spring it on him because we were on the same side and to spring something on Bård, no matter what it was and though my intentions were good as far as our common cause was concerned, I couldn't do it. I had to let him read it first and if he didn't want me to read it aloud, he probably had sound reasons which hadn't crossed my mind, perhaps he thought it wasn't a good strategy to read it aloud. I was in the loo while he read it, I came out and my hands were shaking, he wanted me to read the text aloud. But what if they get up and leave, I said. Then we stay put, he said. When shall I read it, I asked. He told me how he thought the meeting would go. The accountant would start with Dad's businesses. The accountant would review the business side of the estate. Then she would hand out copies of the will and go through it, and there would invariably be one or two things to discuss. Once the will had been read, the accountant would bring up the matter of the cabins and might well mention that she was aware that they were a bone of contention. At this point Mum would probably argue that Astrid and Åsa should have the cabins because Astrid and Åsa had been so nice for so many years and because they had been with Mum and Dad on Hvaler for so many years, and for those reasons it was only natural that they got the cabins. Then you can read your text, Bård said. I drank two big cups of coffee, trying not to spill them, it was a quarter to five, and we walked to the accountant's office, it's about seeing it through, I thought, don't think of anything other than seeing it through, don't think about the consequences, don't worry about how they might react, just see it through because it's absolutely crucial, this is about your life. We went to the offices, they were already there, Mum and Astrid and Åsa, Mum with a glum face and the scarf I had given her one Christmas around her neck. A gesture to me, I thought, a thank you to me and a plea, I thought, which I would ignore.

Right, now we're all here, the accountant said, and asked if we wanted something to drink, she nodded to a tray with mineral water, thermos flasks with coffee and hot water for tea. I fetched a bottle of Farris mineral water, I was restless, I asked if anyone else wanted a Farris, Mum would like a Farris, I opened a bottle of Farris and put it and a glass in front of her. I opened a bottle of Farris for myself, took a glass, then went to my seat next to Bård, sat down, poured the mineral water and drank it. The accountant started, she listed Dad's businesses with which the others, my siblings, appeared to be familiar. The accountant gave a PowerPoint presentation of the business accounts which the others seemed to know about. Someone had to serve as directors, the accountant said, Dad had wanted all four of his children to be directors, probably an expression of a hope of reconciliation once he was gone, he had given up hope of reconciliation while he was alive, wasn't able to, he hadn't been strong enough to reconcile while he was alive—who would have been—but he had hoped for reconciliation after his death, spring in January, that his four children would all be directors of the businesses which carried his surname, our surname, and become friends again. Astrid said that she was happy to be a director, they had probably agreed in advance that she would volunteer, the only one of my siblings who had had any contact with me until two months ago. Bård said that he, too, would like to be a director. Åsa said in jest that being a director probably wouldn't interest me very much, and we all laughed, everyone knew that I wouldn't want to be a director, they knew me well enough after all. Perhaps they had noticed that there were two folded pieces of paper in front of me, they looked pristine, but the blank side was upwards so they couldn't know if there was something on them or whether it was paper I had brought along with me to take notes. The others also had paper in front of them, except for Mum, blank sheets of paper they had taken from the middle of the table where there was a pile of them and several pens, while I would appear to have brought along the pieces of paper which lay in front of me. Did they see the papers in front of me and did they fear them? The accountant pointed to some numbers on the PowerPoint slide, Bård had said that we weren't talking large sums and it didn't look like it either. It took just over an hour, a straightforward review, no one had any comments. Bård had a couple of harmless questions, which the accountant cleared up. That was it, the accountant said, turned off the PowerPoint presentation, leaned slightly across the table and added that she was aware that a dispute had arisen about the cabins on Hvaler. And even before Mum started to protest, I turned over the papers lying in front of me on the table in order to get started, to get it over with, waiting had been unbearable, I had to have my story translated from paper into words, to get it over with, I spread out the papers and looking only at them, I read:

I, and especially my children, have often heard my mother and my sisters talk about the happy times they have had together on Bråteveien and on Hvaler over the years. Heard how nice and kind my sisters have been and so on. As my son Søren observed after having been to Bråteveien some weeks ago for my parents' eightieth and eighty-fifth birthday party, if you didn't know your parents had two other children, it would look like just another happy family.

At this point Mum cut me off. She said she refused to listen to this and got up. That was how bad it was, Mum said, she wasn't going to listen to this, she was leaving, she said, I imagined she knew what was coming. Astrid got up and put her arm lovingly around her, and it was then, at that point in the meeting, that I raised my voice for the first and only time. Are you too much of a coward, I challenged her. You're the coward, Mum retorted, but with Astrid's calming arm around her, she sat down again, reluctantly. Now is not the time or the place, Astrid said, shaking her head, I imagined she knew what was coming as well. I continued, somewhat rattled, but with forced calm and probably rushed it in order to get through my text before anyone else exploded or stormed out, to say out loud something which throughout my whole life, to this day, right up until now, I had felt was absolutely necessary for me to say, so that I could be done with it. And that's how Astrid, Åsa and Mum want it to look, I read on, but there are these other two, troublesome children who ruin the picture. Do they just happen to be unpleasant people? Or is there a reason why the two eldest of Mum and Dad's four children haven't been to Bråteveien and Hvaler like the two youngest?

Shame on you, Mum said, shame on you.

Reconciliation, and my sister Astrid must know this, I carried on, because she works with human rights, I said, can only happen when all parties in a conflict get to tell their story, and she must also know, given that she has worked with the Balkan conflict, that a story doesn't get old. Yet only the other day Astrid told me that

187

she couldn't understand why Bård, who is nearly sixty, couldn't move on from his childhood, completely failing to grasp that his past, his childhood lives in him as the story of his life. His own, the only one he has.

Shame on you, Mum said, what nonsense, what lies!

Now is not the time or the place, Astrid said, Aunt Unni ought to be here.

I've been scared of Dad my whole life, I continued. I didn't realise how much until 17 December last year when he died. I experienced a physical sense of relief. When I was between five and seven years old and repeatedly sexually assaulted by Dad, he told me if I ever told anyone, then he would go to prison or Mum would die.

You're lying, Mum shouted.

I didn't say anything, I said, I repressed it, I was silent, but my life became increasingly difficult, I became increasingly self-destructive and chaotic as everything that I had repressed began to surface. I realised that I needed help and I got it, after several tests I eventually qualified for free psychoanalysis. Twenty-three years ago when I told Mum what had happened, she refused to believe me. As did my sisters. I became an outcast who threatened the family honour. My speaking out in public at various events became a problem and a threat, as Astrid responded once when in despair I said that I felt Mum and Dad would rather see me admitted to a psychiatric ward than become a writer: Well, it would have been easier.

Now is not the time or the place, Astrid said for the third time and shook her head, and with the accountant present!

The accountant sat at the end of the table, speechless.

You're lying, Mum said.

But it wasn't as easy as that, I read aloud, I carried on. Dad is dead. Dad demanded my silence and I've been silent for a long time, but I can't accept that the family silence must be extended to my children. I have, as I said, tried to tell my family my story many times without being heard, but I'm forced to do so now, so that my story as well as Bård's can be acknowledged and form a part of this settlement, which isn't just financial the way I see it, but a moral one. That's why I'm here.

I looked up.

Now is not the time or the place, Astrid said for the fourth time, shaking her head.

When would be the right time, Bård said.

Liar, Mum hissed at me. Pointing the finger at your dad, what do you think it was like for your dad to be accused of something that awful, and then came the i-word with that strange pronunciation of hers, *inchest*, she said, with an h, what do you think it was like for your poor dad, how do you think it was for him and why didn't you confront him, why didn't you go to the police, you should have gone to the police if what you're saying is true, but you didn't, you didn't go to the police, and you never confronted your dad.

I'm not surprised she didn't confront Dad, Bård said, who might have been just as scared of Dad as I was, and who didn't know because I hadn't told him, because I couldn't tell everyone everything, couldn't expose the most intimate details to everyone, for my own sake, for their sake, that I had made an attempt to confront Dad when I realised what he had done to me and was in total meltdown twenty-three years ago.

I had called the Support Organisation for Victims of Incest back then and asked if I should confront my parents, and they said they didn't give advice on individual cases with which they weren't familiar, but advised me that if I confronted my parents, I would lose my family. Ninety-nine per cent of children who confront their family lose their family. But I had already lost my family, or so it felt, so I had nothing to lose, I called Mum and confronted her and she must have spoken to Dad, I don't remember the details, just that some turbulent days followed, some distressing days, some agitated phone calls, then Dad wanted to meet with me in Bråteveien. And I went to Bråteveien, I actually had the courage to go there, I remember thinking on my way to Bråteveien, that I had to see this through, don't back down now, be brave, have the courage to go to Bråteveien and meet with Dad. I remember what I was wearing, a blue silk dress, I remember my footsteps going up to the door, I remember ringing the bell, but I can't remember what I had been expecting. Dad opened the door, he was the owner of the BMW outside the house, he had bought the Volvo for Mum, which was parked next to the BMW, Dad showed me into his study with the green leather Chesterfield sofa in front of the fireplace and the large desk. I walked through the impressive hall, down the hallway and into Dad's study and Dad sat behind the mighty desk and gestured for me to take the chair in front of the desk, and I sat down like a prisoner who was about to be interrogated, I had already lost, I was already beaten and neutralised, I was in Dad's power, and he knew it. But at least I'd had the courage to go there, I was there, at least I had made a fragile, if failed attempt at confrontation.

I didn't commit inchest against you, Dad said in his patrician voice, he uttered the word in that strange foreign way in which Mum had just said it, perhaps that was how the word was pronounced back when they learned it and they hadn't heard it or used it since, they had closed their ears to that word. I was incapable of saying anything, paralysed as I was in my blue silk dress, it

190

was summer, it was warm, and as I sat there in front of Dad, I realised that the silk dress was a mistake, that I should have worn something with more coverage, but instead I had put on my best summer dress, I had made myself look nice before going there, to Dad's, I was so naïve, so trapped, so in Dad's power, I didn't have a Klara in those days, I barely knew Klara back then, I threw away the dress after my meeting with Dad, my favourite silk dress, my meeting with Dad had soiled it. I don't remember much of the conversation, but I do remember that he asked me the same question he had asked when he had stood by my bed the morning after he had read my diary when I was fifteen years old, when he went out and got drunk and came back drunk and sobbing and said that it wasn't easy to be human, and proved it by loving me and caring about me and worrying about me, that was how I had understood him, how I needed to read him, when he asked if I had bled when I first had sex. He must have meant when I first had sex with someone other than him. It never even crossed my mind that I could choose not to answer, that I could say it was none of his business, I said no, that I hadn't bled, and that was progress from the previous time he had asked me when I was fifteen, mortified and had been unable to utter a single syllable. No, I said, because I hadn't bled as far as I could remember, but that wasn't in itself unusual. Afterwards, even as I was leaving, I realised that he might not have been aware that it had gone as far as it had, but that he had been afraid that it had gone as far as it had, that Dad had been so drunk that he couldn't remember what had happened back when he hadn't done what he usually told me to do to him, that on this one occasion he hadn't done solely what he usually did to me, but had got on top of me and had full intercourse with me, but that he feared that he had. And I remember Dad saying as I was about to leave, leave his study, leave Bråteveien, I was walking quite quickly, that if only I knew what had happened to him when he was a child.

Why didn't you just go to the police, Mum screamed, and before you told me it was just the once, and now you're saying it happened over and over.

But it was you who asked me if Dad had ever done something to me when I was little, I said.

And you said no! Mum said.

Then why did you ask me in the first place, I demanded to know, and why didn't you ask my sisters the same question.

This is not on, Åsa stopped us. It's all wrong, Åsa said.

Why would she say it if it wasn't true, Bård said.

To get attention, Mum said, she sits in cafés all over town, drunk, talking about her *secret*, it's dreadful, shame on you!

Do you remember? Mum asked, looking at me with narrow, furious eyes, previously you told me that you didn't remember.

I remember, I said.

Mum got up, Mum wanted to leave, Mum shouted: You would never have got to where you are today if you hadn't had a safe and happy childhood in Skaus vei. And you got so much attention, your siblings were jealous of you because you got so much attention.

Yes, I said, why were you so worried about me?

I wasn't worried about you, she snapped back, but if there was one thing that everyone in the room except the accountant knew, then it was that Mum had always been strangely worried about me, that Mum had had one fit of hysterics after another when I was young and was late coming home from something. Because it wasn't easy being Mum back then, to know what had happened to your oldest daughter, but not what to do about it because Mum was at Dad's mercy in every possible way, Mum had four children, but no education, no money, what could she do? I thought about going to see the vicar, she had said to me back when she asked me if Dad had ever done something to me when I was little, back when my story was useful, back when Mum had hoped to divorce Dad in order to marry Rolf Sandberg because if my story came out, divorcing Dad wouldn't be an act of betrayal on Mum's part, but a virtue. You were so strange when I came back from Volda, she said. I thought about going to see the vicar, she said. But why go to a vicar, what kind of worries do you take to a vicar rather than a friend or relative? But Mum didn't share her suspicion and her worries with the vicar when she came back from Volda after leaving Dad alone with Bård and me in Skaus vei, when I acted so strangely after she had come back. Mum didn't go see the vicar just like I didn't go to the police with a case that had passed the statute of limitations. Instead Mum sent me to piano lessons and ballet lessons, something which she never did for my sisters, probably in the hope that I could be fixed in that way, no wonder she had worried about me. Even back then, when the i-word was pronounced with an h, people knew that children who had been subjected to what I had been subjected to might experience problems in later life, become promiscuous, oversexualised, abuse drugs and alcohol, that was what Mum was scared of, what might happen when I became a teenager, that I might start to drink or sleep around and get pregnant at fifteen and take drugs, Mum sent me to piano lessons and ballet classes, something she never did for my sisters, Mum didn't go see the vicar, but instead gave me a copy of Tove Ditlevsen's novel about child abuse, *A Child Was Hurt*, which I didn't read, which I stuffed into a cupboard, filled with foreboding. Mum watched me like a hawk, scanning me for signs, smelling me when I came home at night to see if she could detect smoke, trying to sniff out if the catastrophe had set in.

I won't put up with this, Mum shouted, as she headed for the door in the meeting room, and Astrid got up to follow her and told me that it wasn't just me who had suffered, she too had suffered, it hadn't been easy for her either, having to cope with two such differing accounts, to be caught between a rock and a hard place.

And you, Mum said furiously, now addressing Bård, you were in France and you didn't come home, you didn't come to Bråteveien, you didn't visit me, your old mother, you didn't give me a hug! Mum had hoped for visits, Mum had hoped for hugs, Mum had hoped for all the things which presumably go on in a normal family, she couldn't see or she wasn't willing to accept that the family she had helped create wasn't like that, normal, but that it was abnormal, destroyed. And you sent a horrible email to Dad, she carried on still addressing Bård, a dreadful, horrible email, and Dad was thinking about replying to that vile email, but never managed to because then he died. Mum went up to the accountant and asked if she could annul the will.

Can I annul the will?

And the cat was out of the bag.

Mum and Dad had been hoping to buy us off, to buy me off, that was why we were told that Christmas three years ago that they had made a will, that everyone would get the same, apart from the cabins, in order to shut me up, to silence my nasty story with money, then that didn't happen, then I refused to be silenced and the intention of the will was lost, it hadn't worked. Can we annul the will, Mum asked the accountant, but the ashen-faced accountant replied that she couldn't. Later I have often thought about it, how trapped Mum suddenly was. The will was lying there and it was valid, and the expressed intention of the will was for the four children to inherit equally so that was what must happen even though the real intention had been that Bård and I would shut up, be silenced, complicit and kind and quiet, but we weren't, so it hadn't played out the way they had planned, so they didn't get to do what they wanted with their money, with their will, and now it couldn't be undone, now it was too late.

I'm disappointed in you, Mum hissed at me on her way to the door.

Do you know the first thing that springs to mind when I think about Dad, Bård said, and carried on without waiting for a reply. I was nine years old, we had gone fishing in Hardangervidda, but I wanted to go home and turned around. Dad came after me, he grabbed a stick and beat the living daylights out of me. That's my most vivid memory of Dad.

He only did it because he was scared that you would get lost, Mum screamed, thus revealing that she was familiar with the story, so Bård must have confronted her or them with it at some point. You would have done the same, Mum screamed at him, you told me so yourself that you would do the same had it been one of your children!

What? Bård said.

Yes, you told me so, Mum said.

No, Bård said.

Oh, yes, you did, Mum said, and looked at me again: I'm really, really disappointed in you!

I've been disappointed in you for years, I said, Mum was standing by the door now, her hand on the handle, Astrid and Åsa had got up to leave with her.

You can't direct us to believe you, Åsa said to me, using the theatrical expression she had also used at the funeral. I'm guessing it was a reference to me directing her as a child when she was in my theatre group, her big sister's theatre group, how she must have hated me even then. I replied that I knew that, but that I wanted

195

my account to have a life. They were by the door now having put on gloves and woollen hats ready to leave, and Åsa said that this whole performance showed exactly why the four of us couldn't share the cabins on Hvaler. She refused to share a cabin with any of us, she said, and then they walked out, the three of them, and Bård and I were left behind with the accountant.

We sat in silence for a while, then the accountant said that this had been a surprise, that this had been unexpected.

If you hadn't been here, Bård said, Bergljot would never have been allowed to finish.

He was right about that. If the accountant hadn't been present, they would have left before I had finished reading.

I was exhausted. My legs were shaking. We sat in the meeting room for a while and the accountant asked us questions, including some about the family, but I was incapable of speaking, all the air had gone out of me. Bård talked, explained our view of our family, how we had experienced our family as children. The accountant listened and was sympathetic, yet Mum was paying her bill, the accountant said that it couldn't be easy to be widowed at the age of eighty, and that was true, the accountant was right about that, it couldn't be easy to be widowed at the age of eighty, we sat there about half an hour, then we left, I've always wondered if the accountant billed Mum for that half hour.

We left. We made our way to Bård's car. Bård said he would give me a lift to the Indian restaurant where I was meeting Ebba. I said that I preferred to walk, I needed to feel the wind on my face.

Klara found a Danish publisher willing to publish her book about Anton Vindskev. Klara is like a cork, Anton said, the longer you keep her down, the higher she jumps back up again. Klara is like a palm tree in a hurricane, he said, it'll bend right down to the ground, but once the wind dies down, it'll jump right back up. Klara celebrated the acceptance of her book at Restaurant Hong Kong in Copenhagen. On her way home, she saw a man who was drowning in a canal. She threw herself down on the ground and grabbed the man's coat by his shoulder pads and called out for help. He probably weighed a hundred kilos and he was wearing a thick coat and heavy boots, she could only just keep him above the surface, she cried out for help and people gathered around her, but they merely looked on as if it were a film. Help, Klara called out, help me keep him up, but the people were drunk and thought they were watching a movie. Help me, she called out, I'm losing him or I'll fall in myself, I'll be dragged into the water, sit on my legs or he'll drown or we'll both drown, she called out, then an ambulance, some paramedics and two divers arrived and got the man out alive.

She called me in the middle of the night. Why do people keep trying to kill themselves? I haven't got the energy for any more suicides! I haven't got the energy to save people all the time, it's robbing me of all my strength.

I found the Indian restaurant although I was beside myself, as if I was an evil robot on autopilot, although my heart was beating too fast, although my ribs were groaning and aching. I gulped, my mouth was dry and parched, I felt nauseous, but I couldn't bear the thought of drinking anything. It was obvious that what I had just participated in, the meeting with the accountant, had affected me mentally, yet what surprised me was how my body reacted independently of my mind which had wanted this, *I* had wanted this. I didn't get to the restaurant on time, I was late, the meeting with the accountant had taken longer than I had expected, I had to talk to someone urgently, to Ebba. I found the Indian restaurant and she was there with a Cola Light on the table, and I ordered a beer and it couldn't arrive soon enough, and I got it and I drank it, it was a disaster, I said. Then Tale rang me, it was a total disaster, I said, they went for my jugular, I said, Mum got up to leave before I'd even got to the second paragraph, I said, and when Bård asked why I would say it if it wasn't true, she hissed that it was to get attention, she actually hissed, but I'm with Ebba right now, I said, I'll call you back, I said, I said the same thing to Ebba, it was a disaster, I said, I drank beer and ordered some food, but didn't eat any, I drank another beer, I won't drink much, I said, you need to look after yourself, Ebba said, perhaps I looked more upset and distraught than I felt, although I felt very upset and distraught, what had I expected, but that was the whole point, I hadn't expected anything, I had deliberately chosen not to think about the consequences, of their reactions. Lars rang and I repeated that it had been a disaster, that Mum had wanted to leave before I even got to the second paragraph, but I'll call you back later, I said, I'm with Ebba. Poor Ebba sat there with her distraught mother, whom she didn't know how to help, caught up in her mother's history, which she didn't know how to handle, but which had invariably become her history. She drank her Cola Light while her mother drank beer and spoke on the phone because then Søren rang, it was a total disaster, I said. Did you read your text aloud, he asked, yes, I said, but beforehand I asked Bård if he thought I should read it, and he thought I should. It was a good idea to ask Bård first, he said, but I'm with Ebba, I said. Ebba asked me to tell her everything right from the beginning and I tried to start at the beginning, I ordered a third beer and asked for the bill at the same time to signal to the waiter and to Ebba that it would be no more than three beers. Then I had a text message from Bård. Well fought, congratulations, he wrote, love, your brother. I showed it to Ebba, she nodded cautiously, poor young, innocent Ebba. Likewise, I replied, love, your sister. Then we left, Ebba took my arm, let's just forget all about the family, she said supportively, to her mother, woven into her mother's story. Yes, I said. She asked if I would be all right for the rest of the evening and said that I was welcome to stay at her place. Lovely Ebba, worried about her mother, just like Astrid and Åsa were worried about and looking after their mother. I'll be fine, I said, I won't go out, I said, I'm going straight home to drink some red wine and then I'm off to bed, I said.

I went home as quickly as I could, first by train, then by bus. Karen rang to ask how it had gone and I repeated yet again that it had been a total disaster, I couldn't say it often enough, that it had been a total disaster, it was as if it made it a little easier to deal with. Karen thought Bård's questions had been spot on. When would be the right time? Why would she say it if it wasn't true? Yes, why would you say it if it wasn't true, Karen said, you're not the kind of person who tells lies. No, I wasn't. They had probably talked about it, my friends, throughout the years, what to make of my story and had concluded, fortunately, that I was credible. That was good, and no wonder that they had presumably discussed in private what to think about my story, you can't swallow whole everything people say about their childhood.

When I got off the train, I went to the station café and had a glass of wine while I waited for the bus. I called Klara. It was a total disaster, I said. She had imagined the confrontation, she said, it was hideous, she said. And I was so pleased that she had met Mum once on Hvaler when Mum had asked if I had given Tale and her friends ecstasy, so she had some basis on which to imagine it all.

It was the fact that she had wanted to let go, Klara said, the day after she had saved a man from drowning himself in a Copenhagen canal. It was the fact that she had felt a wicked desire to let go of the stupid, heavy man and watch him sink to the bottom. It was like that poem by Tove Ditlevsen about the little girl who is tempted to pick up a big, beautiful vase, which she knows she mustn't touch, she wants to pick up the forbidden vase, which is big and heavy and ornate like a piece of jewellery, and because it's forbidden she picks it up and stands for some endless, exciting seconds feeling the weight of the vase in her hands, how heavy it is, how big it is, and the girl is so small and to smash the vase would be wicked and utterly wonderful, and she hears a voice saying: Why not do something awfully dangerous now that you're home alone? And she lets the vase go, and in that moment the world becomes wicked and joyless, and on the floor lie a thousand shards which can never be put back together, and the good angels turn away and weep.

But what if the world had been wicked and joyless all along, only she had to break the vase in order to know it?

One day I'll let go, Klara said.

Before I stopped seeing my family for good, I tried for a time to have a small amount of contact with them for the sake of my young children so that they would get to see my family and because I thought that having a minimum of contact with my family would be less stressful than being subjected to Mum's enormous pressure, her threats of suicide, her accusations: How can you be so cruel? Mum's letters listed everything she and Dad had done for me over the years. In spite of everything, it was easier to show up for a sixtieth birthday party with my boyfriend and children, stick it out for an hour and then collapse afterwards. As long as I did that the pressure eased off, the suicidal phone calls stopped as long as I gave Mum enough to make us look normal to the outside world, enough so that she could say should anyone ask: Bergljot is writing her Ph.D. on German drama. Bergljot has been to Berlin. During one of those periods Mum called and suggested that I might need a car, that Dad would like to buy me a car. I thought about it and accepted the offer because I did need a car, a car would be good for the children, and I regarded the car as an apology from Dad. Or I wanted to believe that it was because I needed a car, and surely Dad wouldn't give a car to someone he felt had unjustly accused him of sexual assault. I accepted the car and considered the car an admission and an apology from Dad. Some months later, at Åsa's fortieth birthday party, which I went to because Mum and Dad weren't going to be there, Astrid told me later that night when everyone was drunk, when I was drunk, when Astrid was drunk, that Dad had asked her and my siblings if they believed my allegation. Bergljot says that I sexually assaulted her, do you believe her? She didn't say what she and my siblings had replied when Dad had asked them the question, but I'm guessing that they replied no. That they had stood in the hallway in Bråteveien one Sunday afternoon, and Dad had asked with a grave face if they believed the monstrous allegation I had made. They had said no because they couldn't say yes, and as they said no, they picked their side, they denied me. Dad forced my siblings to deny me. So the car wasn't an admission and an apology, but a bribe. I staggered out of the function room and deep into the forest, I ignored the coach, which was waiting to take the guests back, I didn't want to share a coach with people who had said no when Dad asked if they believed me. I hated Dad who had given me a car and hated myself, who had bowed and scraped for the car, for being stupid enough to think that it was an admission and an apology, while behind my back Dad had forced my siblings to deny and betray me, I hated myself for accepting the car because I had tried to forgive Dad, because I thought the car was Dad was admitting and apologising to me, and then it was all a ploy and a lie. I got lost on the forest paths in the morning fog, I didn't get home until dawn, out of my mind, overwhelmed, overcome, overwrought and overlooked, to make matters worse I called Mum and told her what Astrid had said, was it really true that Dad asked my siblings such impossible questions behind my back? Mum told me not to be so self-righteous. That morality had wrecked her life, that human beings were nothing but animals. Human beings are nothing but animals, Bergljot. I would appear to be naïve if I thought anything else, I was a naïve moralist who didn't understand that human beings are animals and at the mercy of their urges, a naïve

Sunday schoolteacher, who couldn't get over something as trivial as her father snogging her a few times, and then Mum said something reminiscent of what Dad had said to me back then: If only you knew what happened to me on the boat to America. When Mum and Dad were newlyweds, they had worked their passage to the US on the America ferry. I hung up. Why had I called her? What good had I ever thought would come from calling Mum?

I got on a plane to San Sebastian to get out of the country, to get away from it, but I didn't get away from it although I was abroad, it was eating me up, and then I did something I had never done before, I called Mum from San Sebastian in anger. I called and I screamed at Mum, not at an answering machine, I didn't write a text message, I called Mum and Mum picked up the phone and I screamed at her, for the first time in my life I screamed at Mum, I screamed that her bloody irresponsible behaviour was driving me mad, that she belittled everything I told her, how angry it had made me that she had started talking about herself and the America ferry rather than listen to what I, her daughter, was telling her, and when she tried to reply, I screamed at her to bloody well shut up, it was bloody well her turn to listen to me, I screamed that I felt like the central character in *Festen*, whose family ties him to a tree in the forest so they don't have to listen to him, I screamed as I've never screamed at anyone before, as I've never screamed at anyone since, I screamed that listening to her terrible, corrosive rabbiting drove me mad, I screamed myself empty and dry, then I rang off and turned off the phone. Then I turned it back on and called Klara, I walked along the San Sebastian seafront and told her about my furious outburst at Mum, which had taken me aback and shocked me once it was over, it had left me empty and weak and exhausted and trembling and infantile on the bench at the marina in San Sebastian, I needed comforting. I can't keep on doing this, I sobbed, what am I going to do, it's going to kill me, I sobbed. Oh, no, Klara said. Oh, no, it isn't, she said. You're strong, she said. But you have to realise this is war, not a tea party. It's a matter of life and death. There are no peace negotiations, it's a battle to the death for honour and legacy, she said. I had to give up thinking Mum would ever understand me. I had to give up thinking Mum would ever accept me. I would get nothing from Mum and Dad unless I gave up my truth. Mum and Dad would rather see me dead than acknowledge my truth, they would sacrifice me for their honour. This is war, she said, and I had to become a warrior. Not view myself as a victim, but as a fighter, be devious and tactical like a soldier, not think of appeasement, but war. And as Klara spoke, I began to grasp it, and it changed me. I understood that I wasn't negotiating a peace, I was at war, I understood that I wasn't going to be a peace broker, but a soldier. And slowly my body turned into that of a soldier or so it felt on the bench in San Sebastian where I had collapsed sobbing and from which I now rose. I raised my head and transformed my hysterical, grieving, pleading victim's body into that of a warrior. My feet suddenly connected more firmly with the ground, my legs carried me more safely and my chest lifted, and everything twisted and tangled and soft inside me disappeared, my stride lengthened, I walked along the seafront, brisk and full of purpose, I knew where I was going and swung my free arm as if to hit back and defend myself, as if it were a weapon, as if I had become a weapon. If you want war, war you shall have! I thought. I'm prepared, I thought, when I had rung off and turned off my mobile. I'm sharpening my weapons, I said to myself, I whispered it out into the darkness, and it felt much better to be a fighter than a supplicant child, one you could treat with diffidence because she always came crawling back, in pain or drunk. I had become a warrior, they would finally see what their daughter was made of, they would taste my strength, I'm not scared of you, Dad, I'm not scared of you, Mum, I'm fit for battle!

Morning, 5 January. Darkness, sleet, fog. I lay under the duvet not wanting to get up, reeling as if I'd been in battle. It was how Lars had put it when I had rung him on my way back last night to say I felt battered, that I knew I would be going to war, and in every battle you take some knocks. It was true, that was the other face of war. The desire for war and the excitement you feel when you fight for something you believe in was one face, the exhaustion and shaking that followed was the other. I had been in battle, that was how I felt, dazed, battered and tired to the bone, I had drunk red wine in bed until I fell asleep and woke up, heavy and shaking on 5 January to darkness and sleet. The house was cold, I could tell that from my nose which stuck out from under the duvet, I didn't have the energy to get up, I didn't have the energy to stay in bed, I didn't have the energy for silence, I didn't have the energy for sound, but I needed to talk to Klara. I turned on my mobile, which I had turned off last night so I wouldn't call anyone or take any calls when I was so mentally out of it, I entered the PIN and got a message telling me that it was wrong, I tried it a second time and was told again that it was wrong, although it wasn't, I was sure that it was right, I re-entered the PIN and got a message saying that it was wrong and that my phone had been locked and couldn't be unlocked for another hour, but I had to speak to Klara! I remembered that Søren had recently upgraded my phone contract, had got me a new SIM card, what an idiot I was forgetting that now that it really mattered that I remembered it, what did I do now? My mobile was locked, my mobile didn't work on the very day when I needed it most, that was my punishment for what I had done, making Mum run around the accountant's office, wide-eyed with terror like an animal that knows it's about to be tortured and killed. Poor Mum. I went to my Mac and saw that it was already twelve noon, but my watch showed ten, my watch had stopped again, nothing worked, I emailed Søren asking him what to do about my phone, he told me to go down to Elkjøp and get them to sort it out. I got dressed, I hid behind my clothes. Fido didn't want to go outside in the rain, I forced her outside, I was mean, it felt as though I was staggering, I hadn't eaten anything for a day and a half, I must stop off at Kiwi for some groceries. The rain was pelting down, lashing us, Fido hated it, I dragged her along through puddles, I was merciless, water was thrown back from the road, spraying us whenever a car drove by, wearing water-proofs made no difference. We were soaked, Fido's tail was dripping, I walked right past Kiwi, I didn't have the energy to face people, didn't have the energy to pick out groceries, I wasn't hungry. The rain turned into snow as we walked, we waded through slush, I dragged the dog after me through the cold slush and tied her to a post outside the watchmaker and ran inside to drop off my watch so it could be fixed and continued onwards to Elkjøp where I tied Fido to a fence outside, dogs weren't allowed inside. Fido had to wait in the cold slush, shaking, poor Fido, she looked at me with reproachful eyes. I promised to be as quick as I could and ran inside and found I had to pick a number for the queue and wait although I wasn't able to wait. I waited, I tried my best to cope with it, I waited forever, no one hurried up for my sake, finally it was my turn after what seemed like an eternity and then the assistant said that I had to wait, that they couldn't help me until an hour had passed, that the mobile couldn't be unlocked until then. I'll buy a new one, I said, if he could guarantee that the new phone would work immediately, he said it would so I bought a new mobile. He found me a new mobile that he guaranteed would work immediately and set it up for me as quickly as he could, he could sense the urgency, I paid and went outside and untied the dog from the fence and called Klara and the phone worked immediately. Klara picked up and I headed back in the rain, in the slush, still on the phone to Klara and I didn't have to explain the state I was in, she could tell from my voice. Why did I really do it, I asked. What was I hoping for? Surely I knew all along that they wouldn't accept my version of events? Was I simply being wicked? Did I just want to drop the vase?

No, Klara said.

Had you wanted to be wicked, you could have done much worse. Your words were restrained. You said what they deserved to hear. Why should they get away with swiping those cabins for next to nothing without any negative consequences? They've treated you appallingly for years. Astrid and Åsa have benefited from your parents' generosity for years. They've had more than Bård and you for years, emotionally and financially, why should they get away with that without you, without the two of you, retaliating? It has been five against one for years. You've seen it as five against one for years because you didn't know how Bård felt. Now it's three against two and that's new, they weren't prepared for that, but they're still the majority, and they have each other. You've no reason to feel ashamed. It was a healthy thing to do. Yes, Lars is right, you've been in battle, you're bruised and battered now, but you'll feel better in a few days, it's usually gets worse before it gets better.

~

I went to see Lars. He said that he had warned me that it might go like that, get worse. We mustn't drink. I couldn't be as shaky tomorrow, 6 January, as I was today, the fifth, I had meetings. Bård wrote to me in the evening: How are you feeling? It was a precise question. I replied that our mum and sisters were good at shirking responsibility, that they made me feel as if I was the problem, that the unpleasant scene could have been avoided if only I had behaved differently, I said that I realised that. But, but, I wrote. He replied that he'd had a lawyer go over the will and this lawyer thought that it stated clearly—twice—that the intention was that everyone would inherit equally and that we would win a subsequent court case, if the cabin valuations weren't increased. The question was how to communicate this to Astrid and Åsa. I said that I trusted him, that he would have to do it in whichever way he thought best. He could probably hear that I was exhausted, he was probably exhausted, he said that our mum and sisters probably found this just as exhausting as we did. *I believe that they find this just as exhausting as we do.* Did Astrid and Åsa also find it exhausting, did they feel anything other and more than just anger and outrage? Did they also experience something akin to grief, and which had nothing to do with Dad?

We didn't drink, it took a long time before I was able to fall asleep, I lay in the darkness behind Lars's back, trying to get in contact with Dad. Wherever you are, if you're anywhere at all, we draw a line now, I said, I forgive you, I said. I thought he replied: Well fought, Bergljot, but I think I got that line from *Festen*.

During the period I tried to have at least some contact with my family for the sake of my young children so that they would get to see their family, their grandparents, uncles and aunts, cousins, I would occasionally meet with Mum in town. Mum wanted to see me, and I would meet her in town. Her speech would be rather hectic when we met, rushed, she would chew gum and be restless, squirming on her chair while we sat in Baker Hansen. She worried about the elephant in the room. She wanted to see me so that she could tell other people, friends and acquaintances, that she had seen me, but she actually dreaded seeing me, I could sense her anxiety. She was terrified of accidentally mentioning anything that might relate to the elephant, any mention of media reports about sexual crimes and the mood would instantly become silent and awkward. So she made up her mind, I think, to talk only about safe subjects, the weather or my siblings and their families, it was a rehearsal so that everything would sound normal when she spoke to other people. And yet it wouldn't surprise me if she came to Baker Hansen nurturing a faint hope that our differences might suddenly have evaporated, only to be disappointed that they hadn't. Before we parted, after half an hour, say, she would give me two thousand kroner in cash. I thanked her and took the money with a feeling of unease because I needed the money, and how would she have reacted if I had refused it, it would only have added to the awkwardness. Then we would go our separate ways, each relieved that it was over.

Once during such a meeting at Baker Hansen, Mum said: Many people think that Dad is funny.

Why did she say that? To defend her still being with him? Did Mum deep down find it humiliating that she was still with Dad, that she hadn't managed to leave him? I was only one issue, I could be rejected and dismissed as having an overactive imagination, besides they never talked about me, another matter was the family and friends and acquaintances they had made over time, whom they couldn't have avoided making over time, and that Mum, once she was back with Dad in Bråteveien on his terms after the scandal with Rolf Sandberg, was being beaten up by Dad. They drank and argued and one day Mum had a broken arm, she had fallen down the stairs. One day she had a black eye, she had walked into a door. One day she had lost a tooth, she had slipped on the ice. Many people think that Dad is funny, Mum said.

Another time in Baker Hansen, Mum said: Dad is very clever.

What was I supposed to say that? That it made everything OK, Dad is funny, Dad is very clever, so we'll just forget about the other stuff?

A genuine conversation between Mum and me was impossible.

We left Baker Hansen, sad and relieved.

Because we didn't drink on the evening of the fifth, the morning of the sixth was better, the sky was blue. My meetings before lunch went well, perhaps I should quit drinking, perhaps that was what was needed. Tale called at lunchtime. She had been out with a friend the night before, someone who also had a difficult relationship with their family, someone like Klara. She and her friend had got themselves worked up about how people who could and did put themselves in charge of family gatherings and provided the premises because they were adults and had the power, refused to give up their own power and to give their children choices, regardless of the pain it caused them. Tale and her friend had decided to fight back, to say no, to stop playing along with it, and they had both gone home and written emails. Tale had sent emails to Astrid and Åsa and put the same wording in a letter she had posted to Mum, who didn't have an email address. I was welcome to read it, but I wouldn't be able to change anything as it had already been sent.

A minute later it was on my screen.

To Inga, Astrid, Åsa

After your reaction to Mum's brave account the other day, it has become more important than ever to tell you what it feels like to be Mum's daughter and Inga and Bjørnar's granddaughter.

I've seen Mum as broken and distraught as a human being is capable of without dying; so destroyed that very few would be able to get up again. I've seen Mum struggle to learn to live with her past. I've seen Mum hold on to her pain so as not to pass it on to her children. I've seen Mum seek refuge in alcohol, in literature, to escape reality, to escape her memories. I've seen Mum unable to sleep sober because she still fears the night, the bed, the loss of control. I've seen Mum work her fingers to the bone.

I've seen Mum constantly trying to understand.

I've seen Mum say sorry, it's my fault, not yours, take away my shame like she wishes someone could have taken away her shame. I have seen Mum fight, try, hope and give up.

I've spent time with Granny and Grandad and felt like a hypocrite. I've seen them pretend that nothing is wrong and I've done likewise. I'm ashamed of that.

But I didn't know how deep these self-deceptions went and how far you were willing to go to maintain them. Now I've witnessed you denying events which in every possible way have been so present, so pivotal and so decisive for Mum's life, and thus mine too. I've witnessed you not taking it seriously. I don't understand how that's possible, and it makes me angry. Not only on Mum's behalf, but because it also denies my experiences, my history: I've seen her struggle, her loneliness, how small, damaged, vulnerable and alone she was.

Mum didn't become the person she is today because she had a happy childhood; Mum has all her fine, strong qualities in spite of it. In spite of a father who sexually abused her and a mother who let it happen; by denying this, Inga, you only reveal your own failure to take responsibility. And you lose not only a child, but grandchildren and great-grandchildren as well. How sad.

~

I wept. It was terrible to see it, but it felt so good to be seen. To have someone hold up a mirror that didn't lie, it was so painful, yet so good that she saw everything so clearly. It is terrible that someone who has been destroyed spreads destruction, and how hard that is to avoid. Dad, who had once said: If only you knew what happened to me when I was a child.

I called to thank her, she could hear that I was moved and said that she hadn't written it because she was a good person, but because she was upset and angry; besides she wasn't sacrificing or risking anything because she had a life in Stockholm, she didn't need the family in Bråteveien, they couldn't hurt her, she was no longer scared of them, it was a political act, she said, because what would happen to the world if everyone behaved like the family in Bråteveien and got away with it. She wanted to free me from gratitude, I realised, but I felt it nevertheless.

Once during the period when I had a minimal amount of contact with my family for the sake of my young children, so that they would get to see their family, Mum called and told me that Rolf Sandberg was retiring, she was still in contact with him. Rolf Sandberg was retiring and had to clear out his office where he kept all of his and Mum's letters. He couldn't bring them home and Mum couldn't keep them in Bråteveien, she asked if I wanted them, they must be quite interesting to a theatrical person, she said. Perhaps they might inspire me, perhaps they might make a play one day, could I keep their letters in my basement?

If this had happened before I understood my past, I might have said yes, I usually said yes to Mum, I tended to comply with her wishes although I tried to keep my distance because she had no boundaries, but I still depended on her because she was all I had. Had it been before the moment of truth, I would probably have said yes and Mum would have driven the steamy love letters which she and Rolf Sandberg had exchanged to my home and probably showed me some of the more poetical ones, read them aloud to me, and I would have listened and felt uncomfortable, but I would have listened to her, I was still so enmeshed in Mum's life at that point that I didn't know where hers stopped and mine began.

That was the childhood I had been given and to begin with I never questioned it, never realised that I had become enmeshed in Mum's life because I hadn't had a proper father. Thus Mum's way became the norm, I knew no other, I didn't know what normality was. But it was madness that was presented to me as normality, madness that sprung from desperation, only I didn't know that then.

Astrid had replied to Tale quite quickly. With more of the same, Tale said. Astrid opened by saying no wonder that Tale had suffered, that everyone had suffered, that she and Åsa had suffered, but especially Mum and Bergljot, me, I was suffering now. She had thought hard about it, she wrote, she had thought very hard about it for more than twenty years, and she realised that Bergljot, there I was again, suffered because she, Astrid, hadn't taken a side, but if she had done so, it would have been on flimsy and unreliable evidence. She thought it was time for reconciliation. In conclusion she asked if Tale had also sent her email to Mum. When Tale replied that she had posted a copy to her grandmother, Astrid asked if it was all right if she removed it from Mum's post box. She was scared that Mum couldn't take any more. Tale said they could do whatever they wanted, she wasn't taking the blame for any suicide.

But later that day, on 6 January, having discussed it with her Klara, Tale went home and wrote a furious, unedited email to Astrid saying that her intention was never to present herself as a suffering victim, that she wasn't a victim in this case, but then again, neither was Astrid. Neither are you, Astrid!

She wrote that she had written purely as a witness since they clearly needed one, and Astrid going on about how everyone had suffered terribly was pure provocation because Inga's suffering was

218

self-inflicted, and that rather than offer empty words, Astrid could use her influence to talk Inga to her senses because Inga wasn't going anywhere and wouldn't want to write off any more daughters because she couldn't manage without Astrid. But the truth is you have taken sides, she wrote, you sided with your mother at the expense of your sister, and it beggars belief that you're incapable of acknowledging that.

She received no reply to her last angry email. Just as I got no reply to my angry emails to Astrid. Anger wasn't good. Astrid wouldn't stoop to anger, Astrid wanted to act in a civilised manner, with dignity and without contributing to the escalation of the conflict, which anger might very well do, Astrid wanted to bring about peace and reconciliation by acting calmly and in a conciliatory manner, perhaps she looked down on people who acted in anger, who couldn't control themselves, who were ruled by such a primitive emotion as aggression. Perhaps Astrid might respond to us when we had calmed down.

It was time for reconciliation, Astrid had written.

It sounded all very conciliatory. Simple, as if it were merely a question of pulling oneself together and showing a little good will.

The philosopher Arne Johan Vetlesen has said that the problem with truth commissions and reconciliation processes after wars is that they usually demand just as much from the victims as from the aggressors, and that in itself constitutes an intrinsic injustice.

I had often pondered that statement and concluded that a reconciliation process in our family would demand more of me than of Mum and Dad and my siblings, and that that was unjust. And, besides, in truth and reconciliation commissions set up after wars, to a large extent, there was consensus on who the victims and the aggressors were. How can you possible reconcile when you can't even agree on that?

And besides, if Astrid was serious, if she was genuinely motivated by the desire to reconcile, then surely sharing the cabins on Hvaler with *all* of her siblings would have been a start?

Have you ever noticed, Bo said once when we had seen Woody Allen's *Husbands and Wives*, that the defining characteristic of many of his major female characters, especially those played by Mia Farrow, is their apparent concern for everyone, their apparent sacrifice, that all of Woody Allen's women, the ones who seem to mean well, who strive to solve conflicts, who never raise their voices, who are mildly overbearing when others lose their tempers and raise their voices, that these women who apparently never think of themselves but only ever of others, women you struggle to contradict or disagree with because they're so mild and kind, that those women, he said, usually end up getting what they want. Those women tend to cross the finishing line in front, in some strange way their wishes are granted and their dreams come true. He believed that they had developed an effective but uniquely feminine language of power dressed up as concern.

Have you ever noticed, I asked myself, how you use all of Bo's observations to your own advantage?

Bård had communicated to Mum, Astrid and Åsa that his lawyer believed that the intention of the will wouldn't be met unless the cabin valuations were increased. They in turn contacted a lawyer. Their lawyer disagreed with Bård's lawyer's opinion and said that Bård and I wouldn't win a subsequent court case, they cited some legislation. I didn't understand it nor did I have the energy to even try to understand it, but the last paragraph in the letter from their lawyer got my attention. It said that no one could prevent us taking legal action, but that it would be very stressful for my mother and also thwart 'the cooperation which the testators wanted to exist between the beneficiaries involved with the businesses'. Such cooperation wouldn't work unless the family conflict was resolved.

Mum, Astrid and Åsa would appear not to have told their lawyer how Bård's request to have the cabins shared between the four of us had been brusquely rejected, nor had they explained what my conflict with the family was really about.

Karen called. Astrid had written to her and asked if they could talk and it must be about me because they had no contact otherwise. I told her about Tale's email and said that Astrid was probably worried that I might throw myself out of a window or jump in front of a train. Or she pretended to care and wanted to demonstrate that she cared, but deep down she was hoping that I would throw myself out of a window or jump in front of a train. Perhaps everyone in Bråteveien was hoping that I would throw myself out of a window or jump in front of a train. They dreaded what I might say or write next. Only when I was dead would they be safe, and they longed for certainty. It's natural, it's human.

Karen spoke to Astrid and told me afterwards that Astrid had sounded genuinely concerned. Maybe she did care about me in her own way? Maybe she really had tried, once or on several occasions when she had been alone with Mum, a cautious: Are you absolutely sure there's no truth in . . . ?

And Mum's reaction had been just as terse and aggressive as on 4 January when we met at the accountant's, and she had responded with a furious: What are you saying?! What are you insinuating? How could you think something like that about Dad!

It must have been difficult for Astrid. It must have been difficult for Mum. How high the stakes must be for Mum to activate such a defence immediately, to live in a constant state of alert, when she not only reacted as she had done when we saw the accountant on 4 January, but also for her to never ever in the last twenty-three years approach me with a: Tell me what you think happened to you. Instead there was blind panic and an instinctive reaction of fear. Was she in denial? No, she wasn't because she wasn't choosing not to know, she knew better than that, no, it was what her life would look like if my history came out and was believed. That was what she feared.

Poor Mum who spent years being scared that I might founder because of the unmentionable. Then I didn't founder, then I would appear to be OK, and her fear that I might subsided only to be replaced by her fear that the unmentionable would rise from my subconscious, that I would remember my past. Then she reached a point in her life when she stood to gain if the unmentionable was mentioned, back when her infatuation with Rolf Sandberg was at its peak, back when she wanted to divorce Dad in order to live with Rolf Sandberg, back when she asked me: Are you sure Dad didn't do something to you when you were little?

I didn't understand what she meant. We were in the refectory at the teacher training college where she was a student, I remember it so clearly because what was she saying and what raw nerve in me did her words touch? No, I replied.

Then it didn't work out between Mum and Rolf Sandberg, then Mum went back to Dad, what else could she do, and started dreading once again that the unmentionable would rise from my subconscious, that I would remember my past because it would mean that she was living with a criminal, and she realised that she herself might have sown the seed to my memories surfacing by asking me: Are you sure Dad didn't do something to you when you were little?

Mum was scared, always scared. If it wasn't one thing, then it was another.

Then I got married and had children, and Mum's terror, Dad's terror subsided, they thought the danger had passed, then my older daughter turned five and I started suspecting her father of going to her bedroom at night and I fell in love with a married man and got a divorce and I was in crisis and I happened to mention one Christmas dinner that I was considering therapy, and Dad asserted in his most brusque voice, the one everyone in the

226

family and Mum especially was scared of: You're not having therapy!

I remember it clearly because of what was he saying, and what raw nerve in me did his words touch?
After I had written a one-act play about a romantic encounter, I began to suffer strange, painful attacks and I looked at what I had written before they occurred and came across this sentence: He touched me like a doctor, he touched me like a father. And it all came back to me, it hit me like a blow, it was like fainting. I understood everything and everything fell into place and it was terrible and unbearable and I thought I would die, but I didn't die, I bore it somehow because we're so ingeniously designed that anything terrible, unbearable that we repress surfaces the moment we're ready to deal with it. I called Astrid a few minutes after I had fainted, dazed and falling apart, and I called Mum, agitated and falling apart and Mum came over and I collapsed in spasms on the floor and she said: Now I understand why one shouldn't trivialise such things. And she spoke to Dad and they went to Hvaler in crisis and drank and Dad said to Mum: What if I said that I did it?

And Mum replied, she said when she called me the next morning and told me what he had said, that she had responded: Then I couldn't stay married to you. Mum called me and told me as if to prove how principled she was, that she wasn't the type of woman who could be married to a man who had done such things, while for all those years she had been married to a man she suspected had done such things. Dad was drunk and sobbing on Hvaler saying: *What if I said that I did it?* Dad was drunk and open to a serious, life-changing dialogue, and Mum had replied that then she couldn't stay married to him. Mum thus stifled the possibility of a serious, honest, life-changing conversation. Mum must have

227

realised in some nightmare scenario what an admission from Dad would mean for her, how would she deal with such a confession from Dad? Then I couldn't stay married to you, she said, and Dad shut up. And that was the end of that. They carried on with their shared life, they shut down the crisis, they tried putting it behind them, maybe they never spoke of it again because what would they say? Together they decided, tacitly, to act as if nothing had happened, to put a lid on it and perhaps they hoped that it wouldn't cost them their relationship with me. Or they calculated that their relationship with me was worth less than what it would cost them to enter into the honest dialogue Dad had opened up. *What if I said that I did it?* Whatever had opened up for Mum at that moment must have been so dizzying that she could go no further. How should Mum act if Dad admitted it? Dizzying, dizzying. Perhaps she would talk it through with Dad and then summon me to a meeting so we could talk about it seriously and honestly, the three of us, the triangle. Could they have stayed married after that? Might I then still have been able to see them? And what about Bård and Astrid and Åsa, their other children, would they speak openly and honestly about it with them? And moreover, hadn't a crime been committed, shouldn't it be reported to the police? And should other people be told as well, Aunt Sidsel and Aunt Unni and their families, should it be shouted from the roof-tops? Dizzying and impossible, I could see that, while their relationship with me was but a small thing, their relationship with me could be sacrificed, so who wouldn't have acted like Mum?

Me?

Astrid had taken it seriously twenty-three years ago when I called her in tears, Astrid had been moved, unsure and entered into a dialogue with me and spent more time there than Mum and Dad

228

who, once they had turned away from the dizzying, the impossible, soon picked up their old life, Mum with a show of principles: Then I couldn't stay married to you.

Astrid took it seriously for a while, but then I stopped calling her and sharing with her because I started psychoanalysis four times a week and had a space in which I could bring up the unmentionable. I stopped contacting Astrid, I was mainly absent in the years that followed and the issue became less precarious for Astrid, who slipped into the Hvaler family fold and hoped that the business with me would blow over. She would call me a few times a year, if that, usually to talk about an article, but enough for her to feel like a go-between, a demanding role that had made her see herself caught between a rock and a hard place, as she put it. Which must have meant that Mum and Dad were pressuring her not to have contact with me. Or they were pressuring her by asking her intrusive and leading questions: Surely you don't believe Bergljot is telling the truth? But even that happened increasingly rarely as the years passed and the drama diminished; they grew closer to one another in Hvaler, they saw one another often, at Christmas, the traditional holidays and during the long, sunny summers on Hvaler, and then several times a week as Mum and Dad got older, and it wasn't until now, after Dad's death, after 4 January, that Astrid had understood that perhaps the sum total of her actions during these twenty-three years, each of which individually might have seemed innocuous, was that she had ended up siding with Mum. That everything she had received in terms of money and presents from Mum and Dad over the years had landed her with a debt of gratitude she couldn't ignore, because all presents come with strings attached, everybody knows that, I had found that out for myself. It hadn't dawned on her until now that little by little she had acted as if she had sided with her now late

229

father and perhaps her soon-to-be-late mother, rather than with her big brother and sister and their children.

What if you experience a sudden emptiness on the death of someone you've organised your life around to please and gain acceptance from?

What if on the death of someone whose approval you consciously or subconsciously wanted, you discover that the choices you made, big and small, to gain their approval, have pushed others away?

Sybille Bedford writes somewhere that when you're young you don't feel that you're a part of the whole, of the fundamental premise for humanity, that when you're young you try out lots of things because life is just a rehearsal, an exercise to be put right when the curtain finally goes up. And then one day you realise that the curtain was up all along. That it was the actual performance.

During the twenty-three years that had passed since things first blew up, I strongly suspected Mum and Dad of positioning themselves with a view to things possibly blowing up again. That they had deliberately bound Astrid and Åsa more closely by giving them many big gifts, substantial loans, being generous in every way, creating new traditions, new rituals to shore up and strengthen a sense of family and unity in case things blew up again.

Or was I just being paranoid?

The Norwegian film *Sons* is about a group of young boys who were abused by an adult man. He had met them at a municipal swimming pool and befriended them. They were neglected boys in need of a caring father figure. The abuser became that caring father figure. If the boys didn't have enough to eat, he would feed them. If they were wet and shivering, he would give them warm clothes and affection. If they didn't have anywhere to sleep, they could sleep at his place. The film is about these boys taking revenge as adults. They are repugnant and seem unnecessarily aggressive as they attack their abuser who is now an anxious old man. The boys are tall, overweight and gross, a bunch of losers; watching those raging, moronic, juvenile adults fall upon a frail and elderly man is agony.

Suffering doesn't make you a nice person. Usually it turns you into a bad one. Arguing over who suffered the most is childish. Abused children tend to stay traumatised and their emotional life is destroyed, they often assume the mind-set and methods of their abuser, that's the vilest legacy of abuse, it destroys the abused and makes them less capable of freeing themselves. It requires hard work to transform suffering into something which is useful to anyone, especially the victim.

When the scandal involving Mum and Rolf Sandberg was at its most turbulent, when Mum and Dad were busy shoring up their positions in relation to us children, Dad said to me: Mum says that when the two of you walk down the street, then she's the one men turn to look at.

When the scandal involving Mum and Rolf Sandberg was at its most turbulent, when Mum was shoring up her position in relation to us children, she showed me a picture taken on my eighteenth birthday and said: I don't know why Dad is always saying that you're not pretty. I think this picture makes you look quite pretty.

A few years ago when I took part in a television debate about contemporary drama, Mum called me after the programme had been broadcast and said: You're so tall and your hair is so dark, what a shame, you were so pretty when you were younger.

Perhaps she thought that I was just as vulnerable as she was when it came to looks.

Did she speak like that to my sisters? She couldn't have done, or they wouldn't have loved her or been as close to her as they were. Dad had turned Mum into my rival and Mum didn't understand why, she had trained herself to ignore every inconvenient truth, she had too many of her own wounds to lick to put herself in my place. And how could she ever understand me when she never looked closely at herself?

When we were at the municipal swimming pool, while we were swimming and discussing the meeting with the accountant which I hadn't finished telling her about, Karen said, and it made me so happy, that it wouldn't have taken much effort on Mum's part, that things could have been so very different if she had started to cry. If she had said: I've been so miserable. If she had said: I was so dependent on Dad, I couldn't manage without him. If she had said: I was so young, I was so scared. If Mum had said, as Tove Ditlevsen said not long before her death: My life has become stupid.

I left my newly repaired watch behind at the swimming pool that day, perhaps I did so on purpose; it was time for a new watch, a new era.

I got off the metro at Majorstua on the morning of Saturday, 9 January, and walked down Bogstadveien to the House of Literature to meet Bo to discuss an article he had written about his trip to Israel and Palestine. Then it occurred to me that I might bump into them, Astrid, Åsa or Mum. One or two of them, or all three together, and a shiver of fear went down my spine. What if I bumped into one of them, or all three of them, what would I do? Dear God, please don't let me meet them! What would I do? I imagined them as they had looked on 4 January, at the meeting with the accountant, three terrified women, three women with short, greying hair, two of them with flitting eyes. What if I suddenly bumped into one of them, or all three of them, I started seeing them everywhere that Saturday morning on Bogstadveien, which was teeming with people, women with short, greying hair everywhere, some arm in arm, like Astrid would probably walk arm in arm with Mum, the eighty-year-old widow who was to be pitied, out shopping or out for a walk on Bogstadveien, on their way to Baker Hansen, having ventured further afield, if they dared venture out into the world that is, down Bogstadveien on a Saturday morning, unless they stayed home for fear of bumping into me, didn't travel far so as not to bump into me. Avoiding places where they risked bumping into me, perhaps they walked around with the same physical fear that I was experiencing now, a fear of suddenly seeing me, my figure and my face, a figure and a face which would immediately fill them with dread, I imagined their terrified faces, Mum's terrified face at the meeting with the accountant, like a cornered animal that knows it will be tortured and killed, and a wave of pain washed over me, the agony of compassion, poor Mum.

The problem isn't when you sympathise with one side in a conflict, Bo said, but when you sympathise with both. The problem arises when both parties are victims and adopt the role of victim and need it and milk it for what it's worth, refusing to give it up. It had been difficult, he said, to be in a place where every representative of both sides in the conflict employed Goebbels's propaganda rhetoric and who scanned Bo's face for signs of support or scepticism, and became aggressive, if they thought they detected scepticism. It was a challenging place to be, he said, and lit a cigarette, he had started smoking again. I don't know how it'll end, he said, I struggle to see how it can end well, he said, there doesn't seem to be a way out.

I was about to suggest that they broke away, but of course they couldn't, that was the tragedy, the great tragedy, I said, if you can't break away, if you can't escape, if you can't get out, if you're doomed to stay and be consumed by it.

But you've tried that, Bo said, and you're not free.

I dreamt that Mum and I were walking down Eiketunet, a landscape I remember from my childhood, and I was trying to tell her about all my problems, how much I struggled, but she wasn't listening to me, didn't want to listen, didn't want to understand, she just talked about her own problems and I thought: I *really* have to leave home now! And then immediately afterwards: But I can't, I'm only five years old.

I spent the last weekend in January at a seminar on the role of theatre critics in daily newspapers; I was one of the organisers so I couldn't get out of it. I was on edge. I hoped that people hadn't seen Dad's death notice and associated it with me, I hoped that no one knew that my dad had just died and wanted to express their condolences, I didn't want to talk to outsiders about Dad and his dying and the funeral. I tried to look busy during breaks, hunched over my Mac, writing, I went for walks on my own and dropped out of the gala dinner on Saturday. When the seminar ended on Sunday afternoon, I drove to Lars's house in the woods. I had been looking forward to going there, to getting away from it all, I had no urgent jobs to do, *On Stage* had finally gone to print and the only thing I had to do was prepare for a talk in a week's time about the dramatization of Rolf Jacobsen's poems. I was looking forward to turning on the radiators in Lars's house, for the heating to spread, to be deep inside the woods, far away from everything. I usually felt calm when I went there, I hoped that I would feel calm there.

I reached the house, I switched on the radiators and waited for the heating, the calm, I was hoping for calm and a good night's sleep. I dreamt that I was in Frogner Park, struggling to get two small children and a lot of bags up the steps to the top of the sculpture park where Mum and Astrid and Åsa were waiting so that we could join in the International Women's Day march. It starts at one thirty, Astrid said, when I reached the top and the time was instantly one thirty. But I need to put in my contact lenses, I protested, I need to change the younger one's nappy, I said, I can't get there for one thirty. They looked at one another, and I realised that they would leave without me. We'll go on ahead, they said, and got in the car, we'll probably see you there.

I woke up feeling heavy. Tale rang and could hear that I felt heavy, I told her about the dream and she said: You keep trying to justify to yourself that you don't want to see them, but they're the ones who don't want to see you.

In Jerusalem Bo had seen the Wailing Wall, the security guards, the heavily armed military police and the spot where the wall loomed so high that it blocked out the sky to all sides of this tiny, claustrophobic square which was surrounded by barbed wire and surveillance cameras and megaphones and soldiers in guard towers, it looked like a scary Soviet defence installation from a 1980s James Bond movie, he said. Some Orthodox Jewish boys ran around having fun, it was a public holiday in this creepy place. The guide put his hand on the wall and said that behind it lay a refugee camp. Who lives there, Bo asked, what an idiot he was. Why Palestinians, of course, the guide said, those who were expelled in '67. Behind it, half a metre from Bo and cut off from the rest of the world, they had lived there for almost fifty years. It had been an unpleasant visit. It had been even more unpleasant in Tel Aviv because Tel Aviv looked like a European city, all new and modern with tall, shiny skyscrapers and a big opera house and a huge modern museum, Tel Aviv was familiar and civilised and a success, he had felt safe and at home in Tel Aviv with its fashionable shopping areas and luxury restaurants and a broad seaside promenade where attractive young people in Western clothing drank coffee or beer, while gazing across the Mediterranean; on cloudless and very clear days they could see across to Gaza, it was eerie.

Bård wrote to ask me how I was. I replied that I was well and that I was in Lars's house in the woods, that I hadn't heard from any of the three of them and that was a good thing. He'd had a text message from Mum on his birthday, he wrote, at ten minutes to midnight, just before it wasn't his birthday any longer: Congratulations. A mother never forgets.

Mum might have hoped that Bård had been afraid of not getting a greeting from her. That Bård had checked his mobile throughout his birthday, hoping for a beep and a happy birthday, love Mum. And perhaps he had, I didn't know him well enough to say. But Mum had probably hoped that he was like that, that he had been waiting for his birthday greeting and so she prolonged the agony so that he would realise just how much he yearned to hear from her, just how much he really loved his mother, and then there were no congratulations from her until ten minutes to midnight, just before his birthday was over, and then she wrote: A mother never forgets.

She had probably spent a long time coming up with that. And her intention was that Bård would in turn spend a long time contemplating it. Wonder what it was she couldn't forget. His birthday or his behaviour in the inheritance dispute. There was always a sting in her tail. I remembered that from the old days, how I would often feel ill whenever I had spoken to Mum. The phone would ring, I would answer it, it was her, we would chat about this and that and when the conversation was over, I would be holding the handset, feeling ill. Once, as I stood holding the handset feeling sick after having spoken to Mum, I said to myself: Surely it's not meant to be like this? Shouldn't it be the other way round?

Had it always been like this? No. It got worse after my divorce, after I had managed to get both a divorce and my professor, after I had succeeded where she had failed.

Optimism had reigned in Europe before the gunshots in Sarajevo, Bo said, he had come straight from the National Library. In order to understand today's wars, he had to understand the Second World War and in order to understand that, he had to understand the First World War and the time before that. Before the gunshots in Sarajevo, he said, the most important conversations about politics and art and science were international. Before the gunshots in Sarajevo, the avant-garde from various countries would meet in Gertrude Stein's Parisian salon, the incendiary questions of the day were discussed at the international conventions of the psychoanalytical association, and leading Europeans spoke warmly about cross-border collaboration. The great European war won't come, the leading Europeans said, then gunshots sounded in Sarajevo and the war came and advances in civilisation such as the railway made it easier to move troops, the trains could supply the front with fresh bodies and the arms industry had developed automatic rifles with greater firepower, millions of young men were butchered on both sides, and people were shocked when they realised the horror of it all. But not Sigmund Freud. Freud didn't share people's horror of what Europeans were capable of. He understood the general outrage, he wrote, because he too had shared in the belief that the great nations had developed so much appreciation of what they had in common and such enormous tolerance of the differences between them, that 'foreign' no longer equalled 'hostile'—so in view of their self-image, no wonder the cultured cosmopolitans were disillusioned when faced with the realities of war, when their self-image collided with reality.

Freud wrote that the notion that people could erase all wickedness within themselves and their society through common sense and a certain level of education was a falsehood, Bo said. Psychoanalysis had shown Freud that we are essentially made up of impulses, that we are neither good nor evil, but good in one respect, evil in another, good in certain circumstances, evil in others, that human beings are primarily human, and the danger arises when we deny this fundamental premise. It's the weak point of the European mind, the Western human being, Bo said, summarising Freud, that we were blinded by the triumph of our own civilisation, that we overestimated our cultural abilities and underestimated our urges. And so we were shocked and dismayed at the horrors of war, but the shock and disappointment were unfounded, Freud wrote, we in the West hadn't suddenly plummeted deeply because we had never risen as high in the first place as we had convinced ourselves that we had. People in Western Europe had repressed their fragile egos, he wrote, and Bo agreed, we had chosen to overlook that our intelligence isn't separate from our emotional life, and during wars and crises our otherwise dormant urges would rise to the surface. Civilisation was put to one side, people started believing their own lies and exaggerating the wickedness of their enemy, people in Western Europe didn't realise that they were obeying their passions rather than their interests.

Whenever we squabbled, Mum used to say to us: No wonder there's war in the world when you lot can't keep the peace.

I dreamt that I was with five-year-old Tale in a haberdashery, I had tidied up some bobbins of sewing cotton, but she messed them up again, I told her off and she exploded, not in a childish tantrum, but in a grown-up and sarcastic manner and everyone heard, she spoke to me as if I was the world's worst mother. I had no idea what I had done to deserve such a dressing-down, such lofty condescension from her, she told the shop assistants that I had stolen the bobbins, she betrayed me, she wanted to hurt me, and I was hurt and I felt despair and rage, but was scared to react the way I really wanted to, with outrage and aggression so that everyone would hear, but I couldn't help it, I picked her up and set her down hard on a chair and shouted: How dare you speak to your mother like that!

It was a phrase, I realised to my horror as I blurted it out, that I'd heard many times as a child: How dare you speak to your mother like that!

Tale burst into tears and I could see that her sobbing was convulsive, that her despair was profound, and I felt sorry for her and guilty, and I hugged her and thought that now we could make up and cry together, that I could finally comfort her. We sat like that for a while, me with my arms around her, her head against my chest, her face buried in my chest, then suddenly she looked up at me and hissed: Go away!

She hated me. Why did she hate me, what had I done? Then

her father appeared and told me that she was jealous of his girlfriend.

And then it dawned on me. I was jealous of Mum who was Dad's girlfriend. And furious with Mum because what had she done? Nothing. It was this nothing which Mum did. It was everything Mum didn't see, which I couldn't tell her when I was five years old, everything Mum didn't want to or didn't dare see, my despair and that which made me despair, which made me hate her because she had been unable to protect me.

Jung describes the unconscious as a vast historical warehouse. I admit that I, too, have a nursery, he writes, but it's a small room compared to the huge periods of time, which even as a child interested me more than childhood.

I, too, want to get out of the nursery! Please help me get out of the nursery!

According to Freud, Bo said, there's a link between the collective madness of war and a civilisation that has done its utmost to rein in mankind's urges, whose population has developed the ability to give up satisfying its urges, a civilisation which denies death and the wish for others to die, including those we love, that exists in each of us.

So we're just animals? I said.

No, no, he said with a smile.

Self-awareness is crucial, he said. We shouldn't deny our irrational urges or overestimate ourselves, but see ourselves in a realistic light; we shouldn't deny the destructive urges deep within us, but strive to live wisely with our urges, our conflicts and irrational impulses.

That was the problem with Tel Aviv, he said, everything that was repressed at the Hilton, all the things that had been brushed under the carpet because it was unpleasant to be reminded of them, but which didn't, of course, stop them from existing for that very reason, and they became evident in subtle ways and possibly more strongly as a result, precisely because people sought to eradicate anything that leaked out, anything that found a way out into the body of society like a poison, everything that was repressed by this impressive display of civilisation based on denial. We aren't aggressive, the official spokesman had said, we're simply defending ourselves, but every passionate defence contains an element of lying, Bo said, certain parts of reality are repressed in order to keep painful feelings at bay, and it's demanding and draining to keep up such defences. No wonder they were exhausted, that they looked so weary in Tel Aviv, he said, he saw it when the sun went down and people took off their sunglasses. They build walls, he said, to keep the Palestinians out, he said, and not just for security reasons, but so they won't have to look at them and recognise themselves in them, so they won't be reminded of their own humiliating history of victimhood, they can't stand them because of what they have done and continue to do to them.

What do we repress, what do we deny, that's the question which must be asked over and over, he said, so that we aren't blinded by our technological advances, our scientific progress, our magnificent new architecture, our well-ordered, well-regulated society here in Norway where a prime minister once said something so very un-Freudian: It's typically Norwegian to be good.

On my way home from meeting Bo at the House of Literature, I bumped into some old university friends from my drama course and joined them for a beer. One of them had brought along his girlfriend, a woman I took an immediate dislike to, she spoke too loudly and too much, she acted as if she owned the place, then the penny dropped and I went bright red: She was just like me. She shared aspects of my own personality with which I had an unresolved and ambivalent relationship. *Look how she puffs herself up in order to get attention!* My immediate antipathy pointed straight back at me.

I'll try to remember that, I thought, the next time I have a strong reaction to another person or a phenomenon, that the explanation may not lie with them, but in me.

Åsa and Astrid wanted to go for a walk with Bård in Frogner Park. Bård asked what the point was and they replied that they wanted to speak to their brother at this difficult time. They would appear to have given up on me. Moreover, there were new developments, they wrote. Mum had had her offer on a flat accepted and they wanted to discuss selling the house in Bråteveien. They wanted a constructive dialogue and thought it was best if they met.

The meeting took place in a café in Frogner Park. Afterwards Bård emailed me that Mum had bought a flat, where it was and how much it cost. The house in Bråteveien had been put up for sale.

When I asked, he said that the mood had been fine.

Bård, Astrid and Åsa in a café in Frogner Park. A brother and two sisters at a café in Frogner Park. Deep down they probably loved one another. Maybe deep down we all did. Once we had been squashed together on the green leather Chesterfield in Skaus vei watching Disney movies on Christmas morning and waiting for it to be time for church. And now? People who spend time together often grow close. People who spend time together become involved in one another's lives and take an interest in one another. Human lives are like novels, I thought, when you're quite a way into a novel, even a dull one, you wonder how it will end, and when you have followed someone for a long time, even if it's a dull character, you wonder what will happen to them. Astrid and Åsa had spent the most time together and loved one another the most, they were the most involved in one another's lives, especially now after Dad's death. Astrid and Åsa must then love Bård next because he had spent a lot of time with them throughout the years, not as much as the two of them had, but they had seen each other regularly and at emotionally charged occasions such as Christmas and Easter and Constitution Day and birthdays. Bård must love Astrid and Åsa more than me because he hadn't seen me, hadn't kept in touch with me for years, to him I must seem like a half-read novel, a lost novel, for the last fifteen years I had probably existed merely as a memory, as far as he was concerned. An estrangement is like a death, I thought, it hurts the most at the start, then you get used to the absence and slowly the other, the deceased is phased out, as is their absence within you.

Astrid and Åsa must love me the least, the long-term absentee. Had Astrid and Åsa and Bård had a nice time at the café in Frogner Park, had they felt their sibling love for one another deep down, had they felt the ties of blood?

I sat by the river wrapped up in the big parka Lars wears for smoking, reading Rolf Jacobsen's poems, and came across this one: *Suddenly. In December. I'm up to my knees in snow. I talk to you, but there's no reply. You're silent. So, my darling, it has happened at last.*

I sat at the partly frozen river thinking about how often I had tried to imagine Mum's or Dad's death, how often I had feared that I wouldn't live to see it, that I would die before Mum and Dad. And now it had happened. Suddenly, in December. And I was overcome with gratitude: Imagine that I would live to see this.

And yet.

Did Dad have a grave? Had he been cremated, I imagine he must have been because the coffin was lowered through the floor at the chapel, to an oven so that he could be cremated, incinerated. I hadn't asked. Mum and Dad, Astrid and Åsa had made it a tradition in recent years, Astrid had told me, to light candles on Halloween on our grandparents' graves. I didn't know where they were buried, I hadn't asked. Lighting candles on our grandparents' graves on Halloween wasn't something we had ever done when I was a part of the family. After Bård and I were marginalised, they had started new traditions to strengthen their unity.

~

257

I sat by the river reading Rolf Jacobsen's poem 'Suddenly. In December'. How quickly it can happen, it's like flicking a light switch. Where does it all go, the face of the deceased, the images behind her forehead, the dress she made and everything she brought to the house, it's gone now, under the white snow, under the brown wreath.

Imagine that I would live to see this.

And yet.

I have a portrait of Anton Vindskev in the guest bedroom. Below the portrait is a sculpture of a luscious, chocolate-brown Caribbean lady smoking a cigar, just like the ones he was so infatuated with. One night I woke up and couldn't get back to sleep, I got out of bed and went to the guest bedroom where I hardly ever sleep. I found a book, a conversation between the Danish poet Benny Andersen and the Danish clergyman Johannes Møllehave, which always has a calming effect on me, I started reading it and from time to time, I would glance up at the picture of Anton and remember all the times I'd been with Klara and him in Café Eiffel. I feel asleep in the early morning hours and when I woke up, I saw that Klara had called several times. When I got hold of her, she said that she had some sad news, that Anton was dead. Anton had felt unwell the night before and had gone to an out-of-hours clinic where he collapsed in the waiting room and died.

Later that same day, as I sat working at the dining table, the heavy chandelier above me started to sway. It's Anton saying goodbye, I thought.

I went to Hamar to talk about the dramatization of Rolf Jacobsen's poetry. I felt calm, I was well prepared, I would be staying the night so I took the dog.

As I drove along the River Glomma in beautiful winter weather underneath a blue sky in a bright light that made everything float, I felt light, bordering on happy. The traffic was light, I felt light, I checked into an almost empty hotel and took the dog for a walk, I had a beer in the bar while I reviewed my notes and walked to the theatre. There I spoke to nice people who wanted what was best for one another, who wanted what was best for me, that was how it felt, we discussed the challenges of turning poetry into drama and I became better informed, I thought, and went back to the hotel, it wasn't even nine o'clock yet, the evening was mild and dark. I took the dog for another walk, and sat in the restaurant, the only guest. The kitchen hadn't closed, they put a candle on my table and lit it, I drank red wine, I looked out at the snow which glittered and glistened in the yellow glow of streetlights outside the window, I had Atlantic cod and I relaxed, it was over. I had said my piece, I had got it off my chest, my heart was unburdened, I thought: Imagine that I would live to see this.

I slept well. I woke up to a morning in Hamar just as bright as the one before. I walked the dog in the snow and ate a delicious breakfast in the hotel dining room with three other guests. Fried eggs and fruit with yoghurt, while I gazed at the snow outside and the snow-covered, undulating ridges on the horizon. I drank coffee with hot milk and read the newspapers, I drank more steaming hot coffee with milk and read the newspapers, just to waste time. I had no plans for the weekend except for thinking deep thoughts about the theme for the next issue of *On Stage*.

As I left to drive to Lars's house in the woods knowing that the weekend lay free ahead of me, that the road lay open ahead of me—there was practically no traffic—between calm, white snow-drifts under a shining sun, I thought: Imagine that I would live to see this.

Anton Vindskev was dead, and Anton's many possessions had been orphaned. Anton's purple boots missed him as did all of his funny hats that couldn't be worn by anyone but him. Klara tried to console Anton's purple boots and Anton's fishing hat and all of Anton's clothes and the other things in his flat, but they were inconsolable.

Anton was to be buried in Norway and Klara returned from Copenhagen one cold and miserable day in February. We went to the funeral together. It's a dress rehearsal for our own, she said, and grew sad at the thought that only one of us would experience the other's, it would have been such fun to go to it together. But that's life, or rather, that's death. She was practising the art of losing, she said, given that it was inevitable. You ought to lose in style and with good grace. She listed everything she had lost recently, and I was impressed that she could remember it all, keys and wallets and make-up bags and mobile phones and earplugs and necklaces and her late father's cufflinks and apartments and cabins and cats, and now also Anton Vindskev. Just today, the day of the funeral, she had lost a Visa card, her hearing aid and her glasses so that she couldn't read the words of the hymns we were singing or hear the eulogies which were given. She practised losing with style and good grace and not ruining today by mourning yesterday's losses or fearing tomorrow's potential losses, to be like the lilies of the field and the birds of the heaven, which are present in the now, silent and obedient, to gather moments of joy with which she could warm herself if times got tough, she had a feeling that times might get tough.

Bård called and asked where I was, I had mentioned that I was going to San Sebastian. I said that I was in Lars's house in the woods.

So you're in the country? He laughed, a little forced.

Astrid had called him. They had found an envelope in Dad's safe. On the front it said that it was to be opened with all his children present. They were hoping to open it at eight o'clock the following evening. Bård had said that he thought I was in San Sebastian, but it would appear that I wasn't. I was in Lars's house in the woods and could I, in theory, be at Bråteveien at eight o'clock the following evening?

Yes.

He said that Astrid feared that the contents related to me. That the letter from Dad, which was to be opened with all his children present, was about me. I could see why she was worried, but I didn't think for a moment that it would be.

Bård thought it might say that Dad had killed someone during the war. At times we had wondered about it. I think I might even have overheard something to that effect when I was little, that Dad had hit a child with his car. But later I'd thought that it was displacement, something less dangerous and easier to live with, that he ran over child once, that it was another child and not me.

Bård said it was most likely to do with investments, possibly a secret bank account in Switzerland.

~

They hadn't opened it. Bård had asked them outright if they had and they assured him that they hadn't, that they intended to comply with Dad's instruction that all his children must be present. They had probably found it together. They were clearing out the house in Bråteveien prior to it being sold and sorting out Dad's things, Dad's clothing and Dad's spectacles and slippers and underwear, which might be missing Dad and be inconsolable, it must be strange to go through a close and recently deceased person's most intimate possessions, but perhaps it was also a fine thing to do. I wondered what they had done with his things. They had been sorting through Dad's stuff, found the code for Dad's safe, and had opened it together. If Mum had discovered that letter on her own, she would have opened it regardless of what it said on the front, out of sheer terror, but they found it together and no one had dared to say what the three of them were presumably thinking and wanted to do, which was to open it! So that they could destroy it, in case it said something that reflected badly on them. If Mum had discovered it on her own, she would have opened it, and if it had said something which reflected badly on her, she would have destroyed it. But they found it together and none of them dared to suggest that they open it without Bård and me being present because whoever did so would be admitting to fears about Dad's relationship with Bård and me, and none of them wanted to admit to harbouring such fears. Besides, the envelope might contain information which must be shared with Bård and me, and then it would come out, it would become known that they had opened it against Dad's, the deceased's, expressed wish and that would be awkward. But couldn't they open it in such a way that they could reseal it? Mum was capable of suggesting it, I thought, should it prove necessary to share the contents with Bård and me. And if it didn't prove necessary to involve Bård and me, but the contents still reflected badly on them, then they could destroy it. Mum was capable of suggesting that they open the envelope to see what it contained, and if it was something which had to be shared with Bård and me, they could tear up the envelope and say that they had found the letter in the safe without mentioning that it had been sealed inside an envelope on which it was written that it must be opened with everyone present. But if something in the letter itself referred to the envelope with its instruction that it must be opened with all his children present, then they would have been found out. It was best to follow Dad's instruction, they must have concluded, they still had great respect for Dad's wishes and so would put off opening the envelope until all his children were present. Mum could hardly wait. Bård said that Astrid had said that Mum had gone crazy on discovering the envelope, completely hysterical, she desperately wanted it opened as soon as possible, tomorrow evening at eight o'clock, and luckily I was in Norway so it was possible. What did Mum fear? What did Mum hope for? That the solution to our problems lay inside the envelope? That Dad admitted and apologised for beating Bård and sexually abusing me, but exonerated Mum and said that she had known nothing about it? Tomorrow evening at eight o'clock in Bråteveien. I wasn't doing anything the following day other than pack for San Sebastian, I said that I would be there.

Perhaps it's an explanation, Bård said, as to why Dad was the way he was.

The very thing that Mum might be hoping for was Astrid's and Åsa's worst nightmare. They didn't believe Bård and me, they had had enough of Bård and especially me, their big sister who had always got so much attention, and now on top of everything else they might also be expected to feel sorry for me.

Throughout their childhoods Astrid but even more Åsa had suffered from their love for Mum, who initially rejected them because she was unhealthily obsessed with me, before she fell in love with Rolf Sandberg. Åsa had once said she believed that her life would have been completely different if Mum had sat on her bed, chatting to her every night like she did with me. That was because Åsa didn't know what Mum said to me when she perched on my bed and because she didn't know why Mum apparently favoured me.

Åsa had been jealous of me and no wonder; for years Mum saw only me, cared only about me. Where is Bergljot? Why isn't Bergljot back yet?

Astrid suffered less from Mum's neglect, Åsa suffered more. On the day she finished secondary school, Åsa proudly came home with her school report. She had done extremely well in all subjects, especially in Norwegian, and she was looking forward to showing the report to Mum, who merely glanced at it, before resuming telling me off for being fifteen minutes late coming back from something or other, did I have any idea how awful those endless fifteen minutes had been for Mum? I didn't, nor did I know how hurt Åsa must have been when Mum merely glanced at her school report before turning her attention back to me. I remember that moment, Åsa's sad eyes, young Åsa's crushing disappointment, Åsa on the verge of tears, no wonder Åsa hated me, the domineering big sister who took up so much room in the house, monopolising Mum. But now Åsa had Mum to herself at last. Åsa had yearned for Mum for all these years, and now she had finally got her. Åsa and Astrid had got Mum now and had had Mum to themselves for years. Astrid was exasperated that Bård at nearly sixty was still angry about how Dad had treated him as a child, was still obsessing about his childhood, but she didn't realise that she and Åsa were also stuck in their childhoods, the overlooked younger siblings who at long last had got Mum and Dad's full attention.

What I had hoped for was that they would come to see that the fault lay with Mum. That Mum's obsession with me was her own responsibility, that Mum was a grown-up and I was just a child back then. Even though Mum was childish, infantilised by Dad, at that stage she was our mother and we were her children. I had hoped that they would realise that it wasn't me who had caused them this very real pain, but Mum who had been thoughtless and in thrall to her own fears. But they wouldn't appear to realise or accept that. Astrid and Åsa acted and spoke as if Mum and Dad had been great parents, while Bård and I had been and continued to be wicked and ungrateful children.

Bård was hoping for an explanation as to why Dad was the way he was. It would be easier to accept that Dad had been the man he was if only we knew the reason.

Oh God, Klara said, he probably has other children.

Søren was hoping for a Swiss bank account, Tale for a confession, Ebba wasn't bothered, but thought I should prepare myself for the worst. Lars warned me not to get my hopes up, that I was likely to be disappointed. After all, that's all you've ever had from that front.

I cleaned the house and prepared for the worst. I turned on the dishwasher and imagined how I would enter Bråteveien where I hadn't set foot in fifteen years. Would we sit in Dad's study? Who would sit in the boss's chair, Dad's chair, would Mum? Who would open the envelope, would Mum? I imagined the envelope on Dad's, now Mum's, giant desk with Dad's distinctive, slanted, masculine handwriting: To be opened with all my children present. In the green leather Chesterfield which used to be in the living room in Skaus vei and which had been put in Dad's study when the family moved to the more impressive house in Bråteveien. Unless it had been replaced in the last fifteen years, it might well have been. Mum in the boss's chair behind the mahogany desk, us siblings on the green leather Chesterfield in front of the fireplace in Dad's study. I emptied the dishwasher and hung up the laundry. If it turned out to be about me, if he had wanted to say something to me, he could simply have written me a letter, a letter just for me. To be handed to Bergljot after my death. But it would be unlike him to leave a confession in his safe in case he died unexpectedly, falling down the stairs, say. No, that would be unlike him, I had known him quite well once in my own way. And, besides, what good would a confession do after years of denial, it wouldn't be worth much to me except that I could say: There you are, didn't I tell you so! He was no fool and would have realised that a posthumous confession couldn't compensate for years of denial. Given that he had denied it for all those years, he might as well maintain his denial in death, he didn't believe in God. Or perhaps he wants everyone to know, Tale suggested, that you're not a liar, a mad woman. Perhaps that's what it is. Offer me rehabilitation after his death? It seemed improbable, it was more likely to be paperwork relating to the sale of their house in Italy.

I hoped to dream about the answer but slept without dreaming. I felt calmer when I woke up. I had braced myself for a broken night and expected to feel anxious when I woke up, but I was calm, was that in itself an answer? Did it mean that I didn't have to fear the contents of the envelope? I prepared for the worst, imagined how I would arrive at Bråteveien where I hadn't set foot in fifteen years and be shown into Dad's, now Mum's, study, and sit down on the green leather Chesterfield next to people who a few days ago had berated me most harshly, my enemies who outnumbered me and were on their home turf. We would open the letter. What would be most in keeping with Dad, I asked myself, as I beat the rugs. What meant the most to him, I asked myself, as I scoured the bathroom. Honour and legacy, I replied, and prepared myself for the worst. Some charge levied at me, the liar, the psychopath who had fabricated stories and accused him of the worst crime a human being can be accused of, to get attention, to use Mum's expression or the expression they might have used about me when they were together. Because I clearly wasn't all that interesting to begin with. I had ruined the last twenty-three years of Dad's life with my lies. An aggressive letter directed at me, a closing argument for the defence, I prepared myself for the worst. I noted down a few things to say in the worst-case scenario: He doesn't give up. I'll say that for him. He's consistent to the end, he wants control, even in death, he wants to be right, he fights on even in death. But I'm a fighter, too, and just as stubborn as he is, I guess it's in my genes. Besides, I have the advantage of being alive.

I wrote these things down on a piece of paper. I intended to bring it with me to Bråteveien so that if the worst happened, I could prove that I hadn't been caught unawares, but that I was prepared, that I knew my dad.

The more I prepared myself for the worst, the more likely it seemed to me that yet again my side of the story would be dismissed and denied by everyone present, demolished by my dead father who was right because he was dead. And my mum and my sisters would welcome his attack and rejoice: Look what it says here, what do you have to say to that? The word of the dead has more weight than that of the living. It's also easier to feel sorry for the dead than the living, so now they would pity Dad even more, Dad who had suffered for years because of me, an innocent man convicted by me, the daughter who had lied to get attention, and I would be the outsider, the black sheep once more. I could already visualise it, I started to shake and called Bo. He said: You've already said that you want nothing more to do with those people. You

271

don't have to go there just because your father insists. It's not a legal document.

But won't it look cowardly if I don't show up, as if I'm afraid of what it might contain?

Their opinion shouldn't matter to you. Why subject yourself to more? I think you've put yourself through enough.

I decided not to go, not to comply with Dad's last request. I called Bård, who understood and said he would be happy to represent me but added that he didn't think it was the kind of letter I feared. Astrid had mentioned that the envelope was fat and contained several folders, presumably securities. Dad had once said to Bård that if he and Mum died in a plane crash, he wanted him to know there was something in the safe. I hope, he said, that it's something positive for us children, that it won't result in any more fighting. But, he added, it was odd that the discovery had made Mum so hysterical that she couldn't breathe normally until the envelope was opened. Mum had called Aunt Unni, who had called Astrid and told her that it was vital that the envelope was opened as quickly as possible in view of Mum's mental health.

The anxiety, the hysteria they display, Klara said, merely proves that they've no idea what your dad was capable of.

When I was awarded a travel grant to develop my magazine concept *On Stage*, I got in my car and drove randomly down through continental Europe to think, work and practise being like the lilies of the field and the birds of heaven and gather moments of joy with which I could warm myself when times got hard, I feared that times might get hard. I drove through Germany, through Austria, I reached Trieste in Italy, I saw the sea and the sun was shining, it looked like spring in Trieste and everything felt easier. I continued into Bo's beloved former Yugoslavia, along terrifyingly narrow roads with hardly any traffic, it felt as if I was alone under the sky with little evidence of other people, there was only the odd house with smoke rising from the chimney, I drove through orange groves and saw a rowing boat on a calm lake between willow trees. Then it grew dark and I got lost on a deserted, unfinished, unlit road near Split, I started to worry that I mightn't be able to find Split, I was exhausted, I had been driving for eleven hours. Then I found Split after all, I drove through the suburbs and right into the old town and found a parking space outside a small, venerable and typically Eastern European hotel by the picturesque harbour and got a room in the hotel and a big iron key, and I wandered around the old city, which was full of people out for a leisurely stroll because it was Friday evening, and the smell of the salty sea wafted in from the harbour and New Year's decorations still hung from the trees and the breeze was mild, and I felt mellow inside and sat down in a café with a beer and my notebook, and a feeling of serenity that looked like gratitude came over me. I had no boyfriend to report to back then, I had no one I wanted to call or talk to, I had no desire to share anything because everything had already been shared, I felt a deep sense of being a part of the world and when I look back on that special Friday evening in Split, I can still feel it. Surely that's the goal and the reason to experience many such moments, they balance out the pain, to build a house of such moments in which I can seek refuge during hard times. I had an inkling that times might get hard.

When I broke my leg some years ago and needed surgery, I spent three days in hospital. I liked being in the hospital, there were people nearby who were awake all night, all I had to do was ring a bell and they would come. The hospital didn't sleep, it was sleepless like me, at the hospital they changed my bed linen, brought me three meals a day and asked me how I was. During two of those three days I shared a side ward with an old woman. We didn't talk about what was wrong with us, why we were there, but I guess she could see that my leg was in plaster and raised towards the ceiling in a pulley. Neither of us had any visitors during the two days we spent together at the hospital, but the woman had adult children and grandchildren who lived in Oslo, it emerged, during a conversation she had with a nurse, and which I couldn't help overhearing; later I asked her gently about her children and grandchildren, but she became evasive and uncomfortable so I stopped, I felt sorry for her and sorry for Mum, who probably felt the same when strangers asked her about her oldest daughter. The old woman's children and grandchildren never visited her during the two days we shared the side ward. Perhaps they had fallen out. A nursing assistant came to shower her, but couldn't do it properly, she got just as wet as the naked old lady, and they laughed and they shrieked and they laughed some more and came out from the bathroom to show me how the nursing assistant had got completely soaked and they were still laughing, the wet and naked old woman and the drenched nursing assistant in her uniform. It was hilarious.

One night it rained and there was a thunderstorm and neither of us got any sleep; when the rain and the storm died down, a moonbow was arched outside our windows. The side ward lay high up, on the tenth floor, we had a great view, it was past one o'clock on a long summer's night, most people were asleep, but we weren't, we looked at the moonbow. I've never seen anybody so excited, so awestruck on encountering a natural phenomenon like a moonbow, but not just any moonbow, this one was brightly coloured and broad against the dark sky. Isn't it beautiful! Isn't it amazing! Imagine that I would live to see this, my roommate said, an old woman; you don't need family to visit you, I thought and felt relieved, family isn't everything.

I made up my mind not to go to Bråteveien. And made up my mind not to change my mind and go anyway, to go out of duty and in order to obey Dad. I decided to disobey Dad and pack for San Sebastian. The time was seven in the evening, then it was seven thirty, then eight. Now Bård would be arriving at Bråteveien. The time was now a quarter past eight. The envelope would have been opened. Murder or half siblings, my phone stayed silent. An accusation or securities, Bård didn't call. If the contents had been dramatic, he would have called. He called me at a quarter past nine. There had been no drama. It was a draft will where Dad had recorded the amounts of money the four of us had been given over the years, right up to 1997 when it stopped. Astrid had got the most, Åsa and I about the same, Bård the least.

They had gone through it together, then the contents of the envelope had lain on the desk while Mum, Astrid and Åsa told him about Dad falling down the stairs, about the plumbers, about the time they had spent at the hospital. Before Bård left, Mum had complained that she never saw his children, and he had replied that she knew why.

I imagined Dad revising the draft will, diligently, accurately right up to 1997 when he gave up. He wanted to be fair, he had made it a point of honour, there was much to make amends for, he wanted to be equitable when it came to our inheritance right up until

277

1997 when he gave up. I imagined Dad hunched over the ledgers, conscientious. What he had given me when my ex-husband and I bought our first house, what my sisters got when they bought their first houses, what Bård had got. I thought that originally Dad might have wanted us to inherit the same amount, that it was a way to atone for how he had treated Bård, how he had treated me when we were children. His relatively major assets acquired through hard work would be divided equally between his four children because it was only fair and because anything else would give rise to rumours and speculation. I thought about the mistake Dad had made as a very young man, as a very young dad, which couldn't be undone, which he had to live with, but how? It can't have been easy, it must have been Dad's tragedy, Dad's fate. Dad did something irreparable and lived in fear for the rest of his life that it might come out. Dad was terrified of his oldest daughter, he would glance at her furtively, he never touched her once she turned seven, the oldest daughter was off limits once she turned seven, Dad ended his relationship with her because she under-stood even more once she turned seven, because she grew into a wild, sentient and talkative child, who might let her tongue run away with her. Dad ended his relationship with his oldest daughter and no longer took her on trips in the car as he had done when she was five years old, when she was six years old because her mother, his wife, had so many children to look after, a boisterous son only a year older than the oldest daughter and two little ones, a newborn and a two-year-old. To give his wife a break Dad would take his oldest daughter along in the car with him when he went to look at building plots for the construction company he worked for, and Dad and his oldest daughter would spend the night in a hotel and it was fun to stay in a hotel, in a hotel you were allowed to get into bed before dinner and close the curtains, that's what you do when

278

you're in a hotel, said Dad who knew how you behaved in hotels. And if they weren't staying in a hotel, they could make a bed in the forest, Dad said, he knew all sorts of things. But then his oldest daughter turned seven and one day when she was in the car with her dad, she asked him if he had ever been with a black woman. And Dad was shocked, the daughter realised, but she didn't know why although she could see that he was upset. You mustn't ask such questions, he said angrily, alarmed, she wasn't allowed to ask such questions, he said, still reeling. What, he must have thought in the middle of the 1960s, if the child starts asking people in the lower middle-class neighbourhood of Skaus vei such questions? If his daughter asked him such questions, what might she not ask others, what might she say at school? Dad had a problem now, his daughter had become his problem, what was he going to do? How it must have haunted him, how he must have lived in terror. He was home as little as possible, worked as much as possible, came back in the evening, crossed his fingers and hoped for the best. He studied his oldest daughter furtively, and luckily she behaved as if nothing had happened. Or did she? His oldest daughter did her homework and played with her friends and practised the piano and took ballet classes, surely that was as if nothing had happened? Life went on like that for quite a long time, luckily, perhaps it could be forgotten, perhaps he could breathe a sigh of relief and put it behind him. The years passed, time is on our side, in a hundred years all this will have been forgotten, but then his oldest daughter started writing strange poems and sending them to the newspapers, which published them. His oldest daughter started writing strange plays and staging them in the sports hall at her school and inviting people to watch them. Imagine the terror Dad must have felt, his fear of his uncontrollable, unpredictable oldest daughter. They came, my parents, to such a performance in the sports hall at my school, written and directed by their oldest daughter, they couldn't not go because the other parents were going, the parents of the children their oldest daughter had directed and those children included their youngest daughters, so they had to go although they would have preferred not to. They sat there terrified at what might happen on the stage, at anything which might give it away, poor Dad. And after such a performance when their oldest daughter had gone to bed that night, when she lay in her bed awake as usual, but proud because she thought she had done well, had been a success, while her parents sat in the kitchen, she heard her dad say to her mum, and perhaps she was meant to hear it because her door was open and her parents must have known that it was, but perhaps they thought she was asleep. Her dad said to her mum that one of the other dads had said: Are we meant to be in some kind of strip club?

The daughter didn't understand the implication of that remark, the daughter didn't understand anything, she was just crushed that her dad wouldn't appear to think that she was any good, that she was a success, quite the opposite, her dad didn't like 'what the girl was up to', the daughter realised that one of the other dads hadn't liked her work, that one of the other dads thought she had created something that looked like it could have taken place in a strip club and that her dad was embarrassed. What if nobody had liked her show even though everyone had clapped at the end, what if she had caused a scandal? Instantly she felt as if she were the scandal herself. Her dad was referring to the opening scene when a row of twelve girls aged nine to eleven entered wearing red feather boas and black silk petticoats which his oldest daughter had sat up at night making, when the twelve little girls shimmied out of their silk petticoats which slipped down around their ankles,

280

one after the other from left to right, and on the black gym leotards which they wore under their petticoats there was a letter on each groin which she had sat up all night sewing, which spelled out a cheerful: Welcome.

Are we meant to be in some kind of strip club?

Poor dad.

Dad never touched his oldest daughter once she turned seven, never even cuddled her once she turned seven, never held her hand like Astrid had said he held hers when they went walking in the forest, never hugged her, never expressed any physical affection once she had turned seven. Her dad became increasingly frightened as his oldest daughter grew up and became more bizarre and unpredictable; perhaps he hoped that her behaviour would become so outrageous that no one would take her seriously. He couldn't escape it, his family. Had he wanted to escape, to get a divorce, his wife might have told the world of her suspicions, what she had on him, her husband, and destroyed him, that was the power the otherwise powerless mother had over the father.

Finally his worst fears were realised. His daughter did remember. What would he do?

He briefly considered confessing, putting it out there and unburdening himself, but the mother quickly realised what that would mean for her and shut him up. Then he had to deny it during the crisis and in the time that followed the crisis, day after day, year after year, and denial came at a price. Not just in terms of his relationship with his oldest daughter, but also guilt, a heavy burden of guilt, as well as a lack of self-respect. He demanded respect with his blustering manner, but gradually as he grew older, he lost his self-respect, he wasn't stupid or callous enough not to be tormented by a sense of guilt for what he had done and the way he had behaved when it came out. The least he could do, the only thing he could do to make up for it, even a little, in relation to his oldest daughter, in relation to his only son, his oldest child, whom he had never given the recognition he deserved, who might have worked out what had happened to his sister and whom he therefore feared and avoided, was that they would inherit just as much as his two other children, the younger ones. It would also make him look good in the eyes of the world, which might have heard rumours that not everything was as it should have been at Skaus vei number 22, if the children inherited equally.

A draft will with details of who had been given what began in the early 1980s and stopped in 1997 when keeping a complete set of records became impossible and irrelevant because the oldest daughter had cut contact, the only son had grown distant and the younger ones grew ever closer; birthdays and holidays and frequent visits with grandchildren who wanted to go to language schools and study abroad, who wanted this that and the other, the mother becoming increasingly controlling as the father aged and gave up noting down every single sum, large as well as small. Instead he wrote a new will stating that all should inherit equally. It looked good. A will which declared that when one spouse died, Bråteveien would be sold and the four children would inherit equally. Except for the cabins on Hvaler.

His documented legacy should state that he wanted the children to inherit equally. But how would he go about it? By writing a will. He didn't trust what his wife might do if he simply left everything to her, he didn't trust that she would share equally because she was capricious and impulsive and she no longer had a guilty conscience, she was no longer anxious, but bitter towards her oldest daughter who had cut off contact. His wife might well decide to reward the nicer and more attentive children, but even if she still went ahead and shared equally, the fact that she had a choice would make it appear as her will, and not his. If they died at the same time, in a plane crash, the children would inherit equally, the Inheritance Act would take care of that, but then the Inheritance Act would get the credit for being fair, not him, and Astrid and Åsa couldn't be sure to get the cabins on Hvaler. Dad had to write a will and word it so that he would appear to be fair while showing preference at same time.

Perhaps Dad was never happy after *that*. Perhaps Dad had never been happy before *that*. I wish I knew what had happened to Dad as a child, perhaps he had hoped that I would ask him about it, but I hadn't, and now it was too late.

When I was young, I was obsessed with sex. With intercourse. A girl in my year had done it, she had slept with a boy, I kept looking at her and imagining it. Students who were fifteen years old and in a relationship had sex, they slept together, I kept looking at them and visualising it, the penis going in and out of the vagina until the penis ejaculated. I wouldn't be able to do that, I wouldn't dare. Then I met a boy at a party and snogged him at a few parties, and Karen asked if we were now an item, and perhaps we were. When you're fifteen and you have a boyfriend, you have sex. The boy was having a party one Saturday night when his parents were out, and I wrote in my diary: Dear God, please don't let me die before Saturday. On the Saturday morning I wrote in my diary: It'll happen tonight, the thing that no one forgets, because no one ever forgets their first time. How strange it was to know that in advance of the event, that I would be writing about it here, on these white pages which smelled of anticipation as only white paper can.

That Saturday night Karen and I went to the party, we drank beer, we danced, then the boy took my hand and led me up to the first floor where the bedrooms were. We took off our clothes so we could have sex, he got on top of me, but he couldn't get it in, he couldn't get an erection so nothing happened. I went home that night without having done it, it was exactly as I had imagined: I wasn't able do it. But neither did I want to disappoint the expectant diary so I made up a story for it, twenty-five pages inspired by

285

the boys' porn mags, which they hid in the forest, women's week-
lies and my own imagination so as not to disappoint my diary. One
evening, some days later, Mum came to my bedroom and said that
Dad had gone. Dad had gone out into the night. Mum had read
my diary and showed it to Dad who had walked out. Dad had
become so distraught at reading my diary, so desperately disappointed in his daughter that he had taken himself off out in the
middle of the night, Dad's despair made me want to die of shame
and guilt. He came back later that night, very drunk, Mum helped
drunk Dad take off his shoes in the hallway, she helped him up
the stairs, I stood behind my bedroom door and saw the terrible
sight, my desperate, drunken Dad. Mum helped him up the stairs,
I stood barefoot in my nightie behind my bedroom door and
watched Dad sink into a cross-legged position on the floor. It's not
easy being human, he sobbed.

Mum closed the door to the master bedroom so I wouldn't see any
more, but I'd seen enough. Dad's despair, my guilt, being human
isn't easy.

Early the next morning he came to my bedroom, completely
transformed from the night before, strict and formal and smelling
of aftershave, he was going to the office. He stood by my bed and
asked if I had bled when I'd had the sex I had described in my
diary. I hadn't bled because I hadn't done it, but I couldn't say that
because I was incapable of speaking, I died, I wanted to die, there
was no life after this. He left and I was alone.

The day before I went to San Sebastian, I received an envelope in the post with all the paperwork relating to the probate. The draft will that had been found in the safe as well as the valid will, the cabin valuations and a letter from a lawyer which stated that Bård wouldn't win a subsequent court case. A letter addressed to Bård and me was also included and it was signed by Mum, Astrid and Åsa. The tone was very formal, fortunately. To Bård they wrote specifically that if he disagreed with the lawyer's accounts, he must contact the lawyer directly within two weeks. To me they accounted for the discovery in the safe and said that Dad had kept a file in his study for each child with press cuttings, letters and other bits, and that everyone had been given theirs, but that mine was too big to be sent by post. Astrid would be happy to deliver it to my home.

In conclusion they wrote that they all endorsed a note that Astrid had written and which was included as well. If we objected we had to say so within two weeks. 'We hope that we can now put this dispute behind us and look to the future.'

In the enclosed note Astrid wrote that she would like to use the new, higher valuation for the old cabin. Secondly, she was willing, seeing as she had been given considerably more money as an advance of her inheritance than Bård, to use some of her inheritance to make up the difference.

~

She needn't have done so. Åsa wasn't going to, Åsa didn't accept the higher valuation for the new cabin.

Astrid was trying to right an injustice. Given that Bård wasn't going to get a cabin, given that he had been given the least money as an advance of his inheritance, Astrid was trying to lessen his loss somewhat. That in itself was laudable. Or was it the least she could do?

However, none of it changed what was for me the crucial matter, which was never mentioned, which they totally neglected, which they refused to address.

Had I expected that it would be mentioned in a letter about inheritance?

No.

But I was outraged because they consistently addressed me as if I hadn't said what I had said at the meeting with the accountant. No one believing me was one thing, another that they pretended I hadn't said what I had said, acted as if the meeting with the accountant had never happened. 'We hope that we can now put this dispute behind us and look to the future.'

I couldn't put it behind me. A daughter never forgets. It wasn't like when your trousers get wet and you take them off and hang them up to dry, and when they're dry, you put them back on and forget all about it. It hadn't dried!

I didn't reply. I had no interest in my file.

Bård replied. Once more he reminded them what the dispute was really about. That he wasn't interested in money. That he would have preferred to have inherited half a cabin on Hvaler, which he

288

and his children could use. This request had been rejected outright. However, given that the stated intention of the will was that we would all inherit equally, he had at least expected that he and I would be compensated with what was the true market value of the cabins. That wasn't happening now. He pointed out that if Dad had died or the inheritance advances been made before 1 January when inheritance tax was abolished, they would have been forced to use the actual market value.

Taking the matter to court might well not prove successful, he wrote, but that didn't change the real issue. This wasn't a dispute between two business parties, but a dispute between a mother, her four children and grandchildren, it was about acting fairly and squarely. He wasn't going to take his grievance to court, he wrote. He resigned from all his directorships.

Dad must have loved me a little bit, mustn't he? He worried about his own life, his own future, but perhaps he also worried a little about mine? Mum showed him my diary and he went out into the night and got drunk, possibly because he feared I might founder.

It's not easy being human.

He was right about that, he had learned that lesson the hard way.

What more could I hope for than Dad gaining that insight? If he had been able to get himself out of an intractable situation with every single relationship intact, he wouldn't have been human. He had to choose, and he didn't choose me.

It was early spring in San Sebastian. I worked well. After a productive day I went for a stroll along the beach and reflected on my efforts, far away from everything that had happened at home, enjoying the break from it. I had a beer at the café at the end of the beach while the sun went down; it was warm enough to sit outside until it disappeared into the sea. I enjoyed the sun, the beer, being away from it all and feeling at peace with myself. Then I got a text message from Astrid: Dear Bergljot. I wonder how you're doing. Much has happened and it has been a difficult time. Mum is better. Busy selling the house. Am starting to feel that the worst has passed. Have been thinking a lot about you, Tale and the others. It's hard not knowing how you are. I really need to talk to you soon. Please would you give me a call when you're ready? Astrid

And there was I just thinking how well I was doing, how I was finally able to concentrate on other things, and was I now going to be dragged back into it all again? Oh, I was back in it all right. One text message was all it took. Now I had to decide whether or not to reply. And both options were equally impossible. What should I do, what could I write? What was she thinking? Her message was obliging and pleasant, but she wrote as if everything I had said for years had never happened, as if the meeting with the accountant hadn't taken place, how was I supposed to react, what would we talk about when we clearly wouldn't be talking about the one thing it was imperative for me that we did discuss. Dad falling down the stairs? How upset Mum was? I didn't doubt that Mum was upset, that Astrid was upset, but would our talking about it make it any better? In my experience our talking only made things worse for me, what would we talk about other than Mum's distress, Astrid's distress, seeing as she didn't want to hear about mine or she didn't believe it. What exactly did she have in mind, if indeed she had anything in mind? Surely she must know that it wasn't the same for me as for her. I had tried on several occasions to tell her what it was like for me, but she would usually respond as she had done on 4 January at the meeting with the accountant. She would say: Now is not the time or the place. She would say: Aunt Unni should be here. She would reel off how it was hurting and upsetting Mum. She had got up at the meeting with the accountant to put a protective arm around Mum. She had kept silent during the meeting when Mum accused me of making it all up to get attention. She had kept silent when Åsa said that I couldn't direct them to believe me. You can't direct us to believe you. Åsa had said *us*, not *me*. You can't direct *us* to believe you. Us equalled her, Mum and Astrid. So Åsa knew that Astrid didn't believe me, they had discussed it and decided that they didn't believe me, and so Åsa could safely say *us*, not me. You can't direct *us* to believe you. Astrid had marched out with Mum and Åsa, while Bård and I were left behind with the accountant. Now she wrote that much had happened and that it had been a difficult time. What would I reply, if I were to reply. I ended up replying that I was the same as always. That apart from Dad dying, there was no news. But that my position was much clearer, I wrote. Mum accusing me of making it all up to get attention. Åsa saying that I couldn't direct them to believe me. The three of them storming out together. What would I talk to you about? It's just going to cause more pain.

She replied immediately that it hadn't been the time or the place, that they had been completely unprepared for it and so taken aback. But she appreciated how hard it had been for me. She felt terrible about it all. But she wasn't Mum and Åsa, they were separate individuals. And she and I had always got on OK, and she didn't want what had happened to ruin it. I meant a lot to her, she wrote.

I was back in the fray again. I was having to explain myself again, but she still didn't get it! She didn't want it to ruin our relationship, she wrote, but it already had! I wrote that it had been ruined, that we had never got on OK because I was left feeling agitated and distraught after speaking to her because our apparently agreeable conversations about writing articles meant silence about so much damage, all the time, all the time, every minute and every second when we had talked about editing articles, the silence about the hurt would fill me up and burst out of me when our conversations were over and I was alone and then I would write my angry, accusatory night-time emails to her. We hadn't had a good relationship, we had had a relationship that worked for her as long as the silence about the damage was maintained, but for me that silence was intolerable.

I was out of my mind and rang Lars, who was exasperated. Why had I replied, why had I gone back into the fray? After all nothing good ever came from it.

But what should I have done? Just ignored it?

Yes. Because she's not saying anything new, she's not coming up with any new information, there is nothing concrete, no

293

suggestions for action or change, just the same empty phrases again and again, year in year out, how upsetting it is for everyone, she's a perpetual motion machine, anything unpleasant is filtered out, anything unbearable redacted, everyone is just really upset. The question is whether she's crafty and strategic or naïve and stupid, but ultimately it makes no difference, don't go there, don't argue with her, just reply that you need to be left alone.

I wrote to Astrid that it's tricky to be the servant of two masters, that she couldn't have her cake and eat it, I wrote that when she said that she didn't want to lose me, she was expressing her own need, but what about mine? I wrote that I needed the whole family to leave me alone.

A week of silence followed, then Astrid wrote to me again. Hi, Bergljot. Hope everything is OK? Fancy a chat soon? I replied that too much damage had been done.

I didn't get any work done that day, I was incapable of thinking of anything else although I desperately wanted to. Hope everything is OK, she had written, fancy a chat soon? As if I had never said what I had said, and she and Mum and Åsa had never reacted the way they had.

Can't you talk about something other than *that*, I checked myself, do you only ever want to talk about *that*? No, I don't want to talk about *that*, I replied, but I can't handle talking to Astrid the way she wants me to.

I called Karen and poured out my heart to her, ignoring the cost of the call; she said: She doesn't understand what she has done to you and she doesn't understand what she's doing to you now.

Astrid wrote again, my name followed by an exclamation mark, like a big sister admonishing her little sister. Bergljot! We have to talk! We need to talk and listen to one another. I don't think that too much damage has been done, it has been a difficult time for all of us. We can go for a walk—this afternoon? I can come over to yours?

I wrote that I was in San Sebastian.

Right, then we'll do that as soon as you're back. We need to talk!

My hopes of getting any work done were ruined, I was caught up in and consumed by a furious urge to explain myself and so I wrote that I felt better when I didn't have any contact with her, with them, that was why I had chosen not to have contact with her, with them, in order to take care of myself. And she wrote that we knew one another quite well, that she knew I was in contact with Bård now, not just via emails and text messages, but in person, and that it was much easier to see the other person's humanity when you met face to face, she didn't think it was right of me to avoid communicating with her after everything we had had together. It was a tricky situation for many people, especially Mum, who appeared to have lost two children and five grand-children. It was quite obviously terrible for Mum. And she had a file for me from Dad's study. And she had to talk to me about Tale's letter. Fancy a chat soon?

I called Klara, I screamed at Klara while I walked along the fine, practically deserted beach in San Sebastian in the afternoon sun which warmed me, I screamed: What does she want from me? I don't want to see her, I don't want to talk to her, the thought of talking to her makes me sick, listening to her going on and on about how Mum is suffering. What does she want from me except to tell me how Mum is suffering, make me feel sorry for Mum, make me forget the meeting with the accountant? And if it's not that, then what is it? Does she want to be in contact with me simply because I'm her sister, what's that about? What form does she imagine that contact will take? That our families will get together and have a lovely time?

My whole body protested at the thought of talking to Astrid, listening to her going on about how upset Mum was, why would I talk to Astrid when the starting point for everything she said was: What you claim happened, didn't happen. If she had believed me, she couldn't have treated me the way she had, she couldn't have addressed me in such a demanding and entitled manner as she did!

I bet it's your mum putting pressure on her, Klara said, I bet it's your mum who is pulling the strings.

Or, Klara said, she feels guilty.

Gunvor in Alf Prøysen's novel *A Blackbird in the Chandelier* has a scar on her temple. She will often touch her scar, caressing it.

Am I caressing my scar?

Not to caress my scar, but move on and step out of the stupid victim role, wouldn't that be a relief? Yes.

But that had nothing to do with me reconciling with my family. I didn't think so. How could it be that Mum, Astrid and Åsa would appear to think that it did?

Bård wrote that the house in Bråteveien had been sold.

I had rejected Astrid and I felt bad about it. Had I gone too far?

I entered the Armenian church in San Sebastian to reflect. I stood alone in the twilight and lit a candle for everyone I loved, my children and grandchildren. I was standing in front of the candle thinking about them when the candle started to flicker, then it stopped flickering, then it started again, then it stopped. I turned to see where the draft was coming from. The candle flickered, then it stopped, and I realised that it was my breathing that caused it to flicker. Every time I exhaled, it would flicker simply because I breathed, because I was alive, I existed, I set things in motion, it was a great responsibility, to breathe, to live, too big for me.

Karen had remarked once when I talked about my parents, that I seemed to have more respect for my dad than my mum. She was spot on. I had told myself so many times when I was younger and trying to cheer myself up, that I took more after Dad than Mum. Why would I want to take after him rather than her, have more respect for him rather than her when it was Dad who had abused me?

And how come I had more respect for Åsa than Astrid when it was Mum and Astrid who contacted me and told me that they loved me, while Åsa never did and would appear to hate and despise me—to the extent she had any feelings for me at all? It was because she was consistent, while Astrid was inconsistent, because Dad was more consistent than Mum and it's easier to deal with people who are consistent than those who aren't, who speak vaguely, in stock phrases and with forked tongues and who contradict themselves. Dad withdrew, but Mum didn't, Mum didn't want to let me go. Dad violated my boundaries as a child, then he withdrew because he knew that a line had been crossed. Mum crossed my boundaries year in year out, she didn't know where the line was, she was inconsistent and unpredictable. Mum had visited me in the turbulent early days after the bombshell twenty-three years ago when I had started psychoanalysis, when I had understood that she crossed my boundaries and I had told her so, and she had screamed at me that I was now accusing her of 'inchest' as well and run outside and home to Bråteveien and told Dad and my

301

siblings that I was also now accusing her of 'inchest' with an 'h', painting me as crazy; Mum was at the mercy of her powerlessness and despair, while Dad tried to control his misery, to bear it on his own. Dad's crime was greater but purer, Dad's self-inflicted punishment was harsher, his reticence, his depression more penitent than Mum's fake blindness, Mum who pretended that nothing had happened, who made demands and apportioned blame. Poor inconsistent Mum, poor Astrid so bewitched by years of preaching her own language of goodness that she believed that she was a good person. And she probably was, deep down, as are most people. Astrid crossed my boundaries, that was how it felt when she tried to force me into a relationship based on silencing a betrayal, it was unbearable, her insistence that something, which was abnormal from beginning to end, could ever be normal.

Dad was the root cause of my misery, but the misery spread to everyone and it wasn't within my power to relieve it. It doomed Mum and Astrid to making me even more miserable while they themselves also suffered.

I walked along the beach and into the centre of San Sebastian while the sun set and it grew dark, and I went inside the small church where I lit a candle for my children and one for Dad. I bought a bracelet of black beads, a mourning bracelet, and I wore it from bar to bar in San Sebastian, looked at it and remembered Dad's death and my grief. On my way back a stray black dog started to follow me, I could see that it wanted to come home with me, and I realised that it was Dad. Do you want something to eat, I asked it, are you thirsty, I asked it, do you want to sleep at my place, I asked it, then it ran off, it wants its mother, I thought, because it was Mum who was trapped and hurting.

I sat on the terrace in the darkness in San Sebastian and drank wine and got mad at Dad and ripped off my bracelet. When I woke up the next morning without it, I had forgotten Dad's death and my grief right until I skidded on black mourning beads and had to bend down to pick Dad up.

I was home from San Sebastian. Astrid wrote that she *had* to talk to me. It was of the utmost importance. I thought it might be about clearing out Bråteveien, that she might be wondering if my children would like to take part. If my children wanted some of the carpets, the furniture or artwork, which Mum couldn't take with her to her new flat. When my children's great-grandmother, my ex-husband's grandmother died, her children and grandchildren were invited to her big house to share her things between them. I called my children and asked if they wanted any of the carpets, furniture or artwork from Bråteveien, which Mum couldn't take with her to her new flat. Ebba and Søren said yes. Astrid called, but not to talk about emptying Bråteveien, she *had* to meet me, we *had* to talk about the situation, I owed her that much, the last four months had been the worst of her life.

Bråteveien was cleared without my children or Bård's children being told.

And no wonder, given how we had behaved, given how we had left it to Astrid and Åsa to organise everything.

Astrid wrote that seeing as I didn't want any contact with her, she felt the need to write me a letter. The following week I received a letter from her in the post. Why did she post it rather than email it? So that I wouldn't forward it to anyone like, say, Bård?

I made some coffee, went to the living room and opened Astrid's letter.

Bergljot!

She wrote that recently I had stated over and over that I didn't think she had ever taken my story seriously. Whenever I said that, she got very upset and angry because it just wasn't true. The experience had probably been terrible for me, and Dad's death might well have caused things to resurface. She was sorry for that, but it didn't give me the right to say that she hadn't listened or taken my story seriously. Since I now wanted to end all contact, there was something she felt she had to put in writing. She hoped that I would also show this letter to Søren, Tale and Ebba.

She said that in the years after I first told her that Dad had raped me, she had listened, she had listened and listened and listened.

That was true, I remembered it.

She described the circumstances when I had first told her twenty-three years ago. I had said that I couldn't remember when and where it had happened, but that I knew that it had. Of course I believed you, she wrote. Why wouldn't she believe her own sister? She believed me and had done a lot of soul-searching, she wrote, examined it warts and all, yes, I remembered that she examined it warts and all twenty-three years ago. Her head was filled with horrible thoughts, she wrote, she tried to pretend that nothing had happened in front of Mum and Dad and she began to dread family events. Yes, that was probably also true.

Ever since then she had given the matter a lot of thought, she wrote. How could she not, she asked. Rape is one of the worst crimes. She hadn't kept quiet about it but thought about it a lot and had spoken to many people about it, her husband, her friends, Åsa, Mum. Could it have happened? When? Could she remember me being distressed? Had I had any injuries? Could I be wrong? After all, the first time I brought it up I was around thirty years old and had three children. We had lived on top of one another in Skaus vei, wasn't it odd that no one had ever said anything? Given how many people knew us and spent time with our family. She had no recollection of anyone dropping hints about this until I spoke up as an adult. That didn't necessarily mean that it hadn't happened. After all, it was a different time where incest wasn't something people talked about. She had thought a lot about her childhood, and her conclusion had to be that *she* remembered her childhood as safe and filled with love and joy.

Because the rape of a child is extremely serious, such allegations are treated with the utmost seriousness, she wrote. I drank my coffee and read on, it didn't feel as if it was about me. Because the rape of a child is extremely serious, such allegations are treated with the utmost seriousness, she wrote in a hectoring tone as if to point out to me how serious my allegations were—just in case it hadn't crossed my mind. She used serious and seriousness in the

same sentence, she took it so seriously, with the utmost seriousness. Her problem was, she wrote, that I couldn't remember and
Dad rejected the allegation. And that's exactly what makes incest
cases so complex and wicked. The absence of proof. It's one
person's word against another. As the years passed it had become
clear to her that she didn't know enough to make up her mind.
She wrote in italics: *The information I had—what you had told me
and my own thoughts—wasn't enough for me to know for sure.*

She couldn't know what had happened, she wrote. She realised
that she couldn't verify my allegation any more than she could
know if Dad was telling the truth when he denied having done
anything. This stance became the only one she could live with
without compromising her own integrity.

As she had already told me on the phone, she wrote, I must
know that she had NEVER—in capitals—said to anyone that she
thought I was lying or that what I claimed couldn't have happened.
But neither could she prove that it had. Had she sided with me,
she would have been accusing Dad of a horrific crime on what she
felt were unsafe grounds. She couldn't do that.

Because she loved Dad *and* me, she wanted to be in touch with
both of us and she didn't think that wanting to see her dad as well
her sister was 'having her cake and eating it'.

She was right about that, I agreed with her.

She wrote that Mum and Dad had accepted her position and
been pleased that she was in contact with me.

She thought it was beyond tragic if this was allowed to destroy
the relationship between our children, their cousins, the relationship between the grandchildren and their grandmother, the
relationship between me and Mum. That was why she had kept on
saying that we had to talk. After Dad's death she had asked me
several times if we could meet to talk. She was of the opinion that

the crisis in our family was now so serious that it could result in a permanent rift. So much communication was lost when you couldn't see one another, listen to one another's voices or see each other's body language. That was why she was so keen on a physical meeting. When people don't see one another, the distance and the likelihood of demonisation increase. Perhaps she was afraid that this might happen because she had experienced the same thing close up in the relationship between Mum, Dad and me and seen how bad it had grown. She couldn't bear the thought that we four siblings and our children wouldn't be in contact. We all had our good and bad sides, and it was much easier to see the whole person when we were physically together.

I didn't reply. There was nothing I hadn't heard before, there was nothing I could say that I hadn't said before, and if there was, it would be in vain because she didn't take anything on board.

The experience had been terrible for me, she wrote, and Dad's death had probably caused certain things to resurface.

What experience? What things? She had already concluded that there was no experience, that it must be some sort of construct in my mind. What things could resurface and hurt me after Dad's death, if there was nothing to resurface? She kept returning to my pain, she understood that I was in pain, but if I hadn't experienced what I claimed to have experienced, if it was all made up, what was the nature of my pain?

She wanted it verified, she wrote.

How? DNA evidence, video footage? She who worked with human rights, who dealt with stories that couldn't be verified every day, what kind of proof did she have in mind?

Should I have called her after every therapy session, after every bad dream, every time a new memory surfaced, every time the past caught up with me, in my dreams or in the middle of the day as searing flashbacks, every time a jigsaw piece from my childhood, adolescence and adult life fell into place and made me see even more of the big picture and my part in it? Dad's strange reactions, Mum's strange reactions in otherwise ordinary situations whenever sexuality or sexual assaults were mentioned, whenever dangerous family secrets were mentioned. Should I have called Astrid and supplied her with details, how would she have felt about that, how would she have liked that, would that have been pleasant? After my bombshell twenty-three years ago, I chose to withdraw, to heal myself, to seek professional help. Should I have called Astrid with the physical details, pleaded my case with a sceptical sister who loved her parents and had every reason to, who had a great relationship with her parents, who wanted a happy family, should I have called her and shared my open wounds, exposed my nakedness, so painful, so shameful, so intimate, so difficult to talk about outside the psychoanalyst's consulting room, tell her things I hadn't told anyone other than my psychoanalyst, not even my friends, my boyfriends or my children because it hurt too much and was too physically intrusive, because I didn't want my nearest and dearest to have such images of me in their heads?

That's why, Astrid.

Dad denies it, she wrote, as if that was a decisive argument, as if she believed it was something he would ever confess to. She had thought about it a lot, she wrote, she hadn't kept silent about it, but talked a lot about it, but with whom? Professionals? The Support Organisation for Victims of Incest? No, she had talked to her husband and Åsa, who shared her agenda, and with Mum whose whole life would appear wasted and shameful, if what I said was true. How might their conversation about this have gone?

Mum: Could she be telling the truth? Lots of people used to come to our house. No one ever said anything to me.

Åsa: She'd had three children when she brought it up; if she'd had any kind of physical injury, wouldn't the doctors have noticed?

Astrid: I don't remember her ever saying anything about it, or that she was unhappy. No one ever mentioned anything like that.

Mum: I don't think she could be telling the truth. Dad wasn't like that.

Åsa: No, neither do I.

Astrid: No, it doesn't seem likely.

How could she claim that they had spoken about the subject in earnest, opened themselves up to it in all seriousness, to use the word she repeatedly used? If they had, then Mum wouldn't have reacted the way she had at the meeting with the accountant: You're just saying it to get attention! Astrid claimed that they had talked and talked and thought and thought, all very seriously, but if that were true, they wouldn't have reacted as uniformly, as aggressively, as they had done on 4 January. She claimed that she had been caught between a rock and a hard place, but had she ever put as much pressure on them as she had on me? Had she ever asked Mum and Dad unpalatable and critical questions? Why were you always so anxious about Bergljot? Why did you send Bergljot to ballet classes and piano lessons, and not us? No, she couldn't have. Or there wouldn't have been that harmony and unity between them that my children had so often experienced in Bråteveien, that Søren and I had witnessed at the meeting before the funeral and in their behaviour at the meeting with the accountant on 4 January.

311

Had Astrid, who occupied a particularly influential position in relation to Mum and Dad, ever talked to them in a way that might result in a genuine conversation about the core of the conflict? No, she couldn't have. Instead she had invited me to her fiftieth birthday party, that is to say, she had asked me to play along and put a smile on my face.

She could have influenced Mum and Dad. But she hadn't.

At the meeting with the accountant and on several other occasions Astrid had stated how tough it was to be caught between a rock and a hard place. How terrible it was to be her. Yet now she wrote that Mum and Dad had respected her position, her piggy in the middle position, that they had even been pleased that she and I were in contact. And why wouldn't they be? They had no reason to doubt her loyalty, although on one occasion, a hundred years ago, according to her and in response to Dad's direct question, she had replied: I don't know what happened, Dad. Once the initial turbulence had died down, Mum and Dad never had cause to question her allegiance because she hugged them and spoke flattering words at every opportunity and followed them up with every possible sign of caring for them and gave, but more importantly, received gifts.

So what exactly was the nature of her pain?

Was she hurting because she knew I was right?

The flaw in *Festen* is that it ultimately ends well for the man who confronts his father and his family. In real life it doesn't end well for anyone who confronts their father and family. The problem with *Festen* is that it lets the person who confronts their family produce evidence. In real life there is no evidence. In real life no one who confronts their family has a twin who has killed herself, leaving a note proving the father's guilt. I would like to have had a twin who killed herself and left a note proving Dad's guilt. *Festen* is a great film, but it's wrong.

I met Bo in a café to discuss some poems he had written in Ireland. While I read Bo's Irish poems, he read Astrid's letter. Every now and then I would glance up at him. When he reached the passage about meeting in person and demonisation, he said: That's not true. You don't need to meet in person to have a good relationship. And who is she scared will be demonised? Herself? But that's not what you're trying to do here.

No, I hope not, I said. I just want to protect my boundaries, I said, my boundaries are so fragile, I want to maintain my boundaries, I said, and if I meet with Astrid, she'll intrude on them without me realising it until it's too late. I don't have the energy to tell my story again and again, repeat it ad nauseam, I don't want to plead my case, it's too intimate, it's humiliating, I'm too tired. I forgot Bo's poems in favour of my case, I pleaded my case. Once, I said, I decided to have hypnosis in order to produce the evidence they demanded, remember times and places, every single detail and present it as proof, but my psychoanalyst had said that if I underwent hypnosis it had to be for my own benefit, because when it came to convincing my family, I might as well give up now, there was no form of evidence in the whole world that they would ever accept, if I produced a video, they would say that it had been manipulated. They had said something similar at the Support Organisation for Victims of Incest, that those who confront their family usually lose their family.

Let me get back to your poems, I said.

She has put on her serious face, he said, she writes with that face. She uses 'serious' and 'seriousness' in the same sentence, to prove how seriously she's taking it. And she probably does take it seriously, he added, but she's tangled up in her own language of goodness and virtue, she shows how much she has practised being a good and sensible human being, a kind of officially good person.

Why would I struggle, I interrupted him, forgetting his poems in favour of my case, why would I struggle with everything that has happened as a result, with loss and pain and isolation, how would I have been able to keep up this draining, painful estrangement, if it was all in my mind, what would my motivation be, what would I stand to gain? Who makes up a story like that, for what, for what, what would my motivation be?

What it says between the lines of her letter, he said, although she doesn't realise it herself, is that you're capable of accusing your father of a terrible crime, accuse an innocent man of something horrific, to use her words; indirectly she's saying that you're a terrible human being.

So why does she want to have contact with a terrible human being, I cried out. Why is she so adamant that we stay in touch? If I'm so stupid and wicked that I made up a story of incest to get attention, how can it be that Mum, according to Astrid, suffers much more because of the conflict with me than the inheritance dispute with Bård? Surely it's easier to dismiss an outrageous liar, which is how they view me, than someone who, let's face it, is only after half a cabin on Hvaler?

Astrid's unease stems from her bad conscience, I said more calmly now. She knows that I'm telling the truth, but if she were to acknowledge it, accept it, there would be consequences and she's incapable of dealing with them. She couldn't whisper in my ear one minute that she believed me, and then the next and in every other respect, including publicly, be Mum and Dad's loyal, loving daughter, it would be impossible, but that was her dilemma to resolve. The solution that worked best for her involved being in contact with and talking to me, conversations which weren't about my allegations, but about editing articles, except that those conversations did me no good, in fact they upset me, why should I help resolve her dilemma in a manner which didn't benefit me? I'm glad she wrote that letter, I said, now even more calmly. I'm glad that she writes plainly that she wants proof of something which can't be proved because then there's nothing more I can do. If only she had said twenty-three years ago that she wanted proof, then we could all have saved ourselves a lot of time. Was it any wonder that I had felt troubled and ambivalent towards someone who wanted proof *and* reconciliation at the same time? That was the impossibility, the untruth which had lain unspoken underneath all our conversations, which now turned out to have been nothing but lies.

It was much easier for me to deal with Åsa, who had never believed me, who had cut me off the way I had cut her off, it was a clean break. Åsa didn't demand verification or evidence, Åsa didn't try to force me to see her, Åsa didn't believe me, pure and simple, and wanted nothing to do with me.

She probably takes it seriously in her own way, Bo said, but I don't think that you should take this seriously, he said, waving Astrid's letter in his hand, I don't think you should take her incredible sadness seriously, the one she goes on and on about, her incredible sadness.

It *is* sad, I said, but I can't make it not so.

316

There is, he said, putting the letter aside, every reason to ignore this. She's exaggerating, he said, how awful she feels about this. But I guess she wants her peace-making mission to succeed. Even though the air has already gone out of that balloon.

Jung saw things the way his instinct encouraged him to. If he didn't, his snake would turn on him. I tried to look at things the way my instinct encouraged me to. If I didn't, my snake would turn on me. My mum and sisters had acted in ways and said things which my snake disagreed with. I travel along the path my snake prescribes, I thought, because it's good for me.

Bo had travelled to Ireland to write poems about Ireland but didn't know why. He woke up one morning in Ireland wanting to write a poem about the rain. Or did he just want to be in Ireland? Why couldn't he do that here in Norway, he wondered, we were in a patisserie in Lommedalen. He had met a man in Ireland who had told him to go left through the forest and then take a right. Bo turned left through the forest and then right and reached a church with a poster which read: Imagine how God feels. He realised that he had come too far and was walking back when it started to rain. The rain was directionless, as was he. He had left the main road and got lost, but that was what he had hoped for, he had wanted to get lost, and it was quiet where he was, but not so quiet that he couldn't hear the drone of traffic from the main road. He could always find his way back there. I walk towards new towns full of anticipation, he had written, because they would give him everything he wasn't or didn't have. You learn something about yourself, he had written, when the road forks between hawthorn and lily of the valley and exposes you. Which way will I go, he had wondered, on coming to a crossroads. He reached a town, but after that town lay another, he had arrived bursting with anticipation, but drank himself into a stupor, he had gone to Ireland to seek the protection of the big trees but found only bushes.

The night before 11 March I couldn't sleep. Is there life after death, I asked, is Dad somehow on the other side, I asked myself and tried summoning Dad, but got no reply. When I finally dozed off, I dreamt that I had woken up in my old bedroom in Skaus vei number 22 and got out of bed because my daughter Tale, who was five and wore glasses, was crying her heart out. I went to see her, she was lying in Mum and Dad's double bed. I comforted her and asked her why she was crying, she said: It won't get up.

Her doll's house had been completely trashed. I started to pick up the pieces, small turquoise bits of furniture and sections of walls and roof, I said that we could fix it and she started to calm down. While I was clearing it up, I got mad at Dad who had wrecked the house, I braced myself and opened the door to the living room where Dad was sitting, heavy and limp in the green leather Chesterfield and I said to him that smashing the house was a rotten thing to do. He replied that it was worthless anyway, just some crap from McDonald's. I said it was bad of him to wreck the house when Tale was so fond of it. But as soon as I had said it, I got scared of how he would react and I went back to Tale and we heard him come up from the living room and go to the bathroom where he took a leak without closing the door, and I thought: What's going to happen now? After all, we're alone with him, there are no grown-ups here, anything could happen.

Irish street names are much more cheerful than Norwegian ones, Bo observed. If the street names in Ireland had been more depressing, it would have been easier to throw everything into the sea of oblivion.

He said it was all about letting yourself fall with the fruit and be carried off by the ants.

All the 8mm films Dad took of me when I was little, where I stand, grinning and naked, on a rock on a beach in Volda in a ballet pose, have they been destroyed, what happened to them? I was cute back then or maybe Dad was a talented photographer? Because it looked like love, I took it to be love. Dad couldn't resist me. When he and I were alone, Dad changed completely, Dad couldn't control himself, the mere sight of my naked body turned Dad's head. I discovered, even as a child, that men would drive themselves crazy wanting me, that I could turn their heads, how did I learn that? In my experience, all you had to do was take off your clothes and wrap yourself round a man, then he would go crazy and not be himself anymore. But it was painful as well because it lasted only a short time. When these rushed encounters were over, Dad would grow distant and cold, he would avoid me because we tend to shun those we have hurt. That was my first sorrow, the many, long, bleak days when Dad ignored me, when Dad took even less notice of me than of the others, when Dad didn't see me, didn't touch me, never cuddled me, but would glance nervously, furtively, in my direction, Dad would watch me fearfully and in secret, while I just missed my dad. Dad would go crazy for me. For a brief moment he couldn't control his desire, and the knowledge of her physical appeal isn't without value for a little girl. But with that knowledge the little girl lost her dad and it hurt because she missed him all those long, sad days, all those

322

years when he didn't look at her out of terror and shame, and she was jealous of her mum, whom her dad would show affection in public. It was a ménage a trois, the mum won and the girl lost. But then her mum rejected her dad by falling in love with a professor she didn't get, and the daughter fell in love with a professor and got him. The daughter had the guts and got a divorce and her professor. As if to rub her mum's face in it? Defeat her mum like her mum had once defeated her? Are we caught in such webs, spun in our early years?

My poor, dead dad, my first and greatest tragic love.

The big house in Bråteveien had been sold and cleared out, the sale would be completed by the end of the month and I would get my share of the inheritance during the first two weeks of May, Bård said.

I refused to believe it till it happened.

On 10 May I received a letter with the probate accounts, columns of figures that meant nothing to me. I needed to sign it and give my bank details whereupon my share would be transferred immediately. I could send the signed letter to Mum's address or drop it off in person. She might have hoped that I would drop it off at her new address, an eighty-year-old widow alone in a new flat. I wasn't going to, so I didn't. I signed the letter and sent it by post.

On 14 May the money was paid into my account. That was weird.

I had an unexpected text from Mum. She had come across an article I had written, she wrote, which was called 'Reading, loving'. I vaguely remembered it. She wrote that she loved me very much.

Her message left me cold.

When Dad dies, I had said to her once, then you'll come round. But by then it'll be too late. That was how I felt, that it was too late. And if Astrid were to come round, if Mum died and Astrid came round, it would also be too late. Even if Astrid wept and repented, I would still be cold.

A psychologist quoted in a newspaper said that he had witnessed scenes when someone guilty of betrayal admitted their mistake and started to weep, but the injured party would look away with an unmoved face, rejecting their plea for forgiveness.

When he was less experienced, he had found it painful to watch and had encouraged the injured party to relent and accept the repentance.

But no longer. Because it didn't work, unless it happened in the right order. Someone guilty of betrayal shouldn't be praised for admitting their betrayal until the despair, grief and rage of the injured party had been acknowledged. Without it, their repentance would fall to the earth like a rock. It's the law of nature, he said, it's in our bones, we can't escape that sequence of events.

I was incapable of forgiveness.

But throw it into the sea of oblivion?

Hold it up to the light, examine it, acknowledge it and accept it, and then throw it into the sea of oblivion?

I couldn't do that either. Because it wasn't isolated incidents and a finished story, but a ceaseless exploration, a necessary excavation full of dead ends and distressing flashbacks. And the presence of my lost childhood, the constant return of this loss had made me who I was, it was a part of me, it pervaded even the slightest emotion in me.

Then I felt bad for not having responded to Mum's I-love-you message and called directory enquiries, got Mum's new number and rang her. How are you, I asked. She wasn't well, she replied, because she never saw Bård and his children or me and my children. Why don't you want to see me? Why do you hate me, she asked. What could I say, should I explain myself yet again? I said that she knew why, and she became aggressive and said that I was a liar, that if I was telling the truth why hadn't I gone to the police, and I rang off, my guilty conscience had evaporated.

Emma asked: Granny? Do you have a mum?

Me: Everyone has a mum.

Emma: My other Granny's mum is dead.

Me: Yes.

Emma: Dad's dad is dead.

Me: I know.

Emma: Is your dad dead?

Me: Yes, he died not long ago.

Emma: Will the dead grow big again?

Me: No.

Emma: Is your mum dead?

Me: No.

Emma: Can I meet her?

Me: She lives a long way away.

Emma: I'd like to meet her.